WICKED
WIND

A Sam Larkin Mystery

WICKED

WIND

A Sam Larkin Mystery

Helen
Cothran

*To Kathy, for always expecting
the best from me.*

Thanks to Kathy Najjar, Louise Gerdes, Kyla Stinnett, and Abigail Padgett, whose intelligent critiques made all the difference, and to Joe Bernier, whose creativity turned mere words into a book that someone would actually buy.

Chapter One

Lacy forced me to get out of bed with her pathetic whining. Instead of cursing the beast, I should have thanked her. It was after ten o'clock, hours after I usually rise. That's what happens when you work until two in the morning to try to meet a deadline. It was now too hot to take the dog for a run or to accompany my elderly neighbor Hattie for our thrice-weekly walk. The worst part was that I had lost several hours of writing time, which wiped out any gains I'd realized by working so late last night. My book was due in three weeks, and I was nowhere near finishing the first draft, much less the outline. My editor was going to love me. I could only hope Vince would get offed by a boa constrictor or crocodile during his annual summer vacation to somewhere exotic.

I tossed an unmeasured heap of bargain-basement kibbles into Lacy's bowl and put on a pot of Kona blend for me. While it brewed, I slumped out to the driveway to get the newspaper. The wind blew sand into my eyes and flung my hair over my face. It had to be ninety degrees already—typical idyllic weather for a Desert Rock summer. No mystery why D-Rockians (as I call Desert Rock residents) descend on San Diego and Los Angeles beaches like locusts this time of year. Besides, the drive to either of those cities takes less time (two hours) than waiting for a light to change or getting through the line at the Oasis Shop 'N Save here.

At around forty thousand residents, Desert Rock is a small town, relatively speaking, and is located out in the middle of nowhere. The pace is slow here. Just last week I spent ten minutes in line at Albertson's while the checker and shopper in front of me discussed the enormity of the onions sold in this town. Having just come here from San Diego to live after my mother died, I nearly exploded from impatience. I asked if they could move it along because I had somewhere to be, and they exchanged an eye roll that said, "Stupid out-of-towner. Why be in a hurry? You'll just get hung up at your next stop."

The aroma of high-octane coffee hit my olfactory nerves when I let the wind toss me back inside the house. Ah, I might live to see another day. I sat at the kitchen table drinking my coffee, staring through the window at my mother's deteriorating garden, when my cell phone rang. It was Eddie, an old friend with whom I had reconnected during my mother's losing fight with cancer.

"Have you read the *Desert Tribune* this morning?" He said after I mumbled a greeting.

"Of course," I said, "Right before I jogged five miles, cleaned the house, and finished my book."

I visualized his eyes rolling. "Then you haven't seen the news about Cole Mintock."

"Cole? What about him?" I noticed that tumbleweeds had piled up in the corner of Mom's yard into a prickly pyramid. It was hard to distinguish the debris from the dead and dying bushes on either side.

"He was murdered."

I knocked over my cup. Hot coffee splashed all over the kitchen table and me. Lacy lumbered over and whined. It couldn't be true, Cole couldn't be dead.

I heard Eddie say, "Someone stuffed him into one of those wind turbines of his and let him bake to death."

I felt the cell phone slip off my ear. Baked to death?

"Sam?" Eddie's voice sounded small and far away.

I pulled the phone back to my ear. "I'm here."

"Are you alright?"

I couldn't answer him. No words came.

"Meet me for lunch," he said in a voice that did not brook dissent. "Ming's. Eleven-thirty."

I grunted consent, hit the "end" button with my thumb, and dropped into a chair.

I had first met Cole Mintock on a research trip for the book I was writing for Blue Nest Press, which publishes books on controversial issues for young adults. The book was due in a month, and my editor said that if I missed any more deadlines he'd "terminate our relationship." Like we were married or something. What an ass. Vince was always popping veins over what he saw as my unnecessary field research—"Use the damn Internet, Sam"—but he knew that the extra effort I made to gather firsthand information made my books top-notch. Despite his threats, I decided to tour the local wind farm.

I calculated that the research would take only a day or two, and then I could get back to writing my book. I had arranged to meet with Cole, who owned the wind farm, then I'd join a tour of the farm a few days later. It was odd, really, that I had never met Cole before. He and my mother had worked together over the years in various groups committed to protecting California's environment, especially its deserts. When Cole first proposed to construct a wind farm out by Thomas Pass in the early eighties, she supported his plan despite the concerns of other conservationists, who were concerned about its impact on the land. My mother saw Cole as a visionary, willing to spend his money on developing clean, renewable energy.

The prospect of meeting Cole now, months after my mother's death, made me feel guilty, as if I should have taken more interest in her life while she was still living it. However, when I pulled into the CalWind parking lot on that Monday morning in July, I banished all bad thoughts and let myself feel noble, willing to endure the wrath of Vince to write a good book. What I found when I got there was more than I had bargained for.

Outside the wind farm office I encountered a melee. Two protestors held signs that read: "Stop the expansion! Wind farms kill birds and despoil the countryside!!" One of the protestors, a skeletal guy with wild hair, screamed at a handsome man dressed in a crisp white shirt and tan slacks. The other protestor, a portly woman in her early twenties, gaped at her compatriot from a safe distance away. A teenage boy with blonde spiked hair shoved the skinny protestor until he had him up against the trunk of a mesquite tree. At the entrance of the wind farm office hulked a bald giant, who roared at the man in the dress shirt and slacks. Above the cacophony of voices, the desert wind howled.

I stood in the hot sun, the wind buffeting me, rapt. I had walked into the middle of the kind of dispute that lies at the center of my books. Here I was, seeing it firsthand instead of reading about it. Lured by the violent emotions, I strode over to the combatants to find out what was going on.

As I walked up to the group, the handsome, well-dressed man saw me and put out his hand to stop my forward progress. He asked if he could help me, and I explained that I had an appointment to meet with Cole Mintock. His face relaxed when he told me *he* was Cole Mintock. After glancing around at the angry people in his parking lot, he asked if I'd wait in the office for him. I didn't want to, of course, afraid I'd miss something. But disobeying the man would not make him inclined to talk with me later, so I trudged to the office. As I entered the small building, the wind caught the door and slammed it shut on my right heel.

"Shit!"

"Wind's a bitch," a young woman with enormous breasts said to me. She stood at the window overlooking the parking lot, and after a quick glance at me, resumed her study of the commotion outside.

"What's going on out there?" I asked, leaning against a desk so I could inspect my heel for blood. Despite the pain, all parts looked intact. I limped over to the buxom redhead so I could gawk too. A cooler vent in the ceiling above the window blasted me with cold air that reeked of mold.

She popped her gum. Peppermint, by the smell of it. "Those two tree huggers showed up two days ago with their stupid signs. They don't have a clue that we're *for* the environment."

I studied the protestors. The young woman now sat in the shade of the mesquite tree, her sign listing to starboard. Her compatriot shouted and jabbed his index finger into the teenager's chest.

"Who's the kid?" I asked.

"That's Brandon, the boss's son. Ripped, isn't he?" Her right hand traced the top edge of her blouse where it bisected her cleavage. She had to be ten years older than the teen, but the age difference seemed not to ring any alarm bells in her.

"And him?" I pointed to the back of the bald hulk.

"Richard Sampson. He's worse than the tree huggers."

"How so?"

"He doesn't want the wind farm expanded either. Says the turbines would mess up his million-dollar view. He lives up on Pioneer Hill. You know, where all those hoity-toity homes went up. Cole says Richard wants to buy the undeveloped property so he can build another gated community. Guy owns like half of Desert Rock." She turned toward me and patted down her unruly hair.

"I'm Sierra," she said.

"Samantha Larkin. I talked to you on the phone to set up an interview with Cole."

Her red eyebrows shot up. "That was you? The writer? I thought you'd be older."

"Why?"

"Aren't writers always older?" She said without elucidation. "You're not even thirty."

"When's your next eye appointment? I'm thirty-two."

"Well, go figure," she said, glancing out the window again. "Crap! Here comes Cole." She sped to the reception desk, plopped her butt down in the chair, and plucked up a manila folder.

The door banged open, and the wind deposited Cole into the foyer like a tumbleweed. On his heels was the hulk. "Richard," Cole said, trying to shut the door before the big man could enter, "I don't have time now. I have an appointment at ten o'clock."

Richard Sampson inserted his six foot six frame into the doorway, his body blocking the light like an eclipse. "Cole, don't put me off, God damn it! I want to talk to you!"

"You'll just have to wait, Rich. I won't miss an appointment just to talk to you about something that's not up for discussion anyway."

A growl emanated from Sampson's chest. He took a deep breath, his body expanding like a balloon about to burst. His hands contracted into balls at the ends of his four-by-four arms. The cramped office was so quiet I could hear the sand blowing against the walls outside.

Sampson gradually deflated. "Then I'll wait here until you're finished," he said. The big man lowered himself into the spindly metal chair beside Sierra's desk and folded his arms. Sierra looked at him like he was a rattlesnake.

Clearly, I had come at a bad time, and I thought of asking Cole if he wanted to reschedule. But then again the wind farm owner might be glad of an excuse to get away from Sampson. "I'm Sam Larkin, Mr. Mintock," I said, extending my hand.

He turned to me, smiled, and shook my hand. "I know, Olivia's daughter. Come on back." He led the way toward his office at a brisk pace. Before he closed his office door, Cole glanced back at the reception area. Sampson still sat in the chair, his bulk threatening to snap it into scrap metal.

"You picked an interesting day to come," he said, and sat down behind his desk. "My wind plant has suddenly been besieged by people determined to have my head. Can I get you anything? Coffee, tea? Sierra goes to Coffee Buzz every morning and buys out the place."

I sat down in the chair in front of his scarred desk. The mention of caffeine made my heart race in anticipation. Before I could answer (in the double affirmative), Sierra let herself in carrying two humongous paper cups. "Got you a chocolate mocha this time," she said to Cole and set the cup down on the edge of his desk. "And I brought a latte for you," she said to me. "Both hot from the nuker."

"Thanks, Sierra, how could I live without you?" he said, reaching for the cup and taking a swallow. After she left the room and closed the door, he put the cup down and said, "Actually, I prefer plain black coffee, but she seems to enjoy the ritual so much."

Cole looked at me, ran a hand over his beard, and sighed. Then he stared down at his desk. Finally, in a voice strong with emotion, he said, "I can't tell you how sorry I was to hear about your mother. Such a deeply principled woman. She cared so much about the desert, and she'd help anyone in this town who needed it. Before I'd agree to work on a committee, I'd always ask if Olivia was serving on it.

Unlike some, she always did more than her share, and she brought a sense of humor to it all. I admired her more than I can express. Her loss will be felt by so many in this community."

His words, and the intensity with which he spoke them, caught me off guard. I had always known my mother was an activist, of course, but I had viewed her methods in a negative light. I appreciated the fact that she got involved when she saw a problem, but she was ridiculously careful, always working with the powers-that-be to effect change, even if it took forever to get anything done. My mother always said that that was the best approach, for if you paid homage to the system, the stakeholders would be less apt to get defensive and fight you.

This never made any sense to me. The stakeholders *are* the problem. They want to maintain the status quo because it serves their interests. I never had any patience for stroking egos and playing by the rules. If I see an injustice, I fight it in the most direct way possible, even if it means getting people pissed off at me. Even if it means getting into trouble, which I have, more than once. My mother found this appalling.

Hearing Cole praise her made me wonder if I'd misjudged her. Cole's wind farm was proof that her methods could work. A wave of remorse washed over me. I wished we could have come to respect each other before she died, get past all the old arguments. But we never talked about it, and when she died, things between us were exactly the same as they had always been. Talk about the status quo.

Blinking hard, I mumbled "thanks" or something equally stupid and began gulping my latte. What the hell, I'd only had three cups of regular with breakfast.

Cole sat and stared at his cup. During his mental departure, I studied him. He was a tall man, but where Sampson was built thick, Cole was thin, like a runner. His gray beard and hair were neatly trimmed, and he smelled of Dial soap. A plush layer of blondish gray hair covered his arms and poked through the top of his shirt. I pegged him to be about 53. He seemed to feel my gaze and glanced up.

"Thanks for taking the time to see me," I said. "I can see how crazy things are for you at the moment."

Cole smiled and ran his left hand over his beard. He wore a shiny gold wedding band. Either he had just had it polished, or he was recently wed. "Today you are a most welcome distraction." He reached over and picked up the cup again, sniffing at the contents inside. He took a small sip. "And I like the books you write, Samantha."

I gaped at him.

"That's right, I checked you out. Even though you are Olivia's kin. Not many people write intelligent stuff these days. I've had lots of folks want to talk to me so they can write glowing two-dimensional pieces in their newspaper about wind energy, or critics trying to trick me into saying something they can quote as evidence of my naiveté. I don't talk to those people. But I like the way you write. The balanced view. Here are the facts, the pluses, the minuses, use your brain to decide for yourself."

"I can't take credit for the format. I'm a freelance writer for Blue Nest Press. They created the series I write for."

"But you write the books. You won an award for your book on poverty in America."

I nodded.

He leaned back in his chair and brought his hands together into a steeple beneath his chin, the point disappearing into his beard. "I agreed to see you because I knew that you would cover wind energy fairly. It's important to get accurate information out there on wind farms, especially now."

"Why especially now? I would think times are flush for the wind industry. What I read suggests Americans finally believe in an energy crisis and are embracing alternatives."

He glanced toward the window, which looked out onto the parking lot where the skinny protester still argued with Cole's son. "That, ironically, is the crux of the problem. Now that the public and the government endorse alternatives, the number of wind farms has exploded. More wind plants, more people disgruntled with wind plants. It's human nature." He paused, stroking his beard absently.

"Wind was once considered a green energy source," he continued, "and anyone concerned about the environment was behind it. But now the more radical environmentalists are against it. They claim the turbines kill birds and bats, make noise, ruin the landscape. Greens like those two out there don't like modern life. They want to force us all back into caves, but then I suppose they'd have a problem with the campfires. Too much smoke."

I smiled, thinking how much I liked Cole's voice, which hinted at laughter no matter how serious the words. "How did you come to build a wind farm?" I asked.

He raked his beard with the fingers of his right hand. "I always loved animals and the outdoors, and I got interested in protecting the environment in college. My folks died early, and I bought up land with the money I inherited from them, planning to build a trailer park. But then I thought, who needs the hassle of dealing with all those people? Why not do something with a positive impact? So I decided to put my money where my mouth was and use the land to build a wind plant."

"You've always been a proponent of wind energy?"

"Well, no, like most Americans I never gave energy a thought. You flip on a switch and the lights go on. But I've always been an environmentalist, and once I got educated about how fossil fuel use leads to global warming, I got into alternatives. I installed solar panels on my house and bought a hybrid car. Of course, the wind farm is on a far different scale. One large turbine alone cost me over a half million dollars—and they cost even more today."

I set my coffee cup down. A half million dollars for one turbine? Shit, that was a lot of money. "Your wind farm has been here for a while. Why all the fuss now?"

He smiled, exposing white teeth. He was handsome, that's for sure. It was clear where his son got his good looks. "I've been approached by General Electric. They want to lease out the land I haven't developed and install their own turbines."

"Is that typical?"

"Yes, and I'm definitely considering it. Many wind farms start out small like mine, but eventually the big energy companies want a piece of the action. Wind farm owners often keep a small plant for themselves and lease the remaining land to GE or Halliburton or whoever. It's lucrative."

"And that Sampson character? What's his beef with the expansion?"

Cole ran his fingers through his hair so hard I thought he might pull it off. He reached for his coffee, but before drinking any, put the cup down. "Rich says the new turbines would destroy his view of the valley—he lives up on Pioneer Hill. Neither does he want to see the land used for 'namby-pamby' energy projects, to use his words. He's definitely not into clean energy or any other environmental 'clap trap,' as he'd put it. The real issue, in my opinion, is that he'd like to buy the land so he can build another gated community. He's tried to buy it from me for years."

"Do he or the protesters have any legal means of stopping you?"

"My attorney says no."

This information did not seem to bring Cole peace of mind. He pulled at his beard and stared at the desk.

I said, "But in the meantime, they aim to make your life hell."

"Yes, but it's more than that. I'm attached to this community. I don't want people in Desert Rock believing that what I do here harms them. My wind plant supplies Desert Rock with 95 percent of its electricity—without pollution. It saves the community money. It brings in tourists. And just so you know, the turbines kill very few birds and bats—so many more are killed flying into cars and windows. And whatever Rich says, I think the turbines are beautiful. They represent the energy of the future. Most experts predict that oil production will peak around 2050, then decline—fossil fuels are finite, after all. And then what? I think the only intelligent thing to do is develop alternatives now instead of waiting until it's too late. If we don't act now and fossil fuels run out, the economy will crash. Not to mention the adverse affects on the climate. No, we definitely need to act now."

Cole stood up and laughed. "Sorry about the sermon. You've caught me in a sentimental mood. I wish I had more time to talk, but, as you have observed, several disasters require my attention."

I stood also, scooping up my coffee cup. Damned if I'd let perfectly good caffeine go to waste. "I appreciate you taking the time to talk with me."

He escorted me to the door, a gentle hand on my elbow. "Anything for Olivia's family. I look forward to reading your book, Samantha. If I survive that long." He sighed as he opened the door and gestured for Sampson to come in.

When I rushed into Ming's Mandarin Palace, Eddie was already at our favorite booth, located away from the kitchen with its crashing dishes

(Ming's staff—her family—are all thumbs). The sight of Eddie's face, kind and familiar, brought instant relief. Ever since his call this morning, I'd been shaky, the news of Cole's murder hitting me hard.

He was studying the menu—as if we ever ordered anything but the buffet—when I walked up to the booth. "Hey," I said and slid into the seat across the table from him.

He glanced up from the menu. "Whoa. Nice hair."

I could feel my face pulse with heat. I could well imagine what Eddie saw: Hundreds of electrified tendrils standing out from my head like Medusa's serpents. The dry desert air left everything—blankets, televisions, pets—with enough static electricity to start a stopped heart. Not to mention the wind, which demolished any styling efforts you made within seconds. Though embarrassed, I appreciated his jibe—it made me feel less edgy. Being in the familiar restaurant with him, going through our usual routine, had settled me.

"Nice hair yourself," I muttered and tossed my battered purse into the corner of the booth. "I thought white-walls were out."

Eddie ran a hand up one side of his head and then down the other. "Just clipped. It'll grow."

I would never have admitted it to him, but his hair looked good. He kept it short on the sides and longer on the top, where his thick dark curls showed to best effect. He wore a goatee these days and long sideburns. The look was out of keeping with the man, who was as conventional as it gets. Eddie wore the standard brown "Coffee Buzz" T-shirt that he and his employees wear at his coffee house, only he looked a lot better in it than Mike and Sonia, who together top out at over four hundred pounds. Eddie isn't a tall guy, but he is strong and fit, and the T-shirt clung to his shoulders and chest invitingly.

"Eduardo!" Ming called out as she marched over to our table, order pad in hand. "What you want today?" she asked him with a big smile, grabbing the menu out of his hands. She ignored me, as always. Ming thinks Eddie would be a perfect match for her daughter, Pam, and she's so saccharine whenever we come in it could make you barf. "Buffet, no menu, right?"

"Right," he said and grinned at me. "And two iced teas."

I kicked him under the table. He knows how I hate when men order for me. We got up and filled our plates with the best Chinese food I've eaten anywhere. Ming makes a delicious broccoli beef, but I spooned on the moo shu pork, cashew chicken, and egg foo yung, too.

Once we were seated again, Eddie said, "I'm sorry about the phone call. I didn't think Mintock's death would affect you so much."

"Better a call from you than reading it in the paper."

"Wasn't your interview the first time you'd met him?"

Meaning, why would I get so upset after just one encounter with the man. I nodded. "But he and my mother were acquaintances from way back. I knew that when I asked to interview him, but I didn't realize how strong their feelings were for one another."

"You don't mean—"

"No, nothing like that. I mean they admired one another. Deeply, it seems. They worked on committees together to protect the desert, had done so for years. I had heard her praise Cole all my life. I knew she liked to work with him, but I didn't think much about it. Anyway, the first thing Cole said in the interview was how much he admired my mom. He praised her to the skies, as if she were some kind of saint or something."

"And?"

"I don't know. It just affected me somehow."

"I'm sure it felt good to hear good things about your mom."

I shook my head. "It wasn't like that. I mean, I guess it was a little. Part of me felt proud of her, I guess. That's hard to admit, given how I always looked down on the way she went about things. But mostly I felt bad that she and I never made our peace with one another, that we never tried to respect our differences. Oh, bah!" I waved my hand dismissively. "It doesn't matter. It's all water under the bridge now."

"You sure about that?"

His questions were starting to annoy me. I changed the subject. "Tell me what you know about Cole's murder. I never even opened the paper."

He said, "The article reported that Cole was found early yesterday morning by one of the turbine maintenance crews. They smelled the corpse while driving by on a routine maintenance run. The coroner figures he'd been dead a week, given the extent of decay, which means he died a day or two after you interviewed him. The unofficial theory is that the murderer knocked Cole unconscious, then dragged him inside the turbine and locked him in. Even if Cole regained consciousness, it wouldn't have been for long. The heat inside that tower would have to be well over a hundred and fifty degrees by noon. He probably cooked to death."

This was more than Eddie usually says during an entire day. I shivered. Poor Cole. "Do they have any suspects?"

He nodded. "Yeah, environmentalist, guy by the name of Luke Lewis. Been out protesting Cole's wind farm expansion."

My fork fell from my fingers and clattered onto my plate. Other diners turned to stare. "That skinny protestor? I saw him outside Cole's office the day I went there. Tall, emaciated guy with crazy hair. He was pretty exercised, yelling at Cole about dead birds and unsustainable lifestyles and whatnot. Cole wouldn't engage him, but the guy did get into it with Cole's son. Still, I can't see why an environmentalist would kill Cole. Cole's an environmentalist, for crying out loud. It doesn't make sense."

Eddie forked a mouthful of cashew chicken into his mouth, chewed, swallowed. "According to the article, the FBI—can you believe the FBI is involved in this? The Department of Homeland Security, too. It's because it's a possible terrorist act, I guess. Anyway, the FBI thinks Lewis works for the Environmental Liberation Front. ELF, as the article called it, is responsible for several environmental terrorist acts across the United States in the last decade. Especially out here in the West. The article said it was ELF that torched that ski resort in Vail, and they've burned up some SUVs and houses under construction."

I shrugged. "I know about ELF from some of the books I've written. I grant they're extreme, but killing people has never been their style. From what I've read, they're careful to make sure no people are in the area when they act. Besides, I can't see a wind farm being a likely target. They've hit obvious symbols of environmental destruction. Wind is still associated with environmentalism, despite some greens' problem with it."

"You're saying that in your opinion this guy's possible affiliation with a terrorist group actually clears him of the murder."

I blinked. "That doesn't sound like such a smart theory, does it?"

He shrugged and tucked into his broccoli beef.

"If it were me investigating the case," I said, watching Eddie chew, "I'd be going after someone else. While I was out at the wind farm I saw this guy who seems a lot more likely to kill someone than that scrawny environmentalist."

"Who's that?"

"Guy named Richard Sampson."

"I've heard of him. Big developer."

"True in more ways than one. You wouldn't believe how big he is—almost seven feet tall and big as a barn. Now there's a guy capable of knocking someone cold and stuffing him into a turbine."

"Why would he do that?"

"He's angry that Cole is—was—thinking about expanding the wind farm. Sampson says the new turbines would destroy his view—he lives on Pioneer Hill—and lower his property's value. But his main concern, according to what Cole said, is that he wants to buy that land himself to build another gated community like Pioneer Hill."

"That's what we need, another development in the desert."

"But the point is, the guy has a motive. Why aren't the sheriff's detectives looking at him?"

"Who says they aren't?"

"The article you read didn't say anything about it."

"Doesn't mean they're not. Cops don't report everything to the media."

I took a sip of iced tea and moved water chestnuts around on my plate with Ming's oversized fork. "I'm going to do a little research on ELF and see what they've been up to lately. Been a year or so since I wrote my last environment book. Maybe see if I can talk to the Sampson dude, too, see what he's all about."

Eddie put his fork down and stared at me. "You're not thinking about getting involved in this?"

Back in the kitchen, Ming's family crashed plates together. The pungent odor of ginger and garlic that had smelled so good when I had walked into the restaurant suffocated me now that I had grazed the buffet. Luckily, the air conditioner was cranked to maximum, driving frigid air down on me, keeping the nausea at bay. It was so cold in the restaurant the Naugahyde seat threatened to crack like pack ice under my butt.

"I just want to find out more," I said. "Cole was my mom's friend. She would be outraged that he was murdered. *I'm* outraged that he was murdered."

"Who wouldn't be, Sam? That doesn't mean we should all drop what we're doing and go off investigating this."

I shoved my plate away and sat back in the booth. "You don't understand."

"I guess I don't."

"Look, you didn't know Cole. He saw the country moving toward an environmental and energy crisis, and he did something about it. He put all his money, his life, into the wind farm. He wanted to make a difference. Now someone has snuffed him out, stuffed him in his own turbine, mocked his ideals. And instead of trying to find the psycho who did this, the FBI wants to implicate another environmentalist. It's just wrong on so many levels."

Eddie shook his head vigorously. "Here we go again. Samantha Larkin, righter of wrongs, coming to the rescue. Do you remember the time in high school when you got suspended for punching the captain of the football team—what was his name? Mark somebody— for harassing Hispanic students? Need me to supply more examples? I've got lots to choose from."

I felt myself go still. My face felt hot. That was exactly the kind of stunt that my mother had deplored. She claimed that I reacted without thinking, flailing away in rage the minute I saw a wrongdoing. She was fond of saying that my heart was in the right place, it was my brain that was hard to locate. I remembered well the incident Eddie mentioned, one of many that got me in trouble in school. I recalled how mortified my mom was to have to go talk to the principle about me, especially given that she was a teacher at the same school.

To my surprise, as I thought of how my mother would react to Cole's death—the same way I had, with outrage—I realized that my mom and I shared a common sensibility, even if we did act on our feelings in radically different ways. A vague sense of understanding and connection tingled through me.

In the distance, I heard Eddie say, "Law enforcement, not you, is responsible for this case."

I started to speak but he uncharacteristically cut me off. "You have a deadline to meet. You could get fired. You could get killed. Murderers don't like busybodies."

"Busybodies!"

"All I'm saying is that you should just focus on writing your book. Vince isn't going to put up with missed deadlines forever, Sam. You love your job. I'd hate to see you lose it."

"Eddie," I said before he could go on chastising me. "I met Cole, I was right there in the room with him. I don't know why, but I know as clearly as I've known anything that my mother would not want Cole's murderer to go free."

"How do you know what she would have wanted? It's not like you two were ever on the same page."

"No, you're wrong, we were, I just never realized it before."

He stared at me and shook his head as if he had water in his ears. "She would never have approved of you getting involved in police business."

"Maybe," I said. "But she would want to see justice done. I'm going to see what I can find out. That's all."

Eddie sighed. "I worry about you sometimes."

"Who doesn't?" I said, feeling glad he cared that much.

Chapter Two

The day after I learned of Cole's death, I climbed aboard a bus with seven tourists from out of town for a tour of the wind farm. The tour company, I found out, was not affiliated with Cole's wind plant. It was a separate entity, providing tours of Desert Rock "attractions" to those suckered by the city's Web site, which promises tourists a "unique desert experience." Nothing unique about sweltering heat and thirty-mile-an-hour winds, in my view, but I'm no marketing guru. Without official sanction to be on wind farm property, the grizzled old tour guide merely drove around the perimeter of the farm and pointed out features only visible with high-powered binoculars. His canned lecture was a recap of facts anyone could find on the Web, plus a sprinkling of uninformed opinions (his). The bus had no air conditioning, and I was half-dead when the guide finally stopped to let us out for air. The hot wind blew the skinny tourists into a pile by the chain link fence like so many sticks.

As I stood near the fence, I could see why Cole felt sentimental about his wind farm, and why my mother had endorsed it. The air around the farm was pristine, no smokestacks, no grimy soot, just column after column of graceful towers receding into the distance. I heard a rhythmic swishing sound from the turning blades, but the pulsing noise merely blended with the whoosh of the wind across the desert floor. The turbines rose hundreds of feet into the air, their white blades whirling against the blue sky. They looked human, as if hundreds of white-robed supplicants had thrown their arms up to God.

I turned my attention to the turbine I stood under. Gazing up at its height, I realized how gargantuan the turbines were. This one had to be over two hundred feet tall. I felt tiny beside it. Then, as I gaped up at it, the tower's head rotated toward me, a growl emanating from its bowels. I jumped.

The tour guide chuckled. "That's the computer telling the blades to move into the wind for maximum power," he said. "Each turbine has a computer that reads the direction and velocity of the wind so that the blades can always be kept in an optimal position."

After imparting this factoid, he herded us back into the hot bus and continued with his explanation of turbine computers. I quit listening to him. Instead, I looked up at the turbine, thinking how good it would be to get home, take a cool shower, drink a gallon of cold water. Call Eddie. Or not. Eddie didn't like my field research any more than my boss did, claiming that it would get me fired one day. To hell with them (well, to hell with Vince). I decided to call Sierra at CalWind to find out how I could get a better tour of the wind farm. So what if I burned another day I could have spent writing? Sue me.

When I pulled up to my house after the wind farm tour, I cursed. My sister's white Mercedes SUV was parked out front.

I found Vanessa eating a sandwich at the kitchen table, Lacy hovering at her elbow. On the counter Vanessa had arranged packages of deli meats, cartons of potato salad, and jars of pickles, mustard, and mayonnaise. The house reeked of pastrami and brine and Vanessa's Ralph Lauren perfume.

"I brought food for lunch," she said with a sniff. "But you weren't here."

"Next time, be sure to let yourself in and make yourself at home," I said and tossed my purse on the counter. I flopped into a kitchen chair.

She exposed the tips of her clinically whitened teeth. I took it as an effort to smile. She said, "Where were you?"

None of your damn business, I thought, wondering if she had brought any of Mike's Deli's scrumptious chocolate chip macadamia nut cookies. I said, "Out doing research for my book."

She muttered something disinterestedly, then said, looking over the tops of her eyes, "See Eddie lately?" Vanessa likes Eddie despite the fact that he never got a college degree. She views him as my last hope for marrying someone decent, or, let's face it, for marrying, period. "How is that handsome man?"

"What are you doing here?" I said, changing the subject. I was not going to discuss my marital prospects with her or anyone. I rose to search for the cookies.

"Just a friendly sisterly visit. I had a thought this morning at breakfast that it would be fun to have lunch together."

Yeah right. Vanessa never does anything spontaneous. She had written this "sisterly visit" on her calendar weeks before, scheduled so as not to conflict with her dye job and massage at Le Tete Salon and Day Spa and her tee time at the Desert Rock Country Club. Besides which I knew from long experience that "friendly" and "fun" were ludicrous descriptions of our face time.

As I was making my way to the kitchen, I stumbled over a flip-flop. Looking down I discovered that Lacy, the Rottweiler mutt I had inherited from my mother, had chewed up two of the flip-flops I had just purchased from Oases Shop 'N Save. Not from the same pair, naturally, but one shoe from one pair, and another from another pair (both lefts). I would like to say that I laughed, that I tossed the two intact right shoes to the eighty-pound adolescent to play with, that I thought how nice it was to have a warm body share the house. But I did not. I began to plot ways to get Lacy out of my life.

After glaring at the beast with no apparent effect, I asked Vanessa without enthusiasm, "How are the girls?" Vanessa's two young daughters, Molly and Kaylee, are more terrible than the flu.

Vanessa answered, "I'm tearing my hair out as usual."

I gave her points for not being one of those parents who remain blind to their kids' faults. The only thing Vanessa seemed ignorant of concerning her children was where their obnoxious behavior originated. It didn't come from their father, Thomas, who was serene and unassuming, especially for an attorney. Anyone could see that Molly's and Kaylee's dispositions came straight from my sister. Ha. Served her right.

"Want coffee?" I asked, digging through my disorganized cupboards for a coffee filter. Mom would have been appalled to see her cabinets reduced to such a state.

"Coffee! It's one o'clock in the afternoon!"

"Sorry, didn't realize there was a town coffee ordinance." I poured the beans into the grinder and pressed down hard on the lid, drowning out whatever she said in response.

I heard her saying when the grinder stopped, "I do want to talk to you."

Here it is, I thought. Another sermon, and the real reason she'd come. I found the cookies at the bottom of the deli bag and rummaged through them, staring at the back of Vanessa's head. Her thick sable hair gleamed. People say we look alike, especially our hair, but I know for a fact that those red highlights are put there by a stylist's hand. Mine are natural. Besides, I could never compete with her on the hair level. Hers has always been a sculpture worthy of the Louvre, with enough moose and gel and spray in it to weather even the fiercest winds.

I poured milk into the bottoms of two cups and then filled them with coffee. When I set the mugs down on the table with the cookies, Vanessa's be-ringed hand shot out and grasped a cup handle like a drunk reaching for his first drink of the day.

"I want to talk about you living here," she said and took an unlady-like gulp.

"What's the problem? I bought you and Connor out when Mom died."

"I'm not talking about ownership," she said like I was stupid. "I mean your living here. In Mom's house. In Desert Rock."

"Oh good, my own GPS system."

"I mean, why? You had a life in San Diego. Mom's dead, and your living here will not bring her back."

I put down my coffee cup. "Really? When the séances failed, I felt sure living here would work."

Vanessa sighed, the air rushing out of her nose forcefully enough to rattle the cookie bag on the table. She tapped her red enameled nails on the Formica tabletop and wiggled around in her chair like an antsy toddler. "Go ahead and make your little jokes. I have the perspective as your older sister, and as the one closest to Mom, to see what you are doing. When she died, she left you with all this guilt. But, Sam, picking up her life is not going to work. You've got to forgive yourself and move on."

Against my will, I bit. "Forgive myself? For what?"

"Oh come on! For making her tear her hair out your whole life."

"I don't think she thought I was that bad," I lied defensively.

"Then why are you here?"

I yanked an elastic hair band out of my pocket and pulled my hair back into a ponytail. I was furious with myself for allowing the discussion to get this far, but I couldn't help it. I felt emotion rise in my veins like lava. "Did you ever think I might like it here? You live in Desert Rock, obviously you like it here! And how dare you comment on my life. You don't know anything about me. You have no idea how Mom's death has affected me. Living here is getting me through this." I regretted letting anger give way to sentiment. It made me vulnerable, gave her cracks to probe.

"But Mom's gone! This is just a house now!"

"Well, it's home to me, damn it!" I lurched up from the table, spilling coffee and knocking Lacy away with my knee. I stomped over to the sink where I could look out the window. The wind bent the trees and jangled the wind chimes. It blew down the stovetop exhaust vent, forcing the damper open and closed with a clanking sound I always associate with home.

"Poor little puppy," Vanessa cooed to Lacy and fed the eighty-pound beast the rest of her cookie. Lacy nibbled the morsel out of Vanessa's hand, then turned her body sideways and leaned into my sister's knees. The year-old puppy grunted and whined as Vanessa scratched her all over with those long fingernails. Lacy's hair fell out like pine needles from an exhausted Christmas tree, coating Vanessa's Versace capris and matching silk top. Vanessa didn't mind—she was like Mrs. Doolittle on steroids. "You need to give this poor dog some love," she said to me.

I gave my eyes a good roll and looked up at the ceiling for deliverance. Then I opened the refrigerator and grabbed a beer.

Later that day, as the sun set and the wind died down and the air cooled, I sat outside on the patio and sipped a scotch over rocks. Lacy heaved her body onto the pavement beside me and sighed, apparently wishing Vanessa had stayed and I had driven off in the white Mercedes. Glancing around the yard, which looked increasingly like one of those empty lots in the center of town where paper bags and druggies collect on windy days, I vowed to call a gardener. I couldn't bear to see all Mom's hard work go to pot, and I had no green thumb. Plants withered on the vine when I looked at them just to save me the trouble. Even after Mom grew ill, she'd come out here and clip a branch or pull a couple of weeds. I don't know how she had the strength to even bend over, but it seemed to revive her, if only for an hour or two.

And then she wound up in bed, unable to get up those last few days to use the toilet. She stopped eating. I was glad she could die at home with hospice helping out—she had been adamant about not going to the hospital—but so much fell on us, on Vanessa and Connor and me, because the hospice nurses and aides could not be there all the time. We tried. Despite her screams we turned her to prevent bed sores, we swabbed her cracked dry lips with Listerine and water, we tried not to cry in front of her so that she'd know we'd be alright, that she could go. But it was not enough. She suffered so, the pain of the cancer all she knew at the end. She fell into a coma, but even then she still cried out with every jagged breath, especially at night. I didn't sleep for five days. We kept feeling her arms and legs and feet to see how cold they had gotten, to learn by touch when her pain would end. Then, finally.

I placed my hand on Lacy's warm fur, felt her rib cage rise and fall with every breath. I left my hand there a long time.

Chapter Three

I forced myself to get out of bed at four in the morning in order to get some writing done before heading out to the wind farm. At the very least, I needed to complete the outline and first chapter so I could mail them to Vince. He'd approve the items as he always does and assume I'm further along than I really am, as usual. I'd discovered that as long as I keep sending pieces to him, he pretty much leaves me alone. Well, until the deadline comes up and he realizes he doesn't have the entire book. Then he calls me and throws a tantrum that cannot be believed.

Even after I slugged back three cups of coffee you could chew, the work went slowly. My mind kept going back to Vanessa's visit yesterday and her allegation that I was living in Mom's house to expiate my guilt. What a meddlesome, pompous ass. Forget Vanessa, I told myself, and just write.

Around nine o'clock, I showered, ate a bowl of stale corn flakes, and reviewed my strategy for the day. Late yesterday, I had called the wind farm and given my condolences to Sierra. She talked about how much she had liked her boss, and how she still couldn't believe he'd been murdered. I told her I felt the same way. Before we hung up, I asked her how I could get a more useful tour of the plant. She recommended that I call Donald Van Dorn, the foreman at Mill Maintenance, the firm Cole contracted with to maintain and repair his turbines. When I called Van Dorn and explained what I needed, he said, "If you can get your butt here by eleven tomorrow, I'll give you a tour." This ought to be fun, I thought.

I decided to stop by the wind farm office before driving to Mill Maintenance. I wanted to talk to Sierra to see what the fallout of the murder had been there, and to learn if the Sheriff's Department had any more suspects. I had been disappointed that Cole's family had not held a funeral service and reception, as that would have been a perfect occasion to observe those closest to Cole. But his obituary explained that a small celebration of life would be held only for family and close friends. At this point, the one tie I had to the case was Sierra. To prime the pump, I bought a box of donuts to go with the Coffee Buzz coffees I was sure she would have bought this morning out of habit, even with Cole gone.

Climbing out of my car in the wind farm parking lot, I was disappointed but not surprised to see that the protestors were nowhere in sight. I had hoped to talk to Luke Lewis. I wondered whether he had made himself scarce or whether the Sheriff's Department had taken him into custody. This morning's paper ran a short follow-up to yesterday's announcement of the murder, which covered the history of CalWind, but it made no mention of Lewis.

The article explained that CalWind generates enough electricity to power the city of Desert Rock, population forty thousand, at least when the wind is blowing, which, according to the piece, blows over three hundred days a year at the farm. The wind farm site is located at the terminus of Thomas Pass, which is flanked by Mt. Barton to the south and Smyth Peak to the north. According to the article, the cooler air from Southern California's coast flows in to replace the hot, rising air of the desert. Thomas Pass acts as a kind of nozzle, squeezing the east-flowing air between the mountains, increasing the wind's velocity. Cole's plant was built where it needed to be to get the most out of the wind as it rushes out onto the desert floor.

The article reported that CalWind was built in the early 1980s, after the great oil embargo. U.S. support of Israel in the Yom Kippur war pissed off Middle East oil suppliers, who retaliated by reducing their supply of crude oil to America. The result was an astronomical rise in gas prices and long waits at the pump. The economy plummeted.

My mother used to talk a lot about that time because it inspired her to get involved in the alternative energy movement. It was during that period when she and Cole met. They worked together to help get legislation passed that would encourage the development of alternative energy sources. Their local representatives and state senators were receptive to the idea, eager to avoid having a similar chain of events occur on their watch in the future. Congress eventually passed bills to encourage the development of alternative transportation fuels so that the nation would never again be at the mercy of unpredictable foreign oil suppliers.

My mother had been thrilled when the legislation passed, of course, but she still wasn't satisfied. The oil embargo made clear that reliance on one type of energy for transportation was foolhardy. By the same logic, it wasn't wise to count on unlimited supplies of coal and natural gas—which generate most of America's electricity—either. She and Cole and others in the alternative energy movement continued to press their representatives for even broader energy bills. As a result, the federal government wrote new energy bills expansively enough to spark investment in the development of geothermal, solar, and wind energy. These energy sources can be used instead of coal and natural gas—both finite fossil fuels that pollute when used—to generate the electricity needed to watch reruns of *Friends*, play computer games, and get money from ATMs.

Unfortunately, once the embargo faded from memory and oil prices dropped, the commitment to diversify lessened. I knew from the research I'd done for my book that the United States imports over half of its oil today, and alternatives provide just a fraction of the nation's fuel and electricity. However, interest in alternatives has increased in recent years. The September 11, 2001, terrorist attacks, which again pointed up America's vulnerability to the vagaries of unstable Middle Eastern nations, helped jumpstart this renewed interest. As a result, investment in wind energy has increased. While wind generated only around 2 percent of the nation's electricity in 2010, the industry is growing. And, as Cole confirmed, the big energy players are getting into the game as well.

Cole got into the business when interest first peaked, weathered the bleak times, and made a fortune by staying in the game. His wind farm today produces somewhere around 300 megawatts of electricity, but if expanded by GE and other energy companies, it could grow to 900 megawatts or more, enough to power a city the size of San Francisco and still have some electricity left over. I had no idea how much GE would pay Cole to lease his land, but the price had to be steep. No wonder he thought of expanding. For him, it must have seemed like a win-win proposition. Not only would he benefit financially, he would also help wind energy grow. Having met the man and witnessed his passion for wind power, I was sure he cared more about keeping the United States energy independent and protecting the climate than about making more money.

Was Cole murdered because someone out there was less thrilled than he about the expansion? It looked that way. Last time I was at the wind farm, I encountered two people, Luke Lewis and Richard Sampson, who had an obvious stake in stopping it. The fact that Cole's body was found inside one of his wind turbines suggested that his murderer wanted to make a statement about wind power in general or the wind plant in particular. Then a thought struck me. What if that was just a decoy, a way to point law enforcement in the wrong direction? What if Cole's murder had nothing at all to do with the wind farm? One of the things I learned while writing several books on crime is that most murders are committed for personal reasons by people known to the victim. Someone who murdered Cole because of some personal issue might have locked him in his turbine as a way to implicate Lewis, thereby calling attention away from him or herself.

I still could not believe Cole had been killed. He had seemed such a thoughtful, decent man. I found myself wondering, If Cole could be murdered, why not anyone, even me? But, no, that wasn't right. I didn't believe there was a murderer running around Desert Rock ready to off anyone who stepped across his or her path. Cole had been killed for a reason. Someone with something to gain or an axe to grind—someone Cole knew, and perhaps trusted—had murdered him. I didn't believe it was Luke Lewis, and the fact that the authorities were focusing on the environmentalist frustrated me. If they'd just step back and take their blinders off, they'd see as clearly as I did that Lewis was an unlikely suspect. Even if they could prove he was affiliated with ELF—and I wasn't convinced of the connection because his methods were so un-ELF-like—Lewis would still make a lousy suspect. I knew from researching numerous books on environmental issues that environmentalists simply do not make a habit out of killing people. Extreme greens sabotage and vandalize, but they draw the line at murder. Yet the FBI persists in calling ELF a terrorist group. Law enforcement's focus on Lewis was wrongheaded in the extreme.

Instead of spinning these hypotheses, I knew I should write, spend my energies getting caught up, try to meet a deadline for once in my life. But the case had begun to absorb my emotional and intellectual energies. I wanted to know—no, I needed to know—what occurred before that fateful day at the wind farm that had sealed Cole's fate.

When I entered the wind farm office, I held the door so the wind wouldn't drive it into my heel again. This was easier said than done while holding a box of donuts weakened in the middle by cruller grease. As I struggled to hold the door against the gusts, my purse sliding down my arm and car keys jangling from my right hand, I dropped the box, which landed upside down on the brown carpeting.

"Shit!"

"Wind's a bitch," Sierra said and sauntered over to me, her pendulous breasts swinging from side to side. "You sure know how to make an entrance."

"Ever the ballerina," I said, recovering my poise. "I wanted to bring you something that might brighten your day a bit. I imagine it's been tough around here."

Sierra nodded, then frowned. "It's hard without Cole here." With a sigh, she grabbed the pink box off the floor, righted it, and glanced inside. While she inspected the contents, I noticed that she was not alone. The young man with spiked blonde hair whom I had seen arguing with Lewis on my first visit sat in the chair behind her desk. Cole's son. He had his feet propped up on the desktop, his hands behind his head, watching us. Close up, I could see his resemblance to his father, the thick hair covering his arms, the blue eyes, the tall, slender build. But whereas Cole looked like a marathoner, long and sinewy, Brandon was built like a tight end, lithe enough to run deep routes, powerful enough to block beefy lineman. He was more handsome than Cole, but his face looked less kind. Perhaps it was the effect of the gel-spiked hair, which made his features look sharp and angular. I looked for signs of grief, but he appeared unaffected. Either he was trying hard to be stoic, or the reality of his father's death hadn't hit yet. He noticed me appraising him, and leapt to his feet.

"Brandon Mintock," he said, sauntering over to me. He stood too close, his body heat wafting over me. I had the impression that he adopted this posture so I could appreciate his impressive height. He looked me over, no glint of apology in his blue eyes. His gaze lingered on my breasts, which was my first clue that this was all an act. I am what high school boys refer to as a pirate's dream—equipped with a sunken chest. I suspected his leer was part of a repertoire of ridiculous behaviors intended to get a reaction. I had forgotten how absurd adolescence is. Despite his attempt to act like a middle-aged construction worker, I put his age at about sixteen.

"I'm Sam Larkin," I said to him, ignoring the act. "I'm so sorry about your father." I had the urge to tell him I knew how hard it is—that I recently lost my mother, and that my father died years ago, but I didn't. I found when people said similar things to me after my mother died, I felt angry. How dare they imply that they knew how I felt? My mother was unique, her death a loss to me they could never understand. Their comment made her death seem just part of the normal thinning of human lives.

"Thanks," he said and looked down at the soiled carpet. He was obviously more comfortable engaging in fun and pranks than he was dealing with serious emotions. At his age, who could blame him? Grief was going to be a long and painful process for him.

Brandon turned to Sierra, who still inspected the donut box. "You going to hoard those donuts, or what?" he said, striding over and grabbing the box from her hands.

Sierra giggled and socked him in the arm. Brandon obviously made her forget all about her grief. "Give 'em back."

"Ha!" he said and moved out of her reach.

She clomped after him in her chunky shoes, grabbing for the box. "Brannn-don!"

He swooped the box down around his thighs, forcing her to lunge downwards, exposing her Grand Canyon cleavage. His attention plunged down into its depths like a touring helicopter getting up close to the sights. When she threatened to get the box away from him, the teen pulled it away and held it above her wiry red hair. She leapt up to grab it, nearly snapping her ankles when her heavy shoes reconnected with the floor.

He wagged a finger at her. "No, no, no, these are not for you!"

"Actually—" I started to say but was interrupted by the arrival of a new person.

The appearance of a middle-aged woman from the back of the office froze Brandon and Sierra. "What's going on out here?" the woman said, her voice tight.

Sierra and Brandon looked like two six-year-olds caught playing in mud. I said, "I brought donuts, and—"

"Who are you?"

Not much for small talk, I noticed, my acute perception extra sharp today.

"I'm Sam Larkin. I'm working on a book about wind power—"

"We have no time for that, now," she said and waved her hand at me like a magic wand hoping to make me disappear. Her steel gray eyes, magnified by thick, wireless glasses, focused on me as if I were a rabbit and she a bird of prey. "The owner of this company just died. We don't have time to chat with reporters about windmills. And I for one am not in the mood for frivolous games." She glared at Brandon, Sierra, and me, but particularly at Brandon. I was now in the mud with the two errant tots. I felt the urge to inform her that I was not a reporter, but my brilliant mind reasoned that that was not a great idea.

"Please leave," she said to me. "Brandon, pick up the work orders and leave. I've talked to you a hundred times about interfering with Sierra's work. Sierra, I want to talk to you. In my office."

Before any of these orders could be carried out, another woman emerged from the same office. She was a tall, slender blonde in her late forties. She walked like a model, one foot placed in front of the other with care. No extraneous movements disrupted the perfect angle of her head. When I looked at her I thought of Nordic ski slopes and parkas and hot rum. She said to the owlish older woman, "Diana, I have to go and open up my shop. We'll have to continue this at another time."

Diana quit glaring at us and turned to smile at the blonde. She said, "Of course, Jillian, whenever it's convenient."

Jillian turned to stare at Brandon. "Brandon, soon you and I will have to sit down and discuss the terms of the trust." Her voice was flat and cold and very tense.

His face transformed. From a humble, guilty expression, his features now showed resentment, even rage. His brow drew down low, narrowing his eyes to slits. His jaw clamped shut, the jaw muscles bulging. He held his body still, all mischievous energy now coiled inside like a snake. He scowled at the woman but did not speak to her.

"Very well," she said. Nodding to Diana, she opened the exterior door and glided out into the wind.

Sierra glanced at Brandon and me with big hazel eyes, and then followed Diana to her office. Brandon pitched the donut box down on Sierra's desk, grabbed the pile of papers from her out box, and stomped toward the door. I followed him out.

The wind hit us, nearly ripping the sheaf of papers from his hand. "I feel like that was my fault," I said, trying to maintain contact with him. "If I hadn't brought the donuts—"

"It would have been something else. Don't worry about it. She's just a bitch."

"Which one?" I asked, seeing he disliked both women.

"Take your pick."

"Is Diana the office manager?"

"Yeah, sort of. She does the books. Been with my Dad for years."

"What about the other woman, Jillian?"

Brandon stopped. "What are you? The FBI?" His face was taut, his eyes hard.

I backed off. "You're right, I'm sorry. It's rude of me to drill you with questions when you're clearly upset. I'm too curious for my own good."

His expression shifted. Instead of angry, he now looked sad. He said, "Sorry. Ever since my Dad died, I've been on the edge. And seeing my Dad's wife doesn't help matters."

"You mean Jillian?"

He nodded.

"She's not your mother."

"Fuck, no! My mother died six months ago." He stared down at the stack of papers in his hand as if he did not recognize them.

Shit, I thought. His mom, and now his dad. Within six months of each other. And his dad remarrying so soon after his mother's death. This was all news to me, and I felt off-balance. Would this change the way I viewed Cole? Standing in the parking lot, buffeted by the wind, I became aware of Brandon's brittleness, his raw pain. "I'm sorry," I said, and even though I hadn't planned to, I added, "My Dad died years ago. I just lost my Mom. I kind of know what you're going through."

He eyed me, strong emotions I couldn't read making the muscles jump in his face. After a beat, he asked in a dull voice, "What did they die of?"

"Dad, heart attack. Mom, cancer."

"That sucks," he said and shrugged.

"Yeah."

Brandon rattled the papers in his hand, said, "Well, I gotta go. I was supposed to be back at Mill Maintenance a half hour ago."

"I'm going there too. Can I follow you over?"

He grunted his assent.

Chapter Four

I followed Brandon's white Ford truck for about a half mile down the highway from the wind farm, then onto a dirt road. Dust billowed up behind his truck, making it hard to see, so I just followed the cloud and hoped I wouldn't tear a hole in my car's undercarriage. When we pulled up to Mill Maintenance ten minutes later, I was relieved.

"Thanks for leading the way, Brandon," I said as we exited our vehicles.

"No worries," he said cheerfully, as if we'd not just talked about our parents dying.

"Have to work the whole day today?"

"I started today at five. My boss said I could have time off, and my grandma says I should, but I can't see the point. Who wants to just sit around and mope?"

"Are you staying with your grandmother now?"

"I live with her. I've been living with her ever since my mom died."

Interesting. Some major discord between father and son. Or, maybe it was just that he refused to live with his step-mom. "So, what do you do for Mill Maintenance?"

He walked toward a fenced yard filled with what I took to be turbine parts. Near the fence I saw a stack of some twenty white objects about one hundred feet long. I realized with a jolt that they were turbine blades. The blades didn't look that big when mounted up on the towers.

Brandon said, "The main thing I do is climb up inside the turbines and do maintenance on the motors."

"Inside the turbine?"

"Yeah, those mothers are hollow," he pointed to a row of turbines to the left of our location. "There's a metal ladder inside. The guys pulley me up the tools and parts I need."

"Doesn't it get hot in there?"

"Shit yeah. Well, in the tower it is. Up above, in the nacelle, the temp is controlled. Anyway, it's a freaking long climb through the tower, so we try to get the bulk of the work done first thing in the morning, while its still cool. Well, sort of. Any longer and you cook—"

We glanced at each other. That's how his dad had died. "Well," he said, the cheer completely gone from his voice. "I gotta get back to work."

"Before you go, where can I find Donald Van Dorn? He's supposed to give me a tour."

"He's probably in the office," Brandon nodded toward a small concrete block building about a hundred feet from the yard. "Donald's okay, but if you want the real experience, I'll take you inside one of those things." He grinned, the playful adolescent returning. His flip-flopping emotions were hard to keep up with. I understood. When you can't handle what you're feeling, you just pretend the emotions don't exist, that you feel fine. Whenever the pain breaks through, you just smile harder. Or maybe you yell at someone or crack a joke. Anything rather than feel it.

I thought about his offer to take me inside one of the turbines. Get into a narrow metal tube with no windows? Willingly? I can't even ride in an elevator without hyperventilating. "Uh, I'll think about it," I lied. "See you around."

Van Dorn had the roundest belly I had seen since experiencing Buddha overload during a pleasure trip to Thailand three years ago. Any further similarity to the pacifist seer ended with the gut. Van Dorn's black eyes glared at me above a bulbous nose and grizzled beard. His long, gray hair was pulled back into a ponytail, which hung midway down his back. I noticed his teeth were crooked and slightly yellow.

"Who?" He barked at me when I introduced myself in his office.

"Sam Larkin. I talked to you on the phone yesterday about getting a tour of the wind farm. Sierra at CalWind said I should call you."

Once my words sunk in, his look softened, and he smiled, his mouth opening up like a road in his thick forest of beard. "Well, why didn't you say so, Sam Larkin? People coming in and out of here all day, with this problem and that problem. Drives me up the wall! I'm Don Van Dorn."

He shook my hand so hard I heard my elbow pop. Then the whirlwind tour began. First he marched me out to the yard where I had seen all the turbine parts. He pointed out rotors and blades and hubs and bolts and other parts I can't remember the names of. The stuff on the ground bore little resemblance to the graceful giants spread out before me in every direction. Then we hopped in a new white SUV with a Mill Maintenance logo painted on it and tore down one of the dirt roads between turbine rows. While we jolted about, he gave me some factoids for my book. I took notes as best I could, the pen jumping around on the page, leaving illegible marks that looked like cuneiform. I cursed myself for not bringing my tape recorder.

"See that truck parked beneath that GE 150?" He pointed off to our left at one of the bigger turbines. "When you see a truck parked beneath a turbine, it means work is being done it on. It could be routine maintenance, or a problem with that particular turbine. If you see a whole row of turbines stopped, that means there's a problem with a component common to all the turbines in the row. That's bad, costs big bucks. Or, sometimes it means the turbines are shut down because the wind is blowing too hard. That can bung 'em up but good. Or they're shut down because the wind isn't blowing hard enough. That doesn't happen too often out here."

"Brandon told me that he has to climb up inside those things to work on them," I shouted over the air conditioner and the rumble of the SUV as it jolted over the rough road.

"That's right. He's an apprentice windsmith, which is a fancy name for technician." Van Dorn stopped the SUV in the middle of the road and let it idle so the air conditioner kept running. "See that door at the base of each turbine?" he pointed to the tower closest to us, at the bottom of which was a door. The opening looked doll-size compared to the size of the tower, but I supposed it was the usual size for a door. "The windsmith enters the tower there, climbs up a metal ladder, and works up where the moving parts are. Helluva job!" He laughed again.

I studied the door. Cole, conscious or unconscious, had been shoved through such an opening. Then it was locked from the outside, leaving him to die. The hairs rose on my arms.

"Are the doors kept locked?" I asked, realizing that if so, whoever had stuffed Cole in the turbine had to have keys.

"Oh yeah," Van Dorn said. "Got to protect against vandals and other riff raff."

"Who has keys?" I asked.

He eyed me. "Same question the police asked. You're thinking about Cole Mintock."

I nodded.

"I'll tell you the same thing I told them. Both me and Cole have a master key. The other keys are locked up in the office each night. I'm responsible for 'em, and I can tell you no keys have gone missing. And, no, the office wasn't broken into. I'm stumped as to how someone would have had a key to that turbine door. The door wasn't jimmied, so the guy had a key."

"Weird," I said, wondering whether the term "guy" was accurate. After all, the murderer could be a woman.

"Damn right it's weird, "he said. "Police asking me all these questions. Can't blame 'em. I'd be asking too."

He put the SUV in gear and we rolled on. "It costs over thirty grand a year to maintain one windmill. Even with annual maintenance costs that high, the initial cost to install a windmill is recouped within four and a half years. Don't that beat all? Amazing. Half a million up front, thirty grand a year, and you still make a profit. Shows how much electricity each one of these suckers produces. Hell of a profitable business."

"Did you know Cole Mintock very well?" I asked. As we jolted over a big mound of sand, my body was forced into Van Dorn, and then slammed against the door. I would have to take three Motrins when I got home if he didn't slow down.

"Oh yeah, Cole, he was a great guy. He came out all the time just to see how things were going, never gave us any grief. Just stand around with me and the guys and shoot the shit. Every year at Christmas he sent us this huge basket of shit, salamis and cheese and coffee and some of them smoked almonds and just about everything you can think of. We got over a hundred people working here, so it was a damn big basket!" He chuckled to himself as he remembered Cole's bounty. "Good guy. Good to the community," he said, his gruff voice sounding almost tender.

"You miss him."

"Hell yeah. God knows what will happen now."

"That expansion would have meant more work for Mill Maintenance."

"Most likely. Or a new maintenance shop would open up. But who knows if the expansion will happen now that Cole's gone."

"Do you know who inherits CalWind?"

"Don't have a clue. But if it's that wife of his, Jesus! She don't know shit about wind farms."

"Will the transition have a big impact on you out here at Mill Maintenance?"

He thought a moment. "Hard to say. We're the ones keeping the wind farm running. Once the turbines are in and the transmission lines connected and the substation built and all that, Cole's office doesn't have that much to do. That's why we got over a hundred workers out here and at Cole's office they have three. We give 'em invoices, they sign 'em, and that's pretty much it. Course, if there's a big problem out in the field, like when a row goes down, we have to get approval from Cole's office to go ahead with ordering parts and whatnot. But most of what we do is the same old stuff."

"So, if Jillian were to take over, you guys wouldn't necessary notice the difference."

He grimaced. "Maybe. But she ain't Cole. What does she care about the wind farm? She'd probably sell it, and the new people might not like the fact that there's only one maintenance company out here. Monopoly prices and all that. Maybe they'd encourage another company to set up shop. Or maybe she'd keep the farm and fight us every time we needed to make an expensive repair."

"Are you the owner of Mill Maintenance?"

Van Dorn guffawed. "Me? No, Ma'am, I'm the foreman, in charge of the crews."

"Ever think about breaking with the company, setting up your own shop?"

He spit out the window, eyeing me like I was crazy. "Nah, I got enough problems without that."

As I climbed into the Corolla after my tour with Van Dorn, a Pumice County Sheriff's Department vehicle pulled up in the parking lot. Out of it climbed an old high school acquaintance, Trent Wise, now a Pumice County Sheriff's deputy.

Trent had a crush on me in high school, which caused me no end of embarrassment. At the time he was known as "The Streaker" because of his propensity to strip down and run naked over the football field and basketball court during half-time. Trent was fast, and the authorities never did catch him in order to discover his identity. But all the students knew. The kids in my class thought Trent's antics were hilarious, and a couple of my friends extracted even more enjoyment out of his stunts by teasing me about it. Knowing Trent had a thing for me, they liked to say he ran naked to impress me. Even if Trent hadn't inadvertently made me the object of ridicule, I was never going to return his feelings. I wasn't into dating at all, preferring to spend my time on more important activities such as fighting injustices and spending gobs of time in my room on restriction. I heard that after high school, Trent spent some time at a nudist camp, where he met his wife. I guess old habits die hard.

I called, "Trent!" and extracted myself from the car.

"Sam Larkin! What the heck are you doing here?"

He looked the same way he did when I saw him last, which had to be around seven years ago during a class reunion. He was a little heavier, but weren't we all? He wore a khaki baseball cap with a

Sheriff's patch on it over his cropped blonde hair. "Looking good, Mr. Sheriff Deputy," I said.

He laughed. "Right back at you. You haven't aged a bit. Still the skinny little gal I once had a crush on."

"Not so skinny these days," I said with fake humility. I knew that my body, all five foot two of it, was still in good shape at 32. Hell, I earned it, what with all the running I did, not to mention the tennis matches with Eddie.

"I heard you had moved back to Desert Rock," Trent said. "I'm sorry to hear about your mother."

"Thanks, I appreciate that." Changing the subject, I said, "I'm out here researching a book I'm writing about wind energy."

"I heard you became a writer. I'm not surprised. I remember that article you wrote in high school that got you into so much hot water. You remember the one? You were criticizing the principle for something or other. I think it had to do with the gay students."

Not only did Trent run like a gazelle, he remembered like an elephant. I said, "How could I forget that? The principle had banned gay and lesbian students from forming a group on campus. Mr. Docket—you remember him? He supervised the school paper. He told me not to run the piece, but I snuck it in when he wasn't looking. I got suspended—and kicked off the paper."

Trent laughed and slapped his thigh. "That's what I always liked about you. Your spunk."

"It's a minority view, Trent," I said, then asked, "You out here on the Mintock case?"

He pulled up his gun belt and puffed out his chest. "Yep. I never would have thought the guy would have enemies, but there you go."

"Still thinking it's the ELF nut?"

"I see you've been reading the paper. Yeah, he looks like our man. We're working with the FBI and the Department of Homeland Security to build up a case so we can arrest him. Department would get a gold star for that. Catch a terrorist these days and you get major commendations."

"Well, Trent, I wish you luck with the case. We'll have to get together for a drink some time."

"I'm a married man now, Sam. With a kid and another on the way."

I butted him with my shoulder. "It's just a drink, Trent, I didn't ask you to sleep with me."

He blushed and stuttered then touched the bill of his cap. With one last glance at me, he hurried away.

As I drove out of the parking lot, I saw him striding toward the Mill Maintenance office. I wondered if he was trying to find out how the killer got a key. I'd have to stay in touch with Trent, wife or no wife, nudist or not.

While I had been away at Mill Maintenance, Lacy discovered a way to open the lower kitchen cabinet doors and had gnawed on every piece of Tupperware I own. I stood in the kitchen with my mouth open and stared at all the mutilated plastic bowls. I then turned to glare at Lacy. I swear the devil grinned at me, and she had the gall to wag her tail (it had not been cropped, but I could take care of that now). I made a mental note: Buy and install child guards on cabinet doors. Then I drew a line through that with my mental pen and wrote: Get rid of dog.

Chapter Five

Eddie hit the tennis ball right at me. I pivoted to the left, but despite my Olympic-level athleticism, the ball struck me square in the ass.

"Damn it, Eddie!" I shouted and rubbed my bum, which I feared was now imprinted with the Wilson label.

"Game, set and match," he shouted, his fists held aloft in victory. This obnoxious performance was intended to irk me as much as possible. I ignored him. He sauntered off the court with exaggerated cockiness and plopped his skinny butt on the courtside bench.

I stalked over to the bench and tossed my racquet into my bag. "Nice sportsmanship, Martinez."

"You just happened to be at the exact place I wanted to hit the ball."

"You just happen to be sitting right now in the place I want my fist to be."

He drank some lime Gatorade and said, "Ha ha."

It really ticked me off to lose. "I'm not going to play with you anymore," I announced childishly, toweling myself off. At eight in the morning, the sun was already hot. Fortunately, the wind was only a mild breeze at this point, allowing us to get the set in before Eddie had to be at work.

"You say that every time I beat you."

"Well, I'm serious this time. You tried to kill me."

He snapped me with his sweaty towel. "If I wanted to kill you, I'd have done it long ago. Trust me."

As we collected our gear, I struggled with whether or not to tell Eddie what I had learned on my second trip to the wind farm. I was in no mood for another lecture about how I would get fired or how curiosity killed the cat, but I needed a sounding board. I decided to test the waters.

"Did you know that people climb up inside those giant wind turbines to work on the motor?"

He inspected me. "You learn this on the Internet?"

Here we go, I thought. Sermon pending. "I admit I went out there again. But," I added, to stave off the attack, "you should have seen the guy who gave me a tour yesterday. Typical desert rat. A real character. I thought he was going to kill me when I first approached him, but once I introduced myself, he was nice as pie." I knew I was babbling, but I hoped to forestall Eddie's lecture as long as possible.

"You can get all the information you need for your book off of the Internet," he said.

"That's not true. It's better to get first-hand information, talk to the people involved in an issue. Get a feel for what they care about. My field research is one of the reasons my books are better than anything kids can pull off the Internet."

"She says humbly."

"Well, it's true. I also wanted to talk to that environmentalist, Luke Lewis, but he wasn't there. I'd like to put quotes from him in the book, give his side of the story—provided he doesn't get arrested and sent away for life. And, hey, I saw Trent Wise, he's working on the case. He confirmed that Lewis is their prime suspect. But, they're still investigating, so they must not have much evidence against him."

"The Streaker? Didn't Wise used to have a crush on you?"

Now why would Eddie remember that? I felt my heart race a little. "Ancient history," I said. "I also met Cole's son. I learned that his mother died, about six months ago. His father recently remarried, to a woman who's as warm as a glacier. Brandon clearly despises her. I feel terrible for the kid. Can you imagine? Two parents die in the space of half a year and you're stuck with a step-mom you don't like. He probably hated the idea of his father marrying right after his mom died, so he'd likely hate the new wife anyway, but still, she's not someone a person takes to."

"Cole Mintock did."

Eddie made a good point. I liked Cole, he seemed smart and kind and nobody's fool. He was attracted to this woman. One could only conclude that she had some redeeming qualities. But I sure didn't see them. She was so—what? Remote. Chilly. And beautiful. Did she seduce him to get his money? She would have seen Cole as a good catch. I didn't know for sure, but she must stand to inherit at least some of his considerable wealth. And what a perfect time to off him, while he was embroiled in disagreements over the expansion. Lots of adversaries threatening him, suspects to call attention away from her.

I came out of my reverie to see Eddie staring at me. He said, "What?"

"I wonder if the detectives have questioned the new wife. If I were them, she'd be on my list. I'd like to ask her a few questions myself."

"Sam."

"I'm just saying she's a possibility. Most murders are committed by people close to the victim—family and friends."

"Something you learned during your long career as a police officer."

"Hey, I've written books on crime. The statistics don't lie."

"I thought your suspect of choice was the big guy."

Ah, I thought, Eddie was paying attention. I knew I could get him interested. "Richard Sampson is still my favorite suspect. But we should look at all possibilities."

"We?"

"I just keep thinking how wrong it would be if they hang it on the environmentalist just because it would win them a commendation. It makes me mad to think that Brandon lost his dad, and the real killer might go free."

Eddie reached out and took my shoulder, an unusually intimate gesture on his part. I felt a jolt of electricity where his fingers touched me. I could see sweat beading on his arm, the dark hair matted down with perspiration, and at the end of that arm, the strong, beautiful hand. I breathed hard. What the hell was wrong with me? We were just friends.

He said, "Is it possible that you're over-relating to the kid?"

I knew what he meant. He thought that since I lost both my parents I was being overly sympathetic to Brandon, to the point where I wanted to find his dad's killer. Ridiculous. "Ridiculous," I said.

Eddie took his hand away and slipped his car keys out of his tennis bag. "When do you want to play again?"

"In thunder, lightening, or in rain?"

"Huh?"

"Shakespeare. Macbeth. Never mind. Next week, same time. Provided the wind stays below thirty miles an hour."

He walked off the court ahead of me, and I watched him drive away in his new Ford Ranger. It was white, no pin stripes, standard wheels. It was so Eddie.

When I got home from the tennis courts, ready for a shower and a solid day of work, I found my wayward brother camped out on my family room sofa. He was eating up the deli food Vanessa had brought Monday for our tender heart to heart chat and listening to Led Zeppelin on my stereo. Lacy sat on the floor beside him and nibbled the pieces of pastrami he offered, slobber dripping from her floppy jowls. Please somebody just shoot me. After I get the locks changed.

Chapter Six

I grabbed a bottle of iced tea out of the refrigerator on my way through the kitchen and held it to my forehead. I still felt hot and sticky from my tennis match with Eddie, and the cool bottle felt good against my skin.

When Connor saw me, he said, "Yo, Sam! Looking good!"

I was saturated in sweat and had on a yellowed white visor with a distorted bill. My tennis shirt clung to my body, dark patches spreading under my arms. What a moron he was.

"Why are you here?" I asked, uncapping the tea and taking a gulp. I marched over and turned Zeppelin off. The only positive I could see in his arrival was that I might finally get the money back that he owed me. Right. That was as likely as him keeping a job longer than four months.

"I came to see you." He cocked his head—just as Lacy was doing at the moment—to signal his amazement that I should ask.

"Uh-huh." I plopped down in the chair opposite the couch and studied the two of them. Lacy didn't even bother to greet me, and Connor just stared at me with that goofy smile on his face. He was still boyishly handsome at thirty, I noted with irritation. His dark hair was in need of a cut, but it looked oddly attractive curling around his angelic face uncontrollably. At the moment, he was clean-shaven, and I could see his dimples—a feature we share—from where I sat. Whereas my eyes are almost black, his are light gray, and he can make them look as innocent as a baby's when it suits. The baggy denim shorts, Hawaiian shirt, and flip flops he wore were standard attire for him, even in winter. His beauty was not the worst thing about him, but it made the other things worse. I asked, "How long are you staying?"

"Oh, I thought I'd just hang out here for a while." He grinned, then added, "That is, if it's okay with you. This is your house now."

"A fact everyone seems unclear on."

He looked somber then, an expression alien to his countenance. "It's weird, coming in and Mom not being here. How do you do it? Doesn't it bother you?"

I didn't want to talk about Mom with him. I had always resented how our mother doted on him, her only son. She used to get furious with me for what she called "over-reacting" to perceived wrongdoing of any kind, but at least I cared. All Connor ever cared about was having a good time. Instead of viewing him as appallingly vacuous, our mother praised his even temper and sense of fun. While growing up, I could come home scraped and bleeding from a fight I'd started with some bully, and she'd just throw me a couple of Band-aids while chastising me for my temper. But if Connor cried about a hang nail, she'd hover over him for an hour with a med kit, then take the poor boy out for ice cream. Because she never asked anything of him in return for all this doting, he learned never to give anything. Well, hell. There it is. I was doing it again. Imagine me telling Vanessa that Mom and I had no issues at the end. What a load of crap that was. I was disgusted with myself.

Connor waited for me to say something. It wasn't his fault. So he was shallow and flaky. So he was revoltingly agreeable. How could he have helped being the only son, and the most beautiful child? I decided to answer his question truthfully. "Every time I come in the door, I expect to see her sitting at the kitchen table working a crossword puzzle. I feel hollow when I come in and find her chair empty. But I do feel her here. It's comforting in a way."

"I miss her."

"Me too."

He scratched Lacy's ears. "You want to play Monopoly?"

"She hasn't moved past Chutes and Ladders yet."

He hugged Lacy in that spontaneous way he has, just like a little boy. "Not the dog! You!"

"Connor, I have work to do. Vince is going to call me any day now and pitch a bitch that he hasn't received my outline yet."

"Please, please?"

I sat and looked at him, feeling compelled by his childish enthusiasm to ignore the work that I was increasingly neglecting. I shook my head. This was his power, his ability to get people to do anything by the sheer strength of his charisma. He could convince the President of the United States to play Risk during a national emergency. I said, "Give me three hours of good writing time, and then we'll play."

He looked crestfallen and astonished that he had been denied. He didn't seem to comprehend that this wasn't "home" in the way he had always thought of it, and that I wasn't his mother, the one would have set whatever she was doing aside to play Monopoly with him. Good that I had denied him, then. He needed to know that I wasn't her.

My thirty-year-old brother shrugged, grabbed the remote, and turned on *Scooby Doo*.

Chapter Seven

On my way to CalWind two days after Connor's unwanted arrival, I realized that the grumpiness that had marred my last forty-eight hours was a sign of depression. Connor's presence in the house had me thinking about my mother more than I had since she died, and I began to entertain the notion that Vanessa might be right. What if I were living in Desert Rock because I could not accept Mom's death? Did I think, as Vanessa had implied, that living in Mom's house, visiting her friends, going to her book club, would ameliorate my guilt over having never made peace with her?

Ridiculous! God how I hate Vanessa's psychoanalyzing. Both she and Connor had gotten to me as usual, making me doubt myself. It had always been that way. Vanessa with her prim superiority, doing good works just like Mom did, safely, within the bounds of convention. And Connor, with his placid flexibility, so easy to get along with, contradicting no one, causing no offense. They had no idea what it is like going around in the world constantly wanting to fight against what other people accept. My siblings could never comprehend how I saw things, why I reacted the way I did. But, so what? Why did I let them make me crazy? What kind of power did they have over me? And more to the point, why was my life any of

Vanessa's business, and why did Connor think he could just waltz into my house as if it were still his childhood home? The three of us had pulled together during Mom's illness, but after that, we had exploded apart again like atoms in a nuclear reaction.

And then there was Eddie. I felt confused about our friendship. We had been comrades ever since grade school. I remember playing marbles with him in third grade, competing with one another in math quizzes in sixth, and getting together for tennis in high school. I used to think he had a crush on me, but I never saw him that way. At least, I don't think I did. I can't claim that I've ever been crystal clear on my feelings, at least when they concern personal issues such as romance. I can describe in detail my emotions regarding euthanasia or poverty in Africa, but ask me how I feel about something closer to home and I'm struck dumb.

Eddie and I lost touch when I went to college. While I wrote term papers on familial relationships in *King Lear*, Eddie worked two jobs, saved all his pennies, and started his own business. While he built up his coffee shop clientele, I went to work in San Diego as a freelance writer for Blue Nest Press. During those years, we did not communicate at all. Then, my mother got cancer. I suspended my book schedule and came to stay with her in Desert Rock. I thought I'd only be in town for a few weeks, but here I was, five months later, a permanent resident (at least for now).

That's when Eddie and I reconnected. He came by the house when he heard I was home to take care of my mom. Thereafter, he showed up at the house several times a week, bringing Vanessa and Connor and me coffees from his shop and take out food from Ming's or Mike's Deli. Sometimes he'd convince me to go out to lunch with him, saying I needed a break. Occasionally, he asked Connor out for a beer in the evening—they had been pals, too, growing up. And he would sit in the chair beside my mother's bed and regale her with stories about his wacky family. I never heard him talk so much in my life. Of course, Eddie was there at the funeral in his one good suit, handling his job as pallbearer with the kind of quiet grace I always associate with him.

Now that I was back in Desert Rock to live, we had picked up our friendship where we left off so many years ago. I heard that he had been in a relationship with a woman, but she met someone else and left town. I had had numerous relationships, but none serious enough to tempt me to matrimony. Naturally, when Eddie and I began hanging out again, people wondered if we were romantically involved. Once, while at a barbeque at Eddie's house, his sister Maria said to us, in earshot of everyone there, "So when are you guys going to tie the knot?" Eddie's ears turned red, and he almost dropped the plate he held. I wanted to crawl under the table or hit Maria in the nose, I wasn't sure which. Vanessa always asks about Eddie as though I am asthmatic and he is an oxygen tank.

But Eddie and I had an understanding. We were friends. We were happy with the way things were. Who needed the complications of romance and sex? And yet, occasionally, when we were together, I felt electricity between us. His presence sometimes produced in me a longing to touch him, to be touched by him. Was this sexual attraction or simply a desire for intimacy? And what did he feel for me? I sensed he might want more than friendship, but the man is so reticent, who could tell? It was all so ridiculous.

I forced these thoughts aside as I pulled into the CalWind parking lot. I was in luck: Luke Lewis was there with his compatriot. I got out of the car and ambled over to them. The protestors sat under a mesquite tree, their signs propped against its trunk. The fight seemed to have gone out of them. But as I approached, Lewis leapt to his feet and said with vigor, "Do you know about the dangers of wind power?"

"No," I lied, "But I'd like to hear what you have to say." He looked amazed that anyone wanted to hear him out. I glanced toward the office and saw Sierra at her post by the window, looking out at us. I waved a hand in her direction.

Lewis launched right in. While he talked, I studied him, trying to gauge whether he would be the type to kill. I knew this was fruitless—many murderers are surrounded by people who would never guess that they could axe someone to death—but I couldn't help myself. It was chilling—and, I admit, exciting—to think I might be standing next to a man capable of smashing someone over the head and stuffing him in a metal tube to die.

My overriding thought at the moment was that the man looked too frail to hurt anyone. Lewis was so thin his hip bones protruded, and his green eyes seemed too big for his gaunt face. He was just a few inches taller than I was, which made him short for a man. He was younger than I was, too; he could not have been more than twenty-eight. Despite looking sun-baked and wild, Lewis was oddly attractive, and I could see that in his past, before the outdoor living and moral fervor aged him, he had been handsome.

"The wind farm at Altamont Pass," he was saying, "kills thousands of birds every year! CalWind doesn't kill as many—but it's still a killer. And it kills more bats. Bats are vital—they help keep insect populations under control. Without birds and bats the earth would be overrun with insects. These creatures are a necessary part of this desert ecosystem! If the wind farm expands, even more will be killed—upsetting a balance that has taken thousands of years to evolve. And all for a bit more profit!"

"Exactly how many birds and bats are killed at CalWind each year?" I asked. I glanced over at his sidekick to see how she was responding to his speech. Clearly, she admired—maybe even adored—him. She gazed at Lewis, her young face almost exultant.

"Ha!" He said. "Depends on whom you ask. The owner of the wind farm gives one figure, the EPA another. Their estimates are ridiculously low. My organization—EarthOne—calculates that at least a thousand birds and twice as many bats die here each year."

"How many does CalWind claim?"

"They say just a few hundred! Their lies are egregious! These bird and bat deaths are horrible—reprehensible—but they are not the worst aspect of wind farms. Wind farms represent just one more attempt to sustain an unsustainable standard of living. We never learn as a species! We cannot keep breeding—humans are overpopulating the planet as it is—we're putting too much of an ecological strain on the earth. And everything we do takes energy—more and more energy—to run our computers and cars and factories and air conditioners. And indigent people across the globe aspire to have what Americans have! Do you know that Americans represent one tenth of the world population but we consume one third of the world's energy? One third!! Now, China and India want to emulate us. What will happen when China and India start living as we do?"

He came up for air, and then continued, his voice louder. "So we keep looking for more and more energy—we pump oil and gas out of the earth and dig coal out of the ground and say it's all in the name of progress! All of a sudden people are saying that oil and gas and coal pollute, that they are running out, so now we need green energy! Green! Like a wind farm doesn't contribute to the destruction of the environment. Of course, this wind farm doesn't pollute like a coal plant does, but the electricity it produces is used to support a way of life that will lead to total degradation—it has to stop!"

I felt exhausted as I listened to him. His words came out in explosive blasts. His eyes darted left and right, rarely connecting with mine. He seemed about to cry.

"But what do you hope to accomplish out here?" I asked. "You're just two people."

His body trembled. "Two people can make a difference! One person can make a difference! Look at Gandhi, Martin Luther King Jr.—look at Caesar Chavez, Rosa Parks. One person decides that enough is enough and takes a stand. Others follow, and soon you have a movement, and change. What is the point of thinking that you can't make a difference? As King said, 'We will have to repent in this generation not merely for the hateful words and actions of the bad people, but for the appalling silence of the good people.' When those who see injustice or harm do nothing, nothing gets done!"

Lewis stopped talking for a moment and glanced toward the turbines dotting the desert floor. "Look—I have nothing against Cole Mintock, I personally believe he thought he was doing the right thing by building this, but he did not take his ideals far enough. He wanted to protect the environment by building a green energy plant—but the energy he created is used to power four thousand square foot homes with big screen TVs and hot tubs. Mintock was actually more dangerous than those apathetic people King was talking about. He was full of good intentions—but he knew just enough to get him into trouble—to get him started on a course that would eventually undermine the goal he strove for. He wanted to help save the planet—but he contributed to its destruction! That's the direction the whole nation is going. The government says, 'We need energy to keep our economy growing, but we need clean energy, so let's develop more wind and solar and hydrogen power, but let's not change our lifestyle.' It's lunacy! We just stick our heads in the sand—think we can continue living like we do—without making any sacrifices!"

His compatriot handed him a thermos. He uncapped it and drank for a good minute. While I watched his Adam's apple bob up and down in his skinny neck, I weighed his words against what I had learned during my research. He had summed up accurately what detractors claim are the adverse environmental aspects of wind energy. But he went further than most critics when he started to talk about how any energy source, green or not, was inherently bad because it permitted an imprudent—even immoral—lifestyle to continue. Most energy experts and environmental groups argue over which energy sources to embrace, not how to get rid of all dependence on them. Luke's view was a minority one, shared only by fringe environmentalists.

I also thought about the personality emerging as Lewis laid out his arguments. He was educated, articulate at times, passionate. He could quote by heart Martin Luther King Jr., the poster child for non-violent direct action. Was Lewis a man who would associate himself with a domestic terrorist organization like the Environmental Liberation Front? Would he kill a man for his beliefs? On the surface, it didn't appear so. On the other hand, he was fervent, his ideals fixed. Often a lethal combination. I decided to see how he would react if I brought the discussion down to earth and closer to home.

"I read in the paper that you are the number one suspect in the Mintock murder case."

His compatriot spoke before Lewis could open his mouth. "It's so unfair! They're picking on him because he rocks the boat. And it's not like he's some bigwig or something. He doesn't have any money or connections to people in big places. The police are just a bunch of bullies, if you ask me. Poor Lukie." She reached out and took his hand.

Lewis stared down at their clasped fingers as if he didn't recognize them. He said, Katie is loyal to me. She can't see what others see. Every time I protest, people say I'm a kook because I fight for issues they think are meaningless. I don't engage in popular protests like most people. They jump on the bandwagon, go out and fight for the issue du jour, the one that captures the public's imagination, like save the baby seals. Most activists own houses and cars, they work their 'caring' around entertainment and consumption. They wouldn't want to be inconvenienced or anything."

Lewis ripped his hand from Katie's and used both hands to point to his own chest. "I'm not like that. I don't own a house, which would use electricity, and I don't drive a car, which uses gas. I spend my life traveling to where environmental disasters, however 'inconsequential' they seem to others, occur. I stand up for the unpopular, the animals and plants and places no one cares about. When reporters write about my protests, they say that my efforts are misguided and that I'm deluded. When the police show up, they mock me. They haul me to jail for 'trespassing' or some other trumped up charge just to make my life miserable. They are astoundingly ignorant people, the police."

And I was sure he didn't hesitate to tell them that, I thought. No wonder Lewis was law enforcement's favorite suspect in the Mintock case. The police don't like educated snobs who sneer at their "ignorance." I should know—that attitude got me into trouble more than once.

I said, "The detectives aren't looking at other people who seem to have greater means and motive than you. They seem unable to make a good case against you, yet they persist in thinking you did it. That doesn't sound like good police work to me, or justice either."

His eyes widened and for the first time he looked me square in the face. "Who are you?"

"Sorry, I should have said. I'm Sam Larkin. I write books about controversial issues for Blue Nest Press. Books for junior high school kids."

He digested that. "Why are you involved in this? I cannot imagine why anyone would take my part. Anyway, it is hopeless. The authorities are going to nail me for this."

I thought he wanted to be brave about what he saw as his impending arrest, but I could see he was scared. I said, "Do you know if they've got any evidence against you? Are they moving for an indictment?"

"I don't know. Detectives have questioned me three times so far. They're watching me all the time."

I thought that all that questioning indicated that the detectives were having a hard time making the case. But it also showed that they were determined to do so. I thought of something that I wanted his response to. "The FBI thinks you're affiliated with ELF. Are you?" ELF was a shadowy organization, with no formal structure or hierarchy, and no brick-and-mortar headquarters. ELF operatives networked online and carried out their missions in small self-directed bands. It would be hard for the police to ever prove that Lewis worked for the organization.

He looked angry. "I would never affiliate with ELF! They destroy property—their actions are extreme. I have never been involved in protests like that—I do not approve of them. I told the officers that a dozen times, but of course they don't believe me. As I said, it's hopeless."

I feared he was right. But in my mind, Lewis was not a killer. I was no expert, but it just didn't fit his profile. I wondered: If law enforcement felt less pressure to go after terrorists, or if Lewis had more influence, would the detectives be pursuing this case against him? Would they have investigated big Richard Sampson, asked him where he was on the night of the murder? And what about Cole's icy wife, the person who stood to gain immediate rewards upon Cole's death? Would they have questioned her? In my opinion, law enforcement was not digging very deep. The agencies seemed to have their minds made up. And Lewis was going to pay.

Chapter Eight

The wind blew all night, roaring through the trees and throwing sand against the windows. The stove damper clanked and clanked. Feeling irritable and restless, I had tried to lull myself to sleep by reading, but the minute I turned the light out, my brain went into overdrive. Had my interview with Lewis yesterday convinced me that he was not a murderer? Did Cole's wife marry him for his money? How much could Sampson bench press? What the hell did Connor do with all those bath towels? And why in the world would Ming think Eddie would marry her daughter?

Rather than get up and do something useful like clean the toilets, I continued in this vein, thrashing around in bed with increasing agitation. Needless to say, I was less than perky the next morning when I got up at five. Thankfully, the wind had died down to a breeze by then. Knowing it would pick up later, I took advantage of the lull to take Lacy for a run. Or, to put it more accurately, I allowed Lacy to take me for a run.

My feet had not left the front porch when she took off at full speed, jerking me off the stoop and dragging me behind her. I clutched the expando-leash like a racer in some bizarre Iditarod. I managed to hold on until we got to the middle of the next block, at which point she spotted what she presumably thought was a cat but turned out to be a plastic grocery sack blowing across the road in the freshening breeze. She took off after it, and the sudden force jerked my feet off the pavement. I went down hard. Before my mind registered what had happened, Lacy dragged me for several feet, the asphalt scraping away the skin on my elbows and knees. Finally, I let go, and the expando-leash retracted, the plastic handle speeding toward the fastener on Lacy's collar at seventy miles per hour. When it connected with a loud pop, Lacy levitated, did a three-sixty while suspended, then shot away down the street, the leash handle scraping after her on the tarmac. I envisioned the terrified dog galloping out onto Verbena Avenue and being struck by a car. Not stopping to check my injuries, I lurched to my feet and ran off in pursuit.

When I tracked Lacy down five blocks later, she was standing in the middle of Sage Road like a gazelle run to exhaustion by a hungry lion. Her head was down, her tongue lolled out, saliva dripped off her jowls in slimy ropes. Her sides heaved. She gaped at the leash handle as if it was going to pounce on her at any minute. As I eased up to her and cooed her name, she wagged her limp tail but did not look away from the leash. I bent and retrieved the handle. The second it was in my palm, Lacy looked up at me, ready to resume our "run" as if nothing had happened.

I'm not sure what I felt at that moment. Part of me wanted to drag her off to the animal shelter. But another part felt a kind of tenderness toward her. She had been frightened and in danger. Without thinking, and even though she had hurt me, I came to her aid. We seemed linked in a way that we had not been when the morning began.

Of course, when my adrenaline dissipated and I inspected my wounds, the warm-fuzzies went south. My elbows and knees bled, and the pain had kicked in. Stupid dog. My legs wobbled as we made our way home, Lacy trotting along ahead of me. All I wanted to do was get to the house, drink a big glass of iced water, and go back to bed. But today was Saturday, one of three days during the week that I swing by my 85-year-old neighbor's house to walk with her. She uses a walker and can force the contraption down the road at an astonishing pace. But she feels more comfortable if someone walks along beside her in case she loses her balance or the thing falls apart, an irrational fear of hers. Since I've lived in Mom's house, she has asked me to tighten the nuts and bolts on it three times. I sighed.

But then I saw her leaning on the walker in front of her house, waiting for me. Aside from the big white tennis shoes, she was dressed to the nines as usual. Even for walking, she wore nicer clothes than anything in my wardrobe. This morning she had on a light gray silk blouse, which was neatly tucked into the top of matching slacks. A rose and charcoal fabric belt broke up the monochromatic outfit. I knew she'd smell of Ivory soap and Chanel Number Five when I approached her. She'd also be wearing the pearl earrings her late husband gave her on their twenty-fifth wedding anniversary. Looking at her elegant figure, I felt my face break into a grin.

Hattie had been my mother's neighbor and best friend for over thirty years, and I associate her with all that was good about childhood and Mom. Hattie's husband and my father died around the same time—both of a heart attack—an event that seemed to bond the two women for life. They traveled the world together. They spent months planning their adventures to China, France, South America. Being a librarian, Hattie traced down every book in the county library system about their destinations, and they'd pore over the texts as if studying for exams. They'd whisper about how to control intestinal gas produced by unfamiliar foods and what to do with that strange European device, the bidet. They always came back from these journeys with outrageous stories about ditching fellow tour group members who got on their nerves, or pretending to be fortunetellers just to yank people's chains. While telling of these adventures, they guffawed, finding themselves terribly amusing. Naturally, each of them complained about the other's traveling eccentricities—Mom accused Hattie of sneaking cigarettes while loaded on cheap wine, and Hattie accused Mom of using her superior knowledge of foreign languages to lie to the natives about her—but I knew they would never enjoy traveling with anyone else. Of course, by the time Hattie hit her '80s and Mom her '70s, they had put away their Samsonite and contented themselves with local charity work and book clubs and morning walks.

I knew Hattie and I would never have the friendship those two had enjoyed, but we got along well and enjoyed reminiscing about the good old days. Like my mother, I found it useful to share my problems with Hattie, who saw through to the core of any problem. She never advised—she was way too classy to foist her opinions on other people—just told stories she though might serve to illuminate the solution to your problem. It was helpful, if irritating.

"Good Lord!" Hattie said when Lacy and I walked up. "What happened to you?"

"That," I said, pointing to Lacy. "What possessed Mom to get such a dog? Why didn't she just adopt a nice poodle or something?"

Hattie pulled Lacy toward her, as if the dog could understand what I said and would get hurt feelings. "Your mother adopted Lacy because the shelter told her that big dogs have a harder time getting adopted than little dogs. She didn't want Lacy to die."

I was not in the mood to hear about my mother's saintly ways. "Still, this dog?"

"Lacy is a doll! What could you possibly have against her?"

I looked down at my bloody knees. "I should think the answer to that would be obvious."

Hattie just laughed (laughed!) and began pushing her walker down the street. I enhanced my grip on Lacy's expando-leash, giving her—I admit—a harder jerk than was strictly necessary to get her out of the way of the speeding Hattie. Lacy pulled at the leash in an attempt to pass the old woman, it apparently being a part of the canine creed to lead but never to follow. I was only human and brought up the rear.

Hattie nodded toward the beat-up Escort of indistinct color parked at my curb. "I see Connor's in town."

"Yes, will the thrills never cease."

She eyed me, seemed to want to say something, but changed her mind. "Tell him to stop on by when he has a moment. I'd like to see him."

"When he has a moment? Between reruns of *Scooby Doo* and computer game sessions, he may find time."

Hattie stopped and gawked at me. "You're cranky these days."

I gave Lacy a tug to let her know the parade was taking a break. She stood by Hattie's walker and looked at us, her head cocked. "Well, cripe," I said. "Connor just waltzes into town whenever he needs a place to hang out, lets himself into the house—*my* house!—without asking to be invited. I should get the locks changed."

"It still feels like home to him."

"Ha!" I said, more forcefully than I had wanted to. "Two problems with that. Number one, it isn't his home anymore, it's my home. And number two, he should never have taken advantage of Mom like that anyway, always coming home whenever he got booted out of some apartment or lost his job or needed money."

"You make him sound like a bum."

"The facts speak for themselves."

"All of us get down on our luck some time or another, don't we?"

"I never came running home to Mom when I had a problem."

Hattie started walking again. "Did you ever think she might have wanted you to?"

I stared at her back in disbelief. "Why on earth would she want that?"

"Because sometimes people—mothers in particular—want to be needed."

"Adult children should not need their parents," I said, catching up with her.

Hattie just smiled. It was highly irritating.

I said, "At any rate, I'm not Mom, and Connor needs to learn to get by on his own now."

She was silent, and my comment sat there. I could hear Lacy's nails clicking on the pavement as we moved along. The sun was higher in the sky now, and I could feel the heat intensify. Sweat dripped into my wounds, making them sting like a bitch. I wished Hattie would say something—her silence was surely a judgment against me.

"Vanessa keeps coming around, too," I said, just to goad her into telling me what was on her mind. "She lets herself in with her old key. It doesn't seem to have sunk in that this is my house now, not Mom's."

"Do you feel like it's your house? I notice you've left all the furniture the way it was when your mother lived. Did you put all your things in storage?"

"Well, yes, but—"

"Your mother has only been gone three months. I imagine in time you'll want to bring your own things into the house, make it yours—that is, if you decide to stay in Desert Rock." She looked at me.

I looked down at the asphalt and then at Lacy. "I may stay. I may go back to San Diego. I don't know."

Hattie still stared at me, I could feel her gaze searching my face. She said, "In any event, perhaps right now the house feels comforting just the way it is, like it always was when your mother was alive."

Hattie was really starting to bug me now. "I just wasn't up to redecorating, that's all. It just seemed easier to move in as is."

"Of course," she said, skirting around a pothole. The streets in Desert Rock are always in disrepair. They crack during earthquakes and buckle over shallow tree roots. The City of Desert Rock responds by pouring hot tar over the blemish, no matter what kind, and dumping sand on it, a mysterious process that has no effect whatsoever.

"Processing your Mother's death is going to take a long time, Samantha. You will grieve her always, but right now, when it hurts the most, it seems perfectly normal to me that you wouldn't want too much additional change to deal with. As long as her things are still around, so is she, at least a little."

I knew what she was driving at, I'm no chimp. She was saying that Vanessa and Connor were grieving too, and that maybe they weren't ready to give up the idea of home any more than I was. I was now more irritated at Hattie than at Lacy. On the other hand, at least what Hattie said made my actions appear normal, not psycho in the way Vanessa had portrayed them. I told Hattie what Vanessa had said about my taking over Mom's life so I could forgive myself, a ridiculous—and offensive—hypothesis. I admit my voice dripped with condescension as I described Vanessa's attempt to appear concerned as opposed to meddling.

Hattie said, "I remember when my mother and father died—they died together, in a car wreck when I was twenty-five—my sister Agnes began pestering me to get married. At that time, an unmarried woman my age was considered an old maid! She had never done that before, but Mother had, and Agnes took it upon herself to take over for her. Then, my sisters Beatrice and Rose had a huge fight, something about Rose's fried chicken, and they didn't speak to one another for years.

I was mad at all of them for acting so petty. Here our parents had just died, and all they could think of was marriage and fried chicken. I didn't understand until years later that they were angry, too, angry that our parents had died. What do you do with all that grief and rage? We took it out on each other."

God, one of Hattie's allegories. Why had I brought up Vanessa and Connor with her, anyway? I knew what I would get. I didn't want to understand the situation or gain deep emotional insights into my siblings' grieving processes. Hattie was so controlled and rational, I wanted to shake her just to see if she'd lose her cool. Come to think of it, I'd often felt the same urge with my mother. No wonder those two got along so well.

"Are you coming to book club Tuesday?" Hattie asked as we got to our turn- around point at the intersection of Telescope and Sage. We started back the other way, the wind now in our faces.

"Yes," I said in the dullest voice I could work up. I wanted her to know that her little story had not put me in a cheery mood, and that my anger at Connor and Vanessa was not because of some damn chicken, fried or otherwise.

Chapter Nine

After my walk with Hattie, I took a cool shower and dressed my wounds. Then I made a pot of coffee and sat down at the computer. What I really should have done was work on my book—I now had just two weeks until my deadline—but I decided instead to verify what Lewis said about bird deaths. Determining the veracity of his claims would help me decide how much I could trust him. I also wanted to find out what I could about Sampson and his building company. I looked forward to the research—I loved finding information. And today I felt especially motivated. The pain emanating from under my bandages and memories of Hattie's allegory provided me incentive to focus on something else besides my petty domestic problems. Plus, with Connor still in bed, and Lacy dead to the world (figuratively speaking, unfortunately), the house was quiet and conducive to work.

I took a sip of coffee and brought up my favorite search engine. Unlike the research I had already conducted for my book, today's search would be focused as opposed to general. I had already done background research on wind energy. For the beginning stage in any research project, I start with a database search. Despite kids' love affair with the Internet, databases are the best way to start any research project because they archive reputable periodicals and use refined searching methods. A database can deliver usable, trustworthy articles in a surprisingly short time. In contrast, looking for information on the open Net is like searching for a diamond ring in a municipal landfill—you have to search through a lot of trash to find the treasure.

My original search had netted me useful background material on how wind turbines work and how much of the nation's electricity is produced by wind energy and so on. Some of the articles had mentioned bird deaths, but that subject was not their focus. Now I needed to narrow my search in order to locate pieces on just that topic. In Blue Nest parlance, this is called "filling holes." I had the general information I needed, now was the time to fill in gaps in my knowledge. At this point, the Internet becomes the best tool. If you choose your search terms carefully, you can generate articles focused precisely on what you want to know about. For me, the process is like looking for a diamond ring in a kitchen trashcan. You still have to sort through trash, but the container you search through is small, so the odds of finding what you need are good.

I typed in "wind farm bird deaths" on the keyboard and hit the search button. Within seconds, the search engine brought up documents covering avian fatalities due to collisions with wind turbines. I scrolled down, searching for pieces written by reputable sources such as the wind energy companies, mainstream environmental organizations, and government agencies. I wanted to learn what the major stakeholders had to say and weigh their claims against one another. Only by examining all assertions could I get a sense of the real scope and severity of the problem. Then I could compare what I had learned with what Lewis told me.

Within three hours, I felt that I had what I needed to assess Lewis's claims. He was more right than wrong. I learned that the U.S. Fish and Wildlife Service and the California Energy Commission consider bird deaths to be a serious problem, but mostly at the Altamont Pass Wind farm in Northern California. The CEC had already spent millions of dollars to research the problem. It estimated that the number of birds killed at Altamont each year is around 1000. Half of those are raptors, and all, according to the CEC, are protected under the Migratory Bird Treaty Act.

However, the agencies studying the problem were careful to point out that the situation at Altamont is unique. For one thing, the wind farm is sited smack in the middle of a bird migratory corridor. That was some good planning. For another, Altamont is an old wind farm, using old turbines, which are smaller than those built today. Unfortunately, the height of the old units places the blades at the exact elevation at which raptors like to fly. Newer turbines are taller, thus locating the blades above preferred flying routes. Bird deaths at the Tehachapi wind farm in California are fewer than at Altamont because that farm is sited away from bird migratory routes and uses newer, taller turbines. Another issue at Altamont is the sheer number of turbines. The older turbines produce less electricity, so more were built to get more power. More turbines mean more bird deaths. According to the U.S. Department of the Interior, more needs to be done to mitigate bird mortalities at Altamont Pass. And action was being taken. Half of the smaller turbines are being replaced with larger ones, which should reduce bird fatalities.

When the agencies mentioned Cole's wind farm at all, it was to compare it favorably to Altamont Pass. The California Fish and Game department estimated that less than a hundred birds die at CalWind each year. Cole's farm isn't new, but it isn't as old as Altamont and therefore does not have the bird death problem on the scale that Altamont does.

Based on my research, I concluded that Lewis had the substance of the problem correct but the particulars wrong. He seemed knowledgeable about his subject, so I could only conclude that his error was intentional. He exaggerated the number of deaths at CalWind by using the figures for Altamont in order to make Cole's expansion appear more destructive than it actually would be. Anyone who didn't take the trouble to verify his claims would have been fooled by this sleight of hand. That's why obfuscation is such a common trick employed by those wanting to convince you of something. They are counting on you not taking the time to verify their "facts."

So Lewis had fudged a bit. How did I feel about that? What did it say about his character? I went over the materials I had downloaded again, this time thinking about how Lewis fit into the environmental movement. Was he outside the movement, estranged by his radicalism? Or, were his views consistent with the movement as a whole?

Statements I found from mainstream environmental groups suggested that in general the environmental movement is behind alternative energy sources such as wind. However, environmental groups are concerned about bird deaths at wind farms and have called for more research into the problem. The Center for Biological Diversity actually sued Altamont Pass over its violations of the Migratory Bird Treaty Act. However, the organization was careful to quote the number of bird deaths accurately and to make clear that Altamont is unique. The CBD's call for a moratorium on permits at Altamont seemed consistent with the concerns of the major regulatory agencies.

In contrast, EarthOne, the organization Lewis belongs to, went further. Just as Lewis said, the organization is less interested in stopping bird deaths per se and more in stopping energy companies in general and the modern lifestyles they enable. Lewis's views seemed to echo his organization's. Knowing there were scores of other environmentalists with similarly radical beliefs made me feel better about Lewis. It made him appear less of a rogue. Of course, this was dangerous thinking. Just because lots of people believe a thing does not make it right or true. After all, thousands of people endorsed Nazism and slavery. Still, I felt relieved to discover that Lewis was acting in accordance with EarthOne's principles and objectives. Unlike ELF, EarthOne had never been accused of committing terrorist acts. True, EarthOne was more radical than, say, the Nature Conservancy, but it had not been accused of taking illegal actions. While some might consider its views extreme, its methods—mainly direct mailings and protests such as Lewis was conducting—were definitely mainstream.

That brought me back to the question of whether Lewis's radicalism could have led him to kill Cole. Nothing I read suggested it. The man was acting as a representative of a non-violent environmental group. Certainly he was fervent, and moral fervor made for sloppy arguments. Hence, the fudging of the bird facts to suit his purpose. I wouldn't take Lewis's environmental claims at face value, that's for sure. But zeal did not automatically translate to violence. That transformation required a trigger, and I had not unearthed anything to suggest such an event in Lewis's life. I was satisfied. There was little reason to think Lewis killed Cole to stop the wind farm expansion. In my mind, there was every reason to think he did not.

Before I began my research on Sampson, I needed a break. Luckily, Connor still slept, so I was able to make myself a quick snack without being derailed by an invitation to play Sorry! or computer mahjong. I should have selected fruit or yogurt, but instead I rooted around in the box that Connor had brought home from Desert Donuts yesterday and pulled out a bear claw the size of a Frisbee. The coffee had sat on the burner too long, filling the kitchen with the odor of burning tar, but I poured a cup anyway. After setting out some T-bones to thaw for a barbecue later, I decided I might as well shuck some corn while I was at it.

While I yanked off the husks and pulled the fine silks from the cobs, I marveled as I often did at my choice of profession. Here I was writing balanced books on highly controversial issues. I have strong opinions about most of the topics I write on, but my job requires me to present both sides fairly, keeping my own views invisible. My high school and college journalism teachers would be thunderstruck to learn that I'm actually able to do it.

The incident Trent had remembered about the forbidden article I'd smuggled into the high school newspaper was no anomaly. After I ran my criticism of the principal's decision to ban gay clubs on campus, my teacher told me I'd never make it as a reporter because I couldn't control my passions. My college journalism professor agreed. She said I was too impulsive to be a good journalist. She had one good reason for thinking so.

The thing is, I was a passionate feminist back then, alert to any wrongs committed against people of my gender. So, when I got wind of a purported rape on campus, I felt I had to act. The incident involved a young woman who told campus authorities that three members of the football team had raped her at a frat party. Outraged by this report, I knocked out an editorial lambasting the college for once again turning a blind eye to the outrageous behavior of its male athletes. Unfortunately, I hadn't checked my facts, and the piece came out the exact day the football players were exonerated. The woman, it seems, made the whole thing up to get back at one of the players, who had broken it off with the woman's roommate because he wanted to see someone else. Professor Minden, after spending two hours in the president's office, laid me on the carpet for my irresponsible journalism. Then she kicked me off the paper.

The event, painful as it was, proved fortuitous. Professor Minden pointed out to me that reporters need to be objective, and even editorialists must check their facts and be mindful of the institutions they work for. She said she didn't think I had the ability to check my opinions when necessary, and that I should find another major. At that point, I had to agree with her. I found it excruciating to cover campus issues I cared about without giving my opinion on them. As a reporter, I couldn't get involved when a protest over some policy or event occurred—it was my responsibility to cover the protest objectively, and participating in it would have undermined that neutrality. I felt stifled, frustrated.

About that time, I saw an ad on the bulletin board outside the communications department. It said Blue Next Press was looking for writers to produce books for junior high school students. I called the number, thinking I could use the extra cash, and Vince assigned me a title in the Controversies series. Writing the book was a joy, despite the high learning curve. The process was so much easier for me than writing newspaper articles. While I still felt passionate about the topics I covered, I found I could be objective without difficulty. Perhaps it was because I had the space to cover the subject in depth, lay out both sides of the argument completely. When the view I disagreed with was weak, I felt content knowing that the kids reading my book would likely see that as well. When the view I disagreed with was strong, I found that I developed more of an appreciation for that position and didn't mind presenting it my book as a valid option. Whatever the reason, I knew after that first book what I wanted to do as a writer. I switched my major from journalism to English, and worked for Blue Nest as much as I could around my class schedule.

After I graduated, I began writing for Vince as a full-time freelancer. Unfortunately, like most of its competitors, Blue Nest is hyper aware of the bottom line and does not keep an in-house writing staff. Freelance pay sucks, and I receive no benefits. But, the work suits me. The process of laying out the arguments for each book with an even hand demands fairness and logic, which I, a person ruled by passion, find comforting. It provides a kind of counterbalance in my life that I've come to depend on to keep me sane. I also like the fact that I'm helping young people think more intelligently about the issues of the day. I believe clear thinking can make the world a better place.

As I shucked the corn, the silks sticking to my fingers and the counter and the sink, I realized that my writing was something my mother should have been proud of. She was an educator and should have appreciated the educational value of my books. Not to mention the fact that in writing them, I was exercising the emotional restraint she had urged all my life. But my mother never praised my work. Maybe by the time I began writing for Blue Nest the chasm between us was so vast she didn't know how to bridge it even to say a little thing like, "I'm proud of you." Oh well, what's done is done, she died, and there was nothing I could do about any of it.

After managing to get all the sticky corn silks and unwieldy husks into an empty grocery sack, I grabbed my coffee cup and bear claw and lugged them back to the office to resume my work. Back at my desk, I bit into the bear claw and noted a rare event: Lacy was not staring at me with her "Miss Adorable" look. I haven't been able to nibble a morsel of food in this house without Lacy's breath in my face since I came to live here. Where was she? Was she okay?

I got up from my desk and went in search of her. I finally found the beast hunched over in the corner of the living room, her head bobbing up and down, body convulsing. I rushed over to the dog with visions of rottweiler-sized puke piles being disgorged on Mom's carpet and a rapid trip to the vet. Hopefully, I was not too late, poor thing.

When I got to Lacy, however, my compassion fizzled. She wasn't vomiting, she was polishing off the last of the steaks I had just put out to thaw.

"Out!" I roared, grabbing her collar with both hands and dragging her to the sliding glass door. I shoved her outside and slammed the door, my shoulders aching with the effort, my breathing ragged with rage. The creature had the nerve to stand on the other side of the glass looking back at me, a hurt expression on her face. I glared at her, hoping she'd get the message, but she just stood there, her big head cocked to the side, her big brown eyes wide and wet.

I trudged back to my office. Between Conner and Lacy, it was a miracle I got any work done. I sipped my now-cold coffee and took a deep breath. Time to get back to work.

My next task was to find out all I could about Sampson, then investigate his company. I wasn't sure how much I'd find about either; after all, Desert Rock is a relatively small city, so Sampson's company had to be small, too. Still, you never knew until you researched it.

I typed in "Richard Sampson" and got seventy-six hits. I scanned the articles and discovered a history of the man that surprised me. One *Desert Tribune* article written five years ago announced that Sampson had been selected Community Leader of the Year by the Desert Rock Women's Society. Apparently, Sampson was quite the philanthropist. His company, Sampson Homes, donated money to the Desert Rock women's shelter, and provided computers and building supplies to local schools. He also joined other southern California builders in donating money to build homes in Tijuana for needy families. The reporter claimed that Sampson also contributed both time and money to a number of Habitat for Humanity projects in Desert Rock and nearby communities. Interestingly, the article listed numerous community fund-raising events that Sampson attended along with other community leaders, Cole Mintock being among the other attendees.

The *Los Angeles Times* ran a biographical article about Sampson for a regular feature they call "Movers and Shakers." Sampson had been selected because of his work in the Desert Rock community, and the article covered much the same ground as the *Desert Tribune* piece. However, the focus of this one was more on how he got to where he is today. I found the biographical information they provided intriguing. Sampson was born in South Central Los Angeles six decades ago. His father was not involved in Sampson's life—he seemed to spend a lot of time in prison—so his mother raised him and his two brothers on her factory wages. The family fortunes were not good. Sampson's younger brother was killed during a robbery of the liquor store he worked at, and his older brother was sent to prison for second-degree murder. At the age of twenty-one Sampson himself was accused of killing a man during a bar brawl, but he was never convicted.

Despite such a discouraging start, Sampson got himself together. While working as a framer then as a cabinet installer for a Lancaster construction company, he got his GED, then his realtor and contractor licenses. He bought rundown houses and fixed them up during evenings and weekends, then sold them for a profit. Eventually he used the profits to buy empty lots and build custom homes on them for resale. Within a few years he went into business for himself as a developer. It was about this time that he moved to Desert Rock. He had heard from a buddy of his that the town had become a magnet for retirees looking to winter here to enjoy the sunny, snow-less days. People from colder climes flocked to Desert Rock in the cold months, and many of them never left. Sampson moved to the town twenty years ago and established Sampson Homes as the premier developer in this part of the desert.

When I checked out the Sampson Homes Web site, I learned that *Builder Magazine* had given Sampson's company the Best Builder Award nine years ago. J.D. Powers and Associates reported that according to its New Home Builder customer satisfaction study, nine out of ten customers would refer a friend or relative to Sampson Homes. And apparently Sampson's company did more than build quality homes ("Sampson Homes delivers on its promise to provide quality, value, and service"), it designed environmentally friendly ones as well. The Web site claimed—and I verified the claim by consulting other sources—that Sampson Homes had 100 percent participation in the EPA's Green Building Program, which qualifies Sampson homes for the Energy Star designation. Sampson homes include upgraded insulation, high efficiency heating and air conditioning units, sealed duct systems, and low-emission windows. Most interestingly, many Sampson homes also include built-in solar panels, which enable homeowners to generate almost as much electricity as they use. The Web site even said that the company had traded in a percentage of its fleet for electric-gas hybrids.

I found the news that Sampson was a green builder astonishing given his vociferous opposition to Cole's wind farm. The man seemed to care about saving energy and protecting the environment. The solar panels suggested an embrace of alternative energy sources. Why was he so against wind power? Or, the more provocative question, why was he so opposed to Cole's wind farm in particular? Another strange thing was that none of the articles I found using the search term "Sampson Homes" reported environmental opposition to his development projects. This just didn't sound right to me. Developers—even those installing solar panels—were favorite targets of environmental groups. I decided to try different search terms to see if I could unearth objections to the company's activities.

After typing in "Sampson Homes Urban Sprawl" I hit pay dirt. While Sampson was being awarded the Energy Star designation by the EPA, the Desert Protection Association was lambasting him for attempting to develop land that had been set aside for the protection of endangered plants and animals. The voters of Pumice County had voted for an urban growth boundary, which would make the area southeast of the city off-limits to developers. Four years later, Sampson had gotten enough signatures to put his own measure on the ballot asking voters to open up the land so he could build one thousand green homes on seven hundred acres. To sweeten the deal, he promised to install solar panels on the roof of every new house as well as build miles of trails and two large parks. The Desert Protection Association called Sampson's ploy "green washing."

The majority of voters were not enthused. The measure failed, although not by much. Forty-seven percent of the voters gave Sampson the nod. As one article noted, the pressure to develop open space is high in most areas of California as a result of an expanding population. Because the population outstrips the number of available houses, housing prices have soared, making it nearly impossible for first-time buyers to enter the market. Many buyers from San Diego, Los Angeles, and the Inland Empire were moving to "bedroom communities" like Temecula and Corona, willing to endure a three-hour round trip commute for the luxury of owning a home. While Desert Rock was too far from the urban centers to make it attractive as a bedroom community, a surprising number of people moved here and tried to find work either in the community itself or in nearby towns such as Limestone and Jackson Springs. I understood why many D-Rockians had endorsed Sampson's plan to open the protected area to development. They would have seen it as a way to make home prices more reasonable.

So, was all the green building just show? Just a way to put an attractive face on a company many thought was raping the land? Was Sampson's philanthropic work similarly contrived just to make him—and his company—look good? That assessment seemed to gel with what little I knew of Sampson before the day's research began. He was against the wind farm expansion. Both Sierra and Cole reported that he wanted to buy up Cole's land in order to build a new housing tract. The man seemed angry and hostile, a profile in sync with his violent past.

The main question I had was how all this fit in with Cole's murder. A big guy like Sampson would have no problem dragging Cole's body into a turbine. Moreover, Sampson was driven, a person who would not give up easily to get what he wants. On the other hand, he had come from nowhere and built a lucrative business and a name for himself. Would he risk all that to kill Cole, whose murder could not predictably result in Sampson getting what he wanted? After all, whether Brandon or Jillian Mintock inherited, either one could still lease the land to General Electric or simply refuse to sell it to Sampson. The tenuous benefit seemed too great to justify the risk.

I stared at the computer screen feeling unsatisfied. Maybe I was focusing on the wrong aspects of Sampson's life. Perhaps his attractiveness as a suspect had more to do with his personal life than with his career. Sampson and Cole knew one another, and their relationship seemed strained. Why? Was there more to that story?

I made up my mind to talk with Sampson. There was no way to get answers to these questions without speaking to the man face-to-face. I located the phone number for Sampson Homes on the site's home page and dialed it on my cell phone. When the receptionist picked up, I explained that I wanted to make an appointment to meet with Sampson, and she patched me through to Sampson's personal assistant, Mandy. I explained to Mandy that I was writing a book on energy for Blue Nest Press and hoped to talk to her boss about his green building program. She checked his schedule and said he had an opening on Monday at four. I took it and got directions to the office. I ended the conversation with profuse thanks, thinking a PA would be the ideal person to mine for any information I needed later on down the road.

I felt the satisfaction that always accompanies a productive research session. I thrived on finding answers to questions—it made me feel that anything could be known, understood. It was empowering. My time had been well spent. My initial assessment of Lewis had been validated, and I was more certain than I had been that the authorities were bungling the case. On the other hand, my research into Sampson had raised more questions than it answered. But that's how the investigative process works sometimes. I didn't mind. Eventually I'd find answers to those questions as well. While the information I had gathered thus far may not seem useful, I knew that once I had more context some of those facts would prove vital to my understanding of the case.

I exploited my energized state by doing housework, a chore I often put off until dust chokes the house and algae take over the toilets. I felt especially enthusiastic to vacuum. I dragged Mom's old Oreck out of the closet and plugged it in, eager to get humming before Connor woke up on his own. I decided it would be best to start on the hall carpeting just outside his door.

Chapter Ten

I was late for my Monday appointment with Sampson. The address Mandy had given me was clear across town, and I had forgotten the pace of traffic in Desert Rock. To D-Rockians, a 25-mph zone means you can't go above 15. I got stuck behind some old fart tooling along on McKinley in a hot pink '64 Thunderbird. Eight other people, family members by the looks of them, were packed inside with him. And, of course, I got stopped at all red lights, which were apparently installed without sensors. You can sit at a red light at midnight in this town, with the whole road to yourself, and the light will not change for you. But what nearly sent me over the edge occurred at the intersection of McKinley and Verbena. I had to wait for two old women to roll across the road in motorized wheel chairs with failing batteries. Their progress across the roadway was so slow, the light changed to red, then green, then red again before they made it to the other side. From the back of each of their chairs flapped a triangular orange flag, as if the ladies rode dune buggies. They seemed oblivious to the line of cars that waited for them to cross against the light. And, except for me, nobody else seemed to care either.

I pulled into the R. Sampson building about ten after four. Although other businesses had leased office space in the building,

Sampson's office was easy to find, located as it was front and center. A big green and yellow sign announced that I had located "Sampson Homes—Quality Desert Builders." I rushed inside and told the receptionist that I was there to see Richard Sampson. She sent me back to the office at the end of the hall.

Mandy, a plain woman in her early 30's, sat in an anteroom surrounded by live plants. They looked hale for greenery forced to live out its days under florescent lights.

"Nice plants," I said to ingratiate myself to her in case her good will was needed later. "Every plant I touch dies in seconds."

She laughed. "They seem to like me for some reason. Rich always complains that one day their tendrils will pry through the cracks in his office door and choke him. You know, like in that movie, *Little Shop of Horrors.*"

I laughed, but not for the reason Mandy would assume. I rather enjoyed the thought of Sampson being undone by a philodendron. "I'm Sam Larkin, sorry to be late. I'm from San Diego and can't get used to the way traffic moves around here."

"No problem. Rich is running late himself. He's actually down the hall getting a soft drink. Why don't I just seat you in his office."

We walked into the office, the plush green carpeting threatening to suck the shoes off our feet. Mandy pointed to a chair in front of the huge mahogany desk. "Can I get you anything? Coffee or tea? A soft drink?"

"No, I'm fine, thank you."

"Okay, Rich should be right in."

I was glad he was running late. It made me feel like less of a schmuck for being late myself. Plus, it gave me time to snoop. The mahogany furniture was massive in size, making the capacious office feel smaller than it was. He had hung some unusual watercolors on the wall, abstract renderings of dark emotional storms. Intrigued, I got up to take a closer look. The name R. Sampson was painted in neat script at the bottom of each. Well, what do you know, an artist. It was hard to picture a man of Sampson's bulk and energy sitting before an easel, delicate paintbrush in his paw.

The office's two large windows looked out over the Mule Train Hills, a great place to hike if you enjoy rattle snakes. I turned back to his desk and listened for anyone coming. Not that I planned to pry open his drawers and steal his letter opener, but I didn't want to be caught unawares. I picked up two framed photographs of dogs from his desk, the same trio of black and tan dachshunds in each. Richard Sampson and mini-doxies? I would have thought a man like Sampson would keep pit bulls. Of course, maybe a guy secure in his masculinity didn't need vicious dogs to prove it. The thought made me kind of like Sampson, at least for a second or two. I noted that his dogs had the same coloring as Lacy, the black body with tan markings. They also shared those little tan dots above the eyes where the eyebrows sprout. I shook my head. I couldn't believe I'd even noticed those stupid dots.

I then picked up a photo of an attractive, freckled-faced woman. She gazed at the camera with kindly green eyes. She looked like the all-American mother. The same woman appeared in a photo with Sampson and two teens, a boy and a girl. The kids were also green-eyed and freckled, but I could see their resemblance to their father as well: Both were built like mountains. Fine in the son's case. In the daughter's, not so much. The family photos were so large and numerous they encroached into the working area of his desk. I heard someone at the door and nearly busted my kneecap leaping around the desk into my chair.

Sampson saw me mid-flight. Unimpressed with my acrobatics, he asked in a tight voice, "Snooping in my desk?" As he moved past me and sat down behind the desk, a wave of Polo cologne hit me. He wore tailored navy slacks and a burgundy shirt. A leather belt and loafers completed the ensemble. His bald head was as big and shiny as I remembered, and I noticed that his nose was flat, as if it had been broken multiple times. He didn't appear as huge in his own spacious office as he had in Cole's tiny reception area, but he still dwarfed me. The muscles in his arms and chest suggested long sessions at the gym.

"Sorry," I said, trying to look as abashed as possible. "It's just that the photos of your doxies caught my eye." How the hell could that be true—from my chair, where I was supposed to be, I could only see the backs of the frames. This was going well.

He forgot all about his personal items being rifled through." You have doxies, too?"

"Actually, no, I have a Rottweiler, but her coloring is similar to theirs. I can't resist those spots above their eyes." Well, puke. How repulsive could I get? Like I actually liked Lacy or something.

"They get to me, too." He grinned at the photos, clearly smitten with his three sausage-shaped beasts. "Barney, Travis, and Sam."

"Pardon me?"

"Their names. Barney, Travis, and Sam. They're brothers."

"I'm sorry," I said. "It's just that my name is Sam, and when you said, 'Sam,' I got, well, anyway, hi, I'm Samantha Larkin. I'm the writer from Blue Nest Press." What an idiot!

Sometimes imbecility works in your favor, though. He seemed to relax in the face of my ditziness, which must have convinced him I was harmless. He didn't seem to recognize me from our brief encounter at the wind farm, either, which was just as well. He placed his Seven-Up can on the desk and extended his hand. "Nice to meet you," he said. His hand was cold from the can. "Mandy said you're interested in our green building program. What kind of book did you say you were writing?"

I fudged a little, not wanting him to know just yet that the main focus of my inquiry was the wind farm. "It's a supplemental text book on energy for junior high school kids. It's the kind of book a kid would check out in order to write a research paper in English class."

"You're a published author?"

"Yes, I've written around twenty books."

"All non-fiction."

"Right. Mainly on controversial topics like abortion and the death penalty. We've been doing a lot of stuff on energy lately. I wanted to talk to people who represent the cutting edge of energy conservation. I've been researching the EPA's Green Building Program and came across your name. I also learned that Sampson Homes won the American Home of the Future award a couple of years back. You seemed the right person to talk to about the importance of green building."

He seemed pleased I had done my homework. Picking up his soda can—which looked tiny in his big mitt—he took a long drink, then leaned back in his chair. He observed me for a moment, his eyes an indistinct color, looking gray one minute and brown the next. While he looked relaxed, leaning back in his chair like that, I felt a power surge beneath the surface. "Sampson Homes is committed to building houses that are both good for the environment and good for people," he said in a well-rehearsed script. He then went on to outline the design elements his company used to construct their green homes, all of which I had read about on his Web site. I needed to get him off script, maybe push a few buttons.

"Do all of those features make a four thousand square foot home as energy efficient as a much smaller home?" I asked, trying to sound innocent. "I mean, a home that big would need a bigger air conditioning unit—or perhaps more than one—so it kind of seems like the larger home, even though built green, would still use more energy than the smaller one."

His body grew still, and the power coursing inside him intensified. Ah, he didn't like to be questioned. "I'll make two points about that. Number one: A very inefficient smaller home could very well use more energy than an extremely efficient larger home."

I wondered about the vague terms he used to make this claim. How small was he talking about, and how large? And how inefficient would the smaller house have to be? Would it have to have a thirty-year old air conditioner? No insulation? My research indicated that many people have upgraded their older homes, installing dual-pane windows, putting in more insulation, and purchasing a more energy-efficient air conditioning unit to make their old houses—which are typically much smaller than today's—more energy efficient. These refurbished homes would have to use less energy than those estates Sampson builds. What he said was true, strictly speaking, but you had to be careful to examine his terms. He was a convincing orator though, I'll give him that.

Sampson went on. "Point number two: People just don't want smaller homes anymore, so your question is moot. Oh, and a third point: Don't forget that we install solar panels on most of our homes, which makes each resident virtually self-sufficient."

"What percentage of homes get the solar panels?"

He eyed me, looking irritated. "Right now, about 30 percent."

Thirty percent? Like 30 percent constituted the most of anything. I let it go. "So you're a proponent of alternative energy sources?"

"Of course. Who wouldn't want solar panels, which let you live off the grid most of the year, at least here. You basically pay for no electricity. In fact, during long summer days, you can sell excess power back to the utility company. What's not to like?"

Here was my chance to steer the interview in the direction I wanted. I said, "I just learned that Desert Rock is powered almost entirely by wind energy. I assume you take a positive view of that."

He grimaced to show his disapproval.

"Is it that you prefer solar power over wind?"

He ran a hand over his hairless head. "Actually, I do, if you mean individual solar panels for residences. Building those giant solar facilities like that monstrosity out by Kramer Junction is a ridiculous use of land. Same with the wind farm. You tie up all that land, for what? A few hundred megawatts. And then the big electric companies come in and buy up leases, then ratchet up the price per megawatt. Doesn't sound like energy independence to me."

"You'd rather use the land for development."

"Of course. I'm a developer. I make no bones about that."

I decided to use some of what I'd learned about Sampson's conflict with environmentalists to get a reaction out of him. "That must be a popular stance with the environmentalists. They'd rather set the land aside to protect native species, or at least use it to make green electricity. I'm sure they oppose the building of enormous homes that eat up energy."

He sat up straighter. I heard the leather chair squeak under his rump. "Come on, people have to live somewhere. If the greens had their way, they'd set aside all remaining open land for toad moss and warbler wrens or whatever hell the species du jour is. Setting aside land for endangered species is the least efficient way to protect them. There'd never be enough land to do it, for Christ's sake. We need to develop the land in an environmentally conscious way so people have an incentive to protect animals."

This conversation was taking me nowhere. I decided to steer it into even more turbulent waters. I was interested in his ideas about energy—I was writing an energy book after all— but I needed to get down to business. "I went out to CalWind for a tour of the place so I could write about it in my book. I was surprised to find out that the wind farm is a source of controversy in this town. I was especially amazed to see an environmentalist out protesting it."

He snorted. "You're talking about that kook who murdered Cole Mintock. Those green wackos are never happy. They scream for alternative energy sources, and when you give it to them, they find a half dozen problems with it."

"You're not over-fond of environmentalists."

"What developer do you know is?"

"Backing up a bit, you said Luke Lewis murdered Mintock. Did the police formally charge him?"

"No. They're taking their sweet time about it."

"Maybe they don't have a good case against him?"

"This is Desert Rock. We don't even have our own police force. Have you seen some of those Pumice County Sheriff Deputies? Bunch of incompetents."

I didn't tell him that one of those deputies was an old acquaintance of mine. I doubted he'd be impressed. It was interesting that he had so low a regard for law enforcement in these parts. Might make committing a murder here seem less risky. I asked, "The deputies ever question you about the murder?"

He sat forward and plunked his soda can on the desk. "I thought you were here to interview me about my houses."

I admit that I had to force myself to remain seated. My instincts told me to run out of the room. "I'm just confused about where you stand. On the one hand you take pride in building green homes with solar panels. On the other hand, you detest environmentalists and are working to stop the expansion of the wind farm."

"How do you know about that?"

"I talked to Cole Mintock, and he mentioned it. I saw you at CalWind, looking pretty pissed off at him."

He narrowed his eyes at me. They flashed through several colors, green, then blue, then a hard steel gray. "I remember you now. You were there to meet Cole. Why are you involved in this?"

I threw up my hands, palms up. "I'm not. I'm just conducting research for my book. I'm just trying to find out—"

"I say this politely," he said, the words spoken with a measured amount of silence between each one. "I don't take kindly to people lying to me or snooping into what is none of their business."

It was now or never. Why not? I took a deep breath and asked, "Where were you on the night Cole got murdered?"

He slammed his hand down on the desktop. The 7-Up can levitated two inches off the desk and came down without a splash. Sampson looked as if he wanted to pummel the desk—or me—but he reeled in the impulse, a maneuver clearly mastered after long practice. "You are way out of line. This interview, or whatever the hell it is, is over."

"All right," I said. My voice quavered despite my best efforts to appear calm. I was frightened, I admit, but I was also angry. "But before I go, I want to tell you that I don't believe that Luke Lewis killed Cole. It just doesn't make sense. I also think the authorities have focused on Lewis because it's an easy case to make, and one that would win them kudos. Whoever killed Cole could go free. I liked Cole, he didn't deserve to die. The least his wife and son deserve is that the right person be punished for killing him."

Sampson remained posed as he had been before I spoke, seemingly frozen, his body poised to pound me into pulp or sit back in the chair and agree with me. He inhaled deeply through his flattened nose—it didn't sound good, the passages were obviously obstructed—then let the air out. He said, "I was working on financial reports here the night Cole was killed."

I smiled, threatening to crack my face into several pieces. "Thank you for your time, Mr. Sampson. I'll let myself out."

As I rose to leave, he stalked over to me. His body towered over mine, and I could feel heat radiating from his skin. He grabbed my elbow, squeezed it hard. "I learned long ago how to stop being a bull in a china shop, "he said. "But I still have moments where I want to break some china. Just don't mess with me or mine, Ms. Larkin."

I nodded, shook off his hand, and sauntered through the door.

Luckily, Mandy was not at her desk. I was in no mood for more ingratiating small talk or insincere compliments on the greenery. Once I was out of Sampson's line of vision, I plowed through the thick carpeting as fast as I could without actually running, eager to get outside into air and light. Walking through the windy parking lot to my car, all I could think about was getting home, opening a cold beer, and sitting with Lacy on the patio, looking at Mom's garden.

Unfortunately, when I pulled up to the house, I saw Connor's junky Escort parked out front. Worse, Vanessa's Mercedes was right behind it. I wondered if I had enough beer in the fridge to get me through this.

Chapter Eleven

I felt shaky after my visit with Sampson and was in no mood for any bullshit from Connor and Vanessa. When I walked in the kitchen door from the garage, my plan was to grab a beer, then sneak back to my bedroom and take a shower. Alas, Connor had cleaned out the beer supply, and Vanessa pulled me into a fight already in progress.

"Why didn't you tell me Connor was in town?" She said, standing with her arms crossed in the middle of the family room. Her perfume seemed to suck the air out of the house, leaving me struggling for breath. Connor was slumped on the couch, hands thrust in the pockets of his shorts, eyes focused out the patio window.

I dropped my purse and car keys on the kitchen counter. "What, are you the KGB?"

"I want to know because he owes me money," she said as if Connor were not in the room. "He should be in L.A. working so that he can pay me back. Did you know that he quit his job with Frank?"

"No," I said, looking at my brother. "What's up with that, Connor?"

He continued to stare straight ahead. "Not that it's either of your business, but I quit because Frank is a jerk." When we were young, our mother socialized with Frank's mom, and we kids hung out with Frank and his sisters. Now Frank runs a construction company in L.A. and has hired Connor on several occasions, not, of course, because my brother is the best worker he ever had. Frank is loyal to our family and puts up with a lot from my brother. Especially when Connor quits without notice to go do something else, then comes slinking back asking for a job again.

"You know, Connor's right," I said to Vanessa. "It really isn't our business."

"It most certainly is my business if he owes me money. And he's living here with you for free. For how long?" She turned to level her haughty stare at Connor.

I was interested in the answer, of course, but I thought I should be the one to ask the question. Connor obviously agreed. "That's between Sam and me," he said. "Why don't you leave me alone?"

Vanessa snorted. "If you don't want me in your business, then you shouldn't ask me for money."

I couldn't help myself. "How much money are we talking about?"

Together they said, "It's none of your business!"

"I'm only asking because Connor owes me money, too. I'm trying to calculate the odds of me getting it back."

Vanessa said, "High school genius scores highest in his class on the SAT, gets accepted at Berkeley, and ten years later still hasn't done a damn thing except sponge off his family. I will never understand you, Connor!"

He scowled and said to her, "And what have you done with your precious degree? Cripe, Van, you don't even work."

I said, "She uses her college degree, all right, always psychoanalyzing everyone. But Vanessa's got a point, Connor. You haven't held down a job in a decade. And now Mom's gone. Don't you think it's about time you grew up?"

"Exactly," Vanessa added after glaring at me. "Why can't you keep a job for longer than four months?"

He said, his voice barely audible, "Not that I have to answer to either of you, but I don't like to be tied down. I like doing my own thing."

"Except when the money runs out," Vanessa and I said in unison.

My brother slumped down further into the couch like a little boy. At that moment, I felt like a bully. Granted, everything Vanessa and I said to Connor was true, but it felt as if we were attacking a child. That's Connor's genius. By refusing to grow up, he forces us to deal with him on an adult-child level. Only, Connor isn't a little boy, and treating him like one—even though he deserves it—makes me feel like a patronizing jerk. I wind up feeling worse than he does.

Still, I never seemed to be able to relate to him any other way. I heard myself say, "This is how it always goes. Connor gets in a fix and the women in this family bail him out. Vanessa, do you remember when Connor snuck out that night and took Mom's car joyriding? What was he, about fourteen? When the police called, she just laughed. Do you remember? She laughed? Shit, if I had done that she would have put me on restriction until I collected Social Security!"

Connor groaned and pulled at his hair with both hands. "God! Do we have to hear that story again? You're always going on and on about that stupid joyriding thing."

"Sam seems to forget all the times she got suspended from school and put on restriction," Vanessa said.

I wanted to punch her. Hard. "Well, la tee da, Miss Perfect with her straight A's and math club. Could a person get more nerdy? My point is that I always got punished just for breathing and Connor got away with murder. Mom thought everything he did was so endearing. Me, it was just, 'Go to your room and stay there until you're twenty-five.' She loved Connor better than both of us put together."

"Oh for Pete's sake," Vanessa said. "Would you give it a rest? Mothers always dote on their sons. Get over it."

"Yes," Connor added, "Please, for the love of God, let it go."

"It's making you bitter," my sister said in that tone of hers that alerts listeners that now they will be psychoanalyzed. "You've resented Mom's relationship with Connor and me all your life. Did you ever think if you'd behaved better she might have liked you more?"

That crossed a line and Vanessa knew it. Connor knew it, too. He stopped pulling at his hair and dropped his hands into his lap, his body growing still. He looked at me out of the corner of his eye. Vanessa pretended to be unconcerned, making a show of gazing out the window, but I could see her shoulders square up.

I had a vision of myself going up to her and wrapping my fingers around her neck.

"All I'm saying," Vanessa said, as though she spoke to the window, "is that you alienated us by being so angry all the time. Always making mountains out of mole hills, protesting this or that whatever. It seems unfair to blame Mom—or us—for what you did to yourself."

"Van's right," Connor said. "We all tried with you, but you didn't want to have anything to do with us. You were so angry all the time. At everything."

Red and white explosions flashed across my vision. I looked hard at Connor, then at Vanessa, but neither met my gaze. I said, my voice ripping the air like a chain saw, "Get out of my house."

I couldn't believe I'd said it. It was such an over-reaction. It was as if I had been compelled to prove Connor right. Neither said a word to me, and I found myself unable to speak to them. I stomped down the hall to my bedroom and slammed the door. I could hear Vanessa's and Connor's voices break the silence I had left. They sat out there talking for hours. Eventually, I heard the refrigerator door open and close, dishes clatter, the microwave ping. I smelled the leftover chicken and potatoes I had made Sunday night through the air ducts. And there I was, sitting in my room watching it get dark outside. I felt like a fool, locking myself in my room like a petulant brat. But I could not force myself to open the door and go out. I wanted to cry, but I would not let myself do it. Instead, I held onto the anger like a swimmer holds her breath under water. At first the rage felt life giving, but then it turned toxic. I knew I'd have to come up for air sometime, but I just kept swimming in the cold dark depths. The sense of suffocation, of freezing to death, felt welcome. Numbness was better than feeling.

I had always been a fan of numbness, at least where personal feelings were concerned. I had no problem connecting with other people's miseries and blessings—I could sense fear or humiliation or anguish in someone I hardly knew—but my own emotional landscape could have been the moon for all the success I had navigating it. About the only emotions I seem to feel clearly are anger and outrage. Love and trust are alien to me. I don't know why. All I know is that it has caused me no end of misery. It certainly hasn't helped me develop trusting bonds with my family.

I took a few deep breaths and felt the anger morph into something else, a feeling that left me longing for my mother. But she was gone, she had died in this very room, just months before. I felt tears sting my eyes. No wonder I preferred the cold sea of anger, the way the icy rage stings and aches but finally obliterates all other emotions. Anger can feel exhilarating, empowering. Grief just hurts.

Chapter Twelve

The morning after my brawl with Vanessa and Connor, I had book club at Hattie's house at ten o'clock. Everyone else in the group was retired, as my mother had been when she joined, but they allowed me, a mere working stiff, into the club as an honorary member. I supposed today they might reconsider that decision. I looked like hell. My face was puffy from lack of sleep, and my facial skin, usually olive-hued, looked blanched. I had done what I could with makeup, the result of my inexpert applications a cross between Tammy Faye Baker and a corpse.

When Hattie let me in her front door, I heard a sharp intake of breath. She was too refined to say anything about my appearance and simply studied me with concern.

I entered the house and carried the plate of brownies I had baked that morning to the living room, where the club members would meet. I removed the plastic wrap and set the plate on Hattie's cluttered coffee table.

To her unasked question, I said, "Bad night."

Hattie, dressed in a deep burgundy skirt and billowy ecru blouse, pointed to a chair. "Please, have a seat. Let's talk for a bit."

I weaved around the sofas and chairs and bookcases overflowing with books and carved my way to my favorite seat by the window.

Hattie is so neat about her personal appearance that it always comes as a shock to enter her home. Her abode is crammed with crap bisected by paths just wide enough to accommodate the width of her walker. She and my mother could not have differed more in their views toward housekeeping. Mom lived ascetically, and we used to quip that you could perform surgery in her kitchen without risk of infection. Hattie was fond of saying that housecleaning was a waste of time because everything just got dirty again. The clutter in her house makes me feel closed in and clammy, which is why I always sit close to the window.

The minute my butt hit the chair, Hattie's orange tabby cat, Walter, jumped in my lap and made himself at home in the manner he usually does. The process consists of sharpening his nails on my thighs until I cry out, then he rolls into a ball and goes to sleep.

"I don't want to keep you," I said. "The girls (I was the only one under seventy in the group) will be here any minute."

Hattie lowered herself into the chair opposite me and waved away my concern. "Never mind that. They're always late anyway. You just tell me what's troubling you."

I needed a sympathetic ear, but at the same time I remembered that Hattie has a tendency to allegorize. I wasn't sure I was up to deciphering another of her childhood stories from which I was expected to extract an important life lesson. Need won out. "Vanessa and Connor and I had a big blow out fight last night. First, Vanessa and I laid into Connor for being such a flake, then they turned on me, implying that all the problems between Mom and me were my fault."

Hattie's other cat, Wilma, a fat gray, leapt up into Hattie's lap and went to sleep. The purring of the two cats sounded like lawn equipment. Waiting for me to continue, Hattie stroked Wilma. I wondered why the cat's bulk didn't snap Hattie's thin legs.

"I'm confused about everything," I said. "Maybe I am bitter. Last night Vanessa said my unresolved feelings about Mom and her relationship with Connor and her are making me bitter. Maybe she's right. I don't seem to be letting things go. I'm not moving on. She's probably also right in claiming that my living here is some misguided attempt to make my peace with Mom. All it's done is throw Connor and Vanessa and me together more often, which is like tossing three pit bulls into a ring."

Hattie's stroking had intensified, and an annoyed Wilma glared up at her with one amber eye. Hattie smartly desisted and said, "I always thought a good fight with my sisters was worth ten smarmy moments. People say when we're angry we say things we don't mean. I couldn't disagree more. We mean it all right, but we're too polite to say it. I once told Agnes during a fight that she looked like a Halloween witch. Well, of course I loved my sister, but I sometimes hated her, and at that moment I did. It's natural to feel these things, get them out so they don't fester. Agnes and I laughed about that fight years later."

"Well, you were light years ahead of us," I said. "I can't see us ever laughing about it."

"You will. As long as you keep talking to each other—and, Samantha, fighting is just another way of talking—you leave open the possibility of laughing about it."

"I think just the opposite. I wonder if I should sell the house after all and move back to San Diego. What am I doing here? Clinging to what is gone, going round and round with Connor and Vanessa. At least in San Diego I wouldn't have to see them as much."

"I would miss you if you left," Hattie said. "Samantha, I too cling to your mother. Through you."

My throat felt swollen, and I began rubbing Walter's head. When his claws extended, I took this as my cue to stop.

Hattie added, "I miss your mother so much it physically hurts. But then, I look over at your house and know that you are there. I see so much of Olivia in you, her spunk, her intelligence, her social conscience. I know that you can't replace your mother in my life, but I'm glad that you're here. You've suffered an enormous loss. You may cling to your mother's friends or yell at Vanessa or cry all night. It's okay, you know. You've got to let yourself grieve."

To my horror, I felt tears prick my eyes. I fought them back by biting my lip until I tasted blood. I said, my voice trembling, "I sometimes think I got into scrapes just to be perverse. Just to show I didn't care what she thought. What a shit."

Hattie stared at me with narrowed eyes. "Now, Sam, you know how I try never to advise, but you are sorely trying me! Quit beating yourself up! You have worked yourself into such a state—it doesn't become you. You weren't a 'shit' to your Mom—you were just being Sam. So you and your mother didn't see eye to eye. So what? How many mothers and daughters do? And so what if your mother found Vanessa and Connor easier to get along with—that's personality, not love. You need to stop dwelling on the past and start looking ahead. Of course you're going to be thinking about your Mom, you're still grieving for heaven's sake. But it would do you good to get involved in things that have nothing to do with your mom or Connor or Vanessa. Are any of your old girlfriends still in town?"

I gawked at Hattie, unable to respond. I had never heard her talk so directly—and emphatically—before. Leave it to me to send that reserved woman over the edge. I finally muttered, "Most of my girlfriends moved away to go to college like I did. They're sort of scattered around the country, now."

She compressed her lips together. "Surely one or two stayed here."

I nodded compliantly, not wanting to exasperate Hattie further. "Yeah, a couple stayed or moved back."

"Then look them up."

"I just haven't felt up to it."

"You see Eddie."

"Yeah, well that's different."

"Why?"

"Eddie's a friend of the family. He's always been around."

"He's safe."

I felt my head jerk up. Is that how I saw Eddie, as safe?

I heard Hattie say, "Reconnect with those girlfriends, Sam, and go do something fun. But right now, go get yourself collected before the girls get here."

I got up as if in a trance and placed Walter on the chair cushion. Unamused, he glared at me with narrow green eyes. His look seemed to say, the claw-sharpening routine will last much longer next time you sit down. I felt my body move down the hall toward the bathroom as if I were a zombie.

The doorbell rang. "What did I tell you?" I heard Hattie say. "Twenty minutes late."

Chapter Thirteen

Somehow I got through the book club. I barely participated, but the others were too polite to say anything. Nor did they mention the fact that I looked like road kill. When I got home, I decided to distract myself by working on Cole's murder case. I had had enough of family dramas and was in no mood to write. Besides, the interview with Sampson had unnerved me, which pissed me off. I did not like being threatened. To prove to him—and to myself—that I was not afraid, I decided to investigate the veracity of his claim to be working late the night of the murder. After eating a bowl of Captain Crunch (Connor's purchase) and a shriveled peach, I called Sampson's personal assistant, Mandy.

After announcing who I was and engaging in small talk in which plants figured prominently, I told Mandy that I wanted to get a gift certificate to thank her boss for taking the time to talk to me. Could she suggest a favorite restaurant of his? She seemed to think I was one classy chick, and readily offered up suggestions about where he liked to eat. Mandy seemed unaware that Sampson had written my name on his shit list and would be as thrilled to get a gift from me as he'd enjoy receiving a pipe bomb in the mail. After telling her I'd buy him a gift certificate for two at the French Grille, I segued into what I really wanted to know.

"Don't you find it difficult to work for him?" I asked. "He was perfectly nice to me, but I still felt intimidated. He's so big, and no one to mess around with I'll bet."

Mandy laughed. "All that's true, but he's a gentle giant. I've been working for the man for six years and I can honestly say he's the best boss I've ever had. Respectful, understanding if I need time off."

"Guess he gives you time off to make up for all the overtime you work. I got the impression that you two work a lot of late nights."

"Oh no, actually Rich rarely works late and I haven't logged any overtime in months."

"Oh," I said, making myself sound silly and confused. "I thought he said something about staying late to work on some financial reports. I must have misunderstood him. Last job I had, I did a lot of overtime, which I hated. Really killed my social life."

"I know what you mean. That's one of the reasons I like working for Rich. I've worked as a PA for other people, and you're pretty much on call 24/7. No, Rich has his priorities straight. His company is important to him, but he likes to spend as much time as possible with his family. Rich has other people to do financial reports and bids and stuff like that for him. That's the benefit of being the owner, I guess."

Very interesting. It looked as if Sampson had fed me a lie. I wondered what his wife would say about that night. I said to Mandy, "I saw all those photos he has on his desk of his wife and kids. His wife looks familiar to me. Does she sit on the city council?" Whoa. I had no idea I could bullshit so effortlessly. I was amazed at my hidden talents.

"Oh no," Mandy said. "I can't see Abby doing anything political like that. Maybe you saw her at the library. She volunteers there, running the literacy program for kids. She's always down there helping out. I think she used to be a librarian or teacher."

"That's it, that's where I've seen her. I do a lot of research for my books, so I'm always in the library myself."

I thanked her for all her help and hung up. I now knew—or at least suspected— two important things: Apparently Sampson had not worked late the night of the murder, which, if true, meant he lied to me. I also knew where to find his wife to see what else I could learn about the "gentle giant." Gentle my ass. He'd probably snap my neck like a pencil if he knew what I was up to.

I drove to Desert Rock's public library around two and waited until the reading program ended. Sitting at one of the computer tables near the children's reading room, I watched as Abby Sampson said good-bye to each kid who filed out. I had to hand it to her. She clicked with the little buggers. I had watched the proceedings as she conducted the reading group. The rug rats sat still while she read the story and then ran a tot-level discussion group about it afterwards. All those grubby little hands shooting up and those shrill voices would have sent me screaming from the room, but she seemed to enjoy it.

When the room cleared, I went in, nearly passing out from the overpowering odor of kid—that combination of bubble gum, fruit juice, and dirt. When I approached Abby, who at fifty-something looked polished and authoritative in her gray skirt and white blouse, I said in a quiet, library-friendly voice, "Abby Sampson? I'm Samantha Larkin, a writer for Blue Nest Press. I wonder if you had a moment to talk with me."

She whispered, "Blue Nest Press? Oh, we just love your books. When the junior high kids come in to do research for their reports, we always send them to Blue Nest books. They are the best out there for young people."

I had heard this many times before, but it always pleased me. I liked that my work was important and appreciated. Today, however, her praise made me feel a little guilty. My real goal was not to talk about children's books but to probe her for information on Sampson. Despite my discomfort, I plunged ahead. "I'm writing a book on energy and I wanted to get your view on what kind of book would be most helpful to kids."

"Oh, well, you don't want to talk to me. You'll want to talk to Elsa, the head librarian. I'm just a volunteer here."

I pretended to be discombobulated. "Oh, I see you in here all the time. I just assumed you were a librarian. You're married to Richard Sampson, aren't you?"

"Why, yes, how did you know that?"

"Just yesterday I was out at Sampson Homes interviewing your husband for my book. His PA, Mandy, told me you ran the literacy program here." I omitted the part where Sampson caught me snooping among his private photographs and then told me to get the hell out of his office. "I enjoyed talking with him. He gave me a lot of good stuff on green building I can use in the book. I like getting the widest range of views possible, and he articulated his position well."

"Oh yes," she said. "Richard knows everything there is to know about green building. And when he's passionate about a subject, he can be very persuasive."

She seemed to be poking fun at his size and temperament, and I laughed. "I can't imagine many people saying 'no' to him."

"Unless it's his children. They walk all over him, he's such a softie. And the dogs, too, good Lord. We have three miniature dachshunds and they rule the roost."

"He showed me pictures of them. They're cute," I said to ingratiate myself to her. "I've got a rottweiler, which I inherited from my mother." I lifted up an arm and pointed to the pinkish-brown scab on my elbow. "She's a lot of handle," I said and shrugged.

Abby laughed, her freckled face lighting up. "Maybe a doxie would be more your size. You said your last name is Larkin. Are you by any chance related to Olivia Larkin?"

That surprised me, although I don't know why it should have. My mother was a teacher and a prominent activist in town—lots of people knew her. "I'm her daughter," I said.

Abby nodded, looking closely at me. "I'm so sorry about her passing," she said, touching my arm. "I knew your mother for many years. We worked together on the annual book fair to raise money for literacy. Working on that committee was a joy—your mother was so organized and energetic. She must have also been a remarkable teacher. During the book fair, all her students from the high school would come up to her and say, "Yo, Mrs. Larkin, what's up?" And they'd actually hang around and talk with her. You know how teenagers are, usually so dismissive of adults. It was really something to watch. *She* was really something."

Abby's words produced a sharp pain in the middle of my chest, and I felt tears burn my eyes. It seemed that everywhere I went these days, people were praising my mother to the skies. I was finally beginning to appreciate who my mother really was, and I felt an intense admiration. But I also felt regret so sharp it physically hurt. She was gone, and nothing I learned could change our relationship now.

Abby must have seen the emotion on my face because she reached out and squeezed my elbow. "How are you holding up?" She asked.

I swallowed hard, not wanting to talk about it. How had things gotten so off track? I came here to pump Abby for information about her husband, and here I was going all soft over my mother's death. "Fine," I said briskly and squared my shoulders. I smiled.

Abby said, "I also know your sister. Vanessa is following right in your mother's footsteps."

Okay, while I might appreciate hearing my mother commended, I couldn't stomach hearing about Vanessa's virtues. I felt myself grimace. Ungracefully, I changed the subject. "I was surprised to hear your husband say he wasn't thrilled with the local wind farm, given his commitment to building energy efficient homes. Do you think he'll succeed in stopping the farm's expansion?"

Abby accepted the redirect without question. She seemed to recognize that Vanessa was not my favorite topic of discussion and understood my need to change the subject. Perhaps she, too, had an obnoxious sister she'd be loath to hear flattered. She said, "I regret that Richard has become so invested in stopping the wind farm. He won't talk to me about it, not that that's unusual. He doesn't talk shop very much. I tried to tell him that it didn't look good, a man commended for building energy efficient homes trying to derail a wind farm expansion. Whatever his views on wind power, most people think of it as green energy. He's going to look like he's against protecting the environment. Plus, lots of people in this town like—or, I should say liked—Cole Mintock, and Richard's animosity toward him can only hurt his reputation, one he has worked so hard to build. My husband has had a difficult past, and people take awhile to see the man he really is."

"Do you have any idea why he is so opposed to the wind farm expansion?"

"Part of me thinks he did it just to irk Cole—those two had a falling out years ago, although I never found out why. But there are also practical reasons Rich is against the expansion. Look. I can see his point. People build up on Pioneer Hill because of the view. It's hellishly expensive to build there because the terrain is so steep. Rich spent a hundred thousand dollars just to put in our driveway. But the view is spectacular. You should come to the house so you can understand what a loss it would be if they erected a bunch of wind turbines all over the valley out there. Here, let me give you my phone number. Give me a call and we'll give you a tour." She handed me one of Richard's business cards with her home phone number scribbled on it.

I took the card, thinking fast. I wasn't likely to take her up on her offer, but maybe I could use the opening to obtain the information I came for. I said, "That is very kind of you. But I wouldn't want to intrude. I know how busy Richard is with his business. Sounds like he puts in a lot of long days, staying late at night to finish up the day's work."

She shook her head. "You know, actually he doesn't. He likes to make it home before five or six so he can make a nice dinner for us. He's a gourmet chef, you know."

Ah, so Abby had confirmed what Mandy said about Sampson not making a habit out of working late. The women's assertions didn't necessarily mean that Sampson lied to me about the night of Cole's murder, but it certainly raised questions about his alibi. I said to Abby, "Maybe I'll stop by some evening after dinner, then."

"Just call first. Rich sometimes takes off in the evenings. You know how men are." Abby smiled conspiratorially.

I wasn't sure exactly what she was getting at, but I rolled my eyes, eager to appear like I understood. "Do I ever. Most of the guys I've dated had to squeeze me in between poker nights, league bowling, and Monday night football." Unfortunately, that was true, one reason, I suppose, I haven't gotten married. Who would put up with that shit for the rest of your life?

"Men!" Abby said and waved her hand as if dismissing the entire male population. "I especially get annoyed when Rich takes off on weeknights because on the weekends I hardly see him at all. It's nothing but golf, golf, golf."

I groaned. "Now there's a game that can burn up time. Does he play both Saturday and Sunday?"

"Yes! I'm thinking of instituting a rule that he can't play on Sundays so we get to spend time with him. Actually, I shouldn't put it that way—Rich really does like spending time with me and the kids. But men always seem pulled by other, well, distractions."

Abby had tried for nonchalance, but I heard heat in her words, and her face looked tense. Eager to learn what had her so irked, I said, "It's so true. Sports, beer, the Internet, video games, buddies. Oh yeah, and how could I forget men's favorite distraction, sex. At least they need us for that."

"Well," Abby said. "They need *some* woman for that."

Anger defied her effort to sound humorous and philosophical. The message I was getting was that Richard was having an affair. To confirm my suspicion, I played the empathy card. "Please," I said. "Don't go there. The last boyfriend I had kept saying he had to go see this sick aunt of his. Aunt my ass—excuse the language. How could I be so dumb?"

"Don't blame yourself," she said with force. "It wasn't your fault your boyfriend turned out to be a philanderer."

"I know, it's just that I pride myself on being a good judge of character. I like to think I can't get taken. But he made a fool out of me."

Abby looked at me, but I noticed her green eyes were unfocused, her thoughts apparently far away. "I sometimes think men are just wired differently than women."

Now her voice sounded resigned. Abby clearly wasn't going to get into specifics with me, a virtual stranger, even if I was Olivia Larkin's daughter. However, she'd divulged enough to make me fairly certain Sampson cheated on her. Whether this was significant to my investigation I wasn't sure, but I was grateful for the information.

Our girl talk had run its course. I would probably not talk to Abby again—I sure as hell wasn't actually going to drive up to their house to check out the view; Sampson would kill me—so I decided I might as well ask her what I really wanted to know. Her reaction might reveal something significant.

I took a deep breath, said, "Talking about Richard's late night activities reminds me of a question I meant to ask. When I spoke to him, he claimed he was working late at the office the night Cole was murdered. But you and Mandy have indicated that that was highly unlikely. I'm wondering if you could shed some light on the apparent discrepancy."

It was as though I had slapped her. Her body recoiled, her eyes flew open, and her mouth became a perfect "O." For the first time during our talk, she looked anything but open and nice.

She said, her words sounding choked off, "What kind of question is that? You said you're a writer. Why are you asking about Cole's murder? No, don't answer that, I don't care." She glared at me, then turned her back in order to retrieve her purse. Within seconds, she had rushed past me and sped out of the room. I swear I smelled nervous sweat—an odor like wet pennies, smoke, and turpentine—permeate the room, replacing the kid smell.

Abby hadn't told me where Sampson was the night of the murder—or where she thought he was, anyway—but I had learned one thing: She was loyal. It made me wonder: Given her loyalty, if she knew where Sampson had been that night, wouldn't she have been eager to say so in order to give him an alibi, despite her anger at me? After all, she would want to exonerate him if she could. Perhaps she hadn't because she didn't actually remember that particular night out of all the other nights. But I hardly thought that was the case. It was the night Cole was murdered, and given her husband's long relationship with Cole, she would have remembered the details of that night. So why hadn't she confirmed where Sampson was? Did she know he was not working late and did not want to contradict his claim? Or did she have no idea where he had been and she thought saying so would raise suspicions?

Either way, Sampson's alibi seemed shakier than ever.

Chapter Fourteen

When I got home from my library visit with Abby on Tuesday afternoon, I found a message on my machine. It was from Van Dorn, the foreman at Mill Maintenance. I had expressed interest in observing a windsmith at work, and he was calling to set up a time for me to observe Brandon on his maintenance rounds Friday morning. I looked forward to the visit, hoping to get a feel for what windsmiths do—it seemed a job my young readers would think cool. Climbing up into the turbine tower evoked the specter of falling to your death or suffocating. Kids would love it. The best way to bring the job to life for them was for me to experience it firsthand. Of course, there was one little problem with my plan: I wouldn't get into one of those turbines unless you conked me on the head and drug me into it. Nonetheless, I decided to go, hoping I'd change my mind once I got there.

I used the three days before my Friday appointment with Brandon to work long hours. I was behind on my book and needed a burst in progress. I wasn't going make the deadline, but it was imperative that I turn the book in no later than a week or two late. Vince would accept tardiness of that degree—with lots of grumbling, of course—but anything beyond that and he'd probably never assign me another book.

When I arrived at Mill Maintenance at five on Friday morning, I felt cheerful, despite the hour. Brandon waited for me beside one of the white maintenance trucks with the familiar red MM logo on its door, and after sleepy greetings, we got in the vehicle and drove off. I rolled the truck window down so I could breathe in the cool, sage-scented air. While we rambled over the dirt road, I watched the sun rise over the Silver Mine Range, turning the sky orange. I made a note to myself to get up early more often. I had forgotten how stunning desert sunrises are, and how energized they made me feel.

Brandon seemed less enthralled. He drove without speaking, his face sleepy as he stared down the dirt road as if our journey would go on for days. I noticed that his blonde spikes listed from lack of sufficient mousse support. I wasn't sure if his lethargy was due to the early hour or from grief catching up with him. I remembered how hard it was just to get up in the morning after my mom died. Who cared about looking good?

"Thanks for letting me tag along," I said.

"No problem." He continued to stare at the road, his face stony.

"How do you stand this early start time?"

"You get here early you get done early."

"How do you work this schedule around school?"

He sighed, obviously irritated to have to converse with me. "I just work less—come out here early then go to school. By October it's cool enough to work after school. I get more hours then. And I work the whole summer."

"I assume you had to be trained to be a windsmith."

"I'm not officially a windsmith. I just went to a one-week training course. You have to take more if you want to be, whatever they call it, certified. But I do a better job than the certified guys, I can tell you that."

"You like the work?"

"Pays good. I make way more than my buddies. They're stuck flipping burgers for minimum wage, and I'm out here earning twice that much. Better work, too. Don't have to deal with asshole customers."

"Want to keep working here when you graduate from high school?"

"Fuck no."

"What then?"

I'm going to be a major league pitcher."

I could see it. His height and strength would make him a good starter, I thought. "You any good?"

"Yeah I'm good. One day I'll be pitching for the Dodgers."

"Good for you," I said, thinking he was pretty sure of himself.

When we arrived at the first turbine on his schedule, we found another Mill Maintenance truck parked at its base. Two men in their twenties, who looked like they had just rolled out of bed, stood outside the truck smoking. These would be the workers who would assist Brandon, mainly by using pulleys to hoist tools and parts to him as he worked aloft.

I asked, glancing out over the rows of turbines scoring the desert floor. "How do you identify which turbine you're supposed to work on?"

"Each turbine has a metal plate with its identification number on it. You can't see it because those bozos are in the way."

After exiting the truck, Brandon muttered a greeting to his coworkers and showed me the identification number. Then he began fastening some kind of harness around his torso.

I pointed to it. "What's that?"

"Safety harness. When I climb up, I use clips to tie off to the ladder. Prevents falling."

I looked up to the top of the turbine, some two hundred feet above us. I shivered, thinking about such a fall.

Brandon pulled a key from the retractable key ring on his belt and opened the door to the tower. I looked in. The diameter of the space looked to be about twenty feet. It was dark in there, too, except for the shaft of light from the open door. The space smelled like metal and grease.

"Go on in," Brandon said behind me. I jumped about a foot off the ground and grabbed hold of the doorframe.

He looked at me, amusement pulling up the corners of his mouth. "If you really want to see what it's like, you need to get inside."

I held my ground, my fingers digging into the jam.

"Go on," he said.

I shook my head like a recalcitrant child refusing to eat her spinach. "No."

He laughed harder than I thought was warranted. Then he gave me a little shove.

I wound up a foot inside the shaft, but a quick backward leap took me safely outside once more. "Very funny," I said, although I didn't think it was. I added, just in case he was unclear on my feelings, "I'm not going in. I thought I could do it, but now I don't think so."

"I can help," Brandon said, his eyes bright.

"I don't think so." I was ashamed of my cowardice, but the revulsion I felt was too great to overcome. The door seemed like an open maw waiting to devour me. I could almost feel the mouth closing around me, the esophagus constricting, pulverizing, suffocating me. I was transported to that summer long ago when we kids dug a tunnel in the back yard, out of sight of my mother, who would have skinned us alive had she known what we were up to. We envisioned the tunnel as an underground fortress in which we could hold secret meetings. In reality, it was a deathtrap. One day, while I was scooping out dirt to enlarge the tunnel, the other kids standing watch above while I dug, the roof collapsed, burying me under four feet of dirt. I remember the weight of the earth pressing down on me, immobilizing my body, shutting out all noise and light. I remember how the air whooshed out of my lungs, and when I breathed in, the feeling of dirt clogging my nose and mouth. I knew that I was going to die. The experience was pure terror.

Fortunately, the other kids were able to dig me out before my last gasp, but I have never been able to be in closed spaces since without panicking. The prospect of entering the turbine made my heart race.

"You all right?" Brandon said, trying to sound concerned. But when I looked at him, his eyes betrayed his amusement. "You look like you saw a ghost."

I forced a laugh and waved my hand as if shooing away a fly. "I'm fine. Why don't you just go about your work. What's on the agenda?" I moved aside so he could enter. The two smokers finished their cigarettes.

"Just routine stuff. Change the gearbox oil, tighten bolts, adjust the brakes."

"Sounds like you work for Jiffy Lube."

He smiled again, showing most of his perfectly aligned white teeth. No doubt the girls at his school thought he was hot. I had seen how he used his good looks and charm to advantage when he and Sierra flirted. Sierra had to be eight to ten years older than he was, but she seemed honestly flattered by his attention. What Brandon had was sex appeal, and a lot of it.

The teen entered the chamber, and to my surprise the space instantly flooded with light. That rascal—he purposely left the lights off to scare me. I hadn't even known the turbine had lights, although that made sense—why work in the dark? The inside of the tower definitely seemed less ominous once illuminated, but it was still too scary for me. I glanced inside as Brandon began climbing the metal ladder, which was illuminated all the way up with fluorescent lights. The jangles from his safety harness and key ring echoed in the hollow tube. His boots clanged on the metal rungs as he ascended. After a while, he became a tiny speck, barely visible as he reached the top.

I studied the chamber from my safe location outside the tower. At least I'd be able to put some details about the space in my book. There wasn't much to see, though. A thick bundle of cables ran alongside the steel ladder, and a steel control panel the size of refrigerator sat on the concrete floor, its doors open. The panel contained a grid of shiny copper and dull steel components, numerous small fans—presumably to keep the panel cool when the tower heats up—and many yards of conduit. I hadn't studied the schematic of wind turbines in great depth, that being outside the scope of my book, but I remembered vaguely that the cables transmitted electricity from the generator to the control panel. They also transmitted communications from the control panel to the blades, telling the unit when to turn on and off.

Since there was nothing else to see in the small shaft, I withdrew and let the workers go about their business. With relief, I went to sit in the shade of the tower. I felt like an ass for backing out, but the trip out here had not been a total waste. I was relieved to see that Brandon could still laugh despite his woes. All in all, he didn't seem to be doing too badly. He still showered and went to work. And I felt that our connection, forged by our parentless status, had strengthened. Maybe I gave myself too much credit, but I figured that my empathy made him feel that at least someone understood. I hoped so anyway. Brandon was running short on people who cared about him. Except for his grandmother, he was essentially going through this alone. I thought with a jolt: At least I have loved ones to go through the loss with. Maybe all the fighting is just our way of saying how we feel about what has happened to us. Considering the last blow-out, I'd say that what we were feeling was anger. No, make that rage. The deep, shaking, primal rage of those who have lost what they loved most. How on earth was Brandon, an only child, dealing with that alone?

As I gazed out over the desert, I noticed a plume of dust signaling a vehicle rumbling our way. I watched as it approached, recognizing the SUV as belonging to the Mill Maintenance fleet. The driver came in fast and slammed on the brakes at the last possible moment, spewing gravel over my feet. Van Dorn. He jumped from the vehicle with surprising agility for a man with so big a girth. With his long gray hair and massive curly beard, he looked like an ancient desert prospector just come from the mines.

"Howdy," he called. "Brandon treating you all right?"

"Hard to complain. He's up there sweating while I'm down here sitting in the shade."

"Couldn't get you to go in?"

"Not a chance."

He laughed and laughed, as if I'd said the funniest thing he ever heard. I revised my image: Not a prospector but Santa Claus.

"So what brings you out here?" I said.

"Thought I'd give you a ride back to the office. It's hard enough getting Brandon to do his work without a pretty gal distracting him."

The "pretty gal" bit was embarrassing, but I smiled. "Sounds like a plan. Thanks."

Van Dorn stuck his head in the tower and told the guys that he was driving me back to the office. We got into the SUV, and he tore off down the dirt road toward the maintenance yard. The interior of the truck smelled of old coffee and cigarettes.

"Brandon seems like he's doing okay considering his father just died, " I said.

Van Dorn shrugged. "Hard to tell with him. He's always been a moody cuss, one day joking around with everyone, the next day cranky as a mule. I told him to take as much time off as he needed, but he didn't want to."

"Some people find it easier if they keep busy," I said, like I was some grief expert. That was rich.

Van Dorn said, "Yeah, well, it surprised me 'cuz the kid doesn't seem to like to work too much when he's here. I'd a thought he'd jump at the chance to get time off."

"Really?" I said, surprised. Brandon had left me with the impression that he liked his job and worked as much as he could to make more money. "Why keep him on then?"

The minute I asked it, I knew. Van Dorn confirmed my supposition. "Cole asked me to work with the kid, as a kind of favor to him, you know? Brandon's got some problems. Probably needs some of that psycho stuff."

"He getting counseling?"

"Don't know. Not that I know of, anyway."

We drove on awhile in companionable silence. Van Dorn was the type of guy I'd enjoy splitting a pitcher of beer with: He would laugh at everything you said. On the other hand, if he had one beer too many, he might just split your gourd open. As the truck rattled along the dirt road, every now and then his cell phone would ring and he'd attend to some problem or other. He barked out orders and growled about schedules. The communications involved terms like sensors and rotors and nacelles and other words that made me feel that I was in a *Star Wars* intergalactic bar scene without a universal translator.

I said, "I'm surprised you get cell phone reception out here. I've read that the turbines can sometimes interfere with television reception, interrupt cell phone calls, even disrupt military radar."

"You been doing your research, I see. The military radar thing *is* a problem, although they're working on it. But with the newer turbines, the TV and cell phone thing isn't a big deal. We never had a problem out here."

I nodded, then asked, "Sheriff been by the office any more?"

"Haven't seen hide nor hair of them since you was here."

"Think they found out how Cole's killer got the key to the turbine door?"

"If they did, they didn't tell me about it. Between me and you, I think they're convinced they got their man."

"You agree with them?"

He started to answer, then embarked on a coughing fit. I was running through the Heimlich steps in my mind when he stopped hacking and wiped his eyes.

"Damn smokes. Wife threatens to leave me if I don't give 'em up. But, hell, I can't seem to do it, hard as I've tried. Where was I?"

"I asked if you thought the environmentalist killed Cole."

"Right. Well, in my opinion that runt couldn't wring a chicken's neck, how's he going to kill a grown man?"

"So, if not him, who?"

He scratched his beard, his fingers disappearing into its wiry strands. "I say follow the money."

"Richard Sampson?"

His head jerked toward me, surprise and something else—alarm? Offense?—in his eyes. "Hell, sugar, I meant the wife. She's gonna get a good chunk of change outta this."

"You don't like Jillian Mintock?"

"That's putting it mildly. I got no use for her."

I said, "Guess it doesn't matter what we think anyway. The authorities are still trying to make a case against Lewis. I wonder how they think he got keys to the turbine."

"Hell, we got po-dunk Pumice County Sheriffs on the case. Don't get me wrong, some of them deputies are buddies of mine, but this ain't some big city police department. I think it'd be real easy to murder someone in this town and get away with it."

As we pulled into the Mill Maintenance parking lot, I realized that I had to agree. Much as I liked to think the city of Desert Rock was safe from serial killers and rapists, I had to admit that law enforcement here resembled Mayberry RFD more than the NYPD. I thanked Van Dorn and headed for my car.

After leaving Mill Maintenance, I decided to head over to the Cal-Wind office to see if I could finagle some information about Jillian Mintock out of Sierra. The chilly wife who disliked Cole's son and stood to inherit the wind farm intrigued me. I'd been spending a lot of energy on Richard Sampson, but his possible gains from the murder were much more nebulous than Jillian's. Even if he killed Cole, he couldn't be sure that Cole's death would stop the expansion. And, would anyone kill over a view or a development? Abby Sampson had suggested some bad blood between her husband and Cole, so maybe the motive had nothing to do with the expansion per se. Still, it all sounded pretty vague.

In contrast, Jillian stood to inherit, what? How much would the wind farm and the surrounding land be worth? Just looking at the number of turbines now installed—which if I remembered correctly was around a thousand—at a half million a pop that came out to be fifty million dollars. Shit! Could that be right? Of course, I was sure that Cole did not own all of the turbines outright, surely he had loans out, but even then, the possible worth of the farm was astronomical. And that didn't take into account his annual earnings from the electricity he sold. Nor did it include future income from land leases. My respect for Cole intensified. The guy started out buying up parcels of land for a trailer park and wound up a multi-millionaire.

The pertinent question was, How much would Jillian get? Most likely she would split the assets with Brandon. Even though Cole and Brandon did not get along, I was certain Cole would provide for his son. Surely he would not give everything to Jillian. Nor could I imagine that he'd cut her out of his will. Of course, even if Jillian inherited the lion's share, it didn't prove she killed her husband. But it definitely provided her with a motive, a fact the Sheriff's Department seemed content to ignore. The more I dug into the case, the more irritated I became with law enforcement. I would have to have a talk with my friend, Deputy Trent Wise.

When I pulled up to CalWind, I noticed that Lewis was nowhere in evidence. His compatriot, Katie, held down the fort on her own. Unlike the passionate Lewis, her protest seemed half-hearted at best. She seemed withered from the hot sun and blown to bits by the wind. Her blonde hair was tied back in a straggly ponytail, and her shoulders drooped as if preventing the ruination of the planet had become an insupportable burden. I wondered, not for the first time, if she cared about the causes that Lewis espoused. I suspected Lewis himself was the real reason she was here.

I made a mental note to talk with her on my way out to find out why Lewis wasn't with her. Right now, I was intent on finding out who inherited Cole's estate. And I was in luck: The silver BMW sedan I had seen Jillian Mintock get into the other day was parked out front. My timing usually sucks, so I felt pretty smug at this stroke of good fortune.

When I walked through the office door, Jillian was standing in the lobby talking to the accountant, Diana Oliver. Sierra lurked in the background, pretending to be engrossed in a letter on her computer screen. I could see that her hands poised over the keyboard did not move. When Diana saw me come in, she frowned, obviously associating me with something unpleasant but unable to recall exactly what. Jillian didn't register anything one way or another. Her pale face remained expressionless.

"Hey, Sierra," I said. Belatedly, I realized I had no plan, no purported reason to be there. Oh well, I'd just have to b.s. the best I could.

"Hello," she said, abandoning all pretense of work. "Managed to come in without dropping anything I see."

I laughed. As a way to wedge myself into Diana and Jillian's conversation, I said to them, "I've been out here twice. The first time I caught my foot in the door, the other time I dropped a box of donuts on the carpet." I smiled like the ignoramus my comment painted me to be.

Diana screwed up her face like she just got a whiff of dog poo. "You're that writer person."

Writer person? Yes, a writer person who disliked redundant phrases like "writer person." I said, "Sam Larkin, we met the second time I was here, the day of the donut incident." I thought I was being witty, but she wasn't amused.

"What do you want?" she demanded.

"Well, I was just, I came by to, my God, that is the most beautiful pendant I have ever seen." I fixed my gaze on a large sandstone trinket hanging from a chain around Diana's neck. "Beautiful" was too strong a word for it. "Big" would have covered it. The thing was the size of a softball. It's a wonder she could hold her head up.

"I made that," Jillian said. "I gave it to Diana on her birthday last year."

Ah, so Diana and Jillian were friends. That knowledge might come in useful. Well, provided I could hack a lead through the ice floe that was Diana Oliver. "You made it?" I said in overemphatic awe. Jillian had buffed and polished the stone and then engraved a series of tiny petroglyphs on its smooth face. The chain was silver.

"Jillian has a shop on Feldspar," Diana said, warming up a tad. "It's right by the bookstore."

"I know where you mean," I said, though I hadn't a clue. I hadn't lived in Desert Rock for a long time, and I no longer knew what stores were here and which had gone kaput years ago. "I'll have to stop in and look at what you have. My sister's birthday is coming up and I think she'd love one of your pieces." Lots of bull there. For one thing, Vanessa's birthday was in January. For another, she would hate anything with a southwestern theme, which, in her mind, was associated with crystals and Sedona and all that "new-age claptrap," as she puts it. Lastly, I was certain I did not want to buy my sister a present of any kind any time in the future.

Jillian said, "You should stop by. I can show you some new pieces I've made. I also carry the work of other local artists, but most of the jewelry for sale is mine."

"You design all your pieces yourself?"

"Yes."

"Amazing," I said, meaning it. I have as much artistic talent as Lacy. I make those elephants that draw pictures with their trunks look like The Masters.

Sierra watched this exchange with a displeased look on her face. Her irritation seemed to be directed at me. I supposed she thought I was being disloyal to her since I was cavorting with her crabby boss and sucking up to Jillian, whom Sierra had made clear she despised. Knowing I needed to keep Sierra agreeable for when I needed her next, I said, "Well, I don't want to keep you all. I just stopped by to ask Sierra what I could do to thank her for all the help she's given me. Sierra, I know you bring Coffee Buzz coffees in every day, could I spot you some morning? Or, maybe I could bring something to go with all that great coffee?" I smiled at her.

It worked. She was pleased to be acknowledged in front of her hard-to-please boss and Jillian, who for all we knew was now the owner of the wind farm. "Those donuts were pretty good," she said, then smiled. "Even though they were pretty smooshed."

"Donuts it is, and I'll try to maintain control of the box at all times. Well, I'll be on my way then. It was good seeing you all again. Ms. Mintock, I'll definitely stop by your shop."

"Please do," she said. "We can have a cup of coffee after you make your purchase."

I supposed I wouldn't get the coffee if I turned out to be a looky-loo. Even if I had to take out a small loan, I'd buy some over-priced bauble just so I could drill her for information over a cup of hazelnut blend.

I exited the wind farm office and sauntered over to where Katie stood beneath the mesquite tree with her sign. The temperature had risen a good twenty degrees since I had stood with Brandon at Mill Maintenance at five this morning. Summer hot spells of over one hundred and ten are common enough in Desert Rock. They are often accompanied by storms that knock out transmitters, shutting down the city's air conditioners, a disaster of high magnitude. When I was little, the outages sometimes lasted for days, necessitating extreme measures like sleeping outside where it was comparatively cool, and eating up all the stuff in the freezer as quickly as possible before it rotted. But these days, with better equipment, the brownouts lasted hours instead of days. I would trade a couple hours without electricity for a chance to see a wicked thunderstorm break up the monotony of sun and wind.

"Hi Katie," I said, as I entered the shade of the tree. "Fighting the good fight alone I see."

She seemed glad to have an excuse to put down her sign and plop her butt down beneath the tree. "Luke's in town being grilled by the cops. Again," she said in a flat voice. "I told him that this protest was a mistake, but he wouldn't listen. They're going to put him away. And for what? Being in the wrong place at the wrong time."

"You're convinced he didn't do it?"

She looked up at me like I was asking whether she believed the earth is round.

"Of course he didn't do it. I mean, Luke does get a little carried away sometimes, but it's only 'cuz he cares so much. He would never hurt anyone. The cops are, like, so wrong. I happen to know for a fact that he wasn't anywhere near Cole Mintock on the night he was killed."

That surprised me. "Did you tell the sheriff deputies that?"

She rubbed a hand over her eyes and shook her head. "No! I didn't. Luke told me not to, he swore me to silence, and I would never do anything he didn't want me to. He's protecting someone. But if I could just tell the cops where he was, this whole mess would be over. He has, what do they call it, an alibi, he just won't use it."

I tried to absorb this information, attempting to get a feel for her credibility. She was loyal to Lewis, that was certain. Could this be a lie to try to save him? If it was the truth, she had been put into a terrible position. On the one hand, Luke had extracted a promise from her that he knew she'd keep because she loved him. On the other hand, she possibly held his ticket to freedom in her hands. What would I do in her place? Maybe I'd tell a third party, hoping that person would relay the information to the detectives. That way, she could keep her promise of not telling law enforcement, and at the same time deliver Luke from a life in prison or a death sentence.

"What did Luke tell the detectives about where he was that night?" I asked.

"He said he was out sleeping in the desert alone, like he does a lot when he needs space. But, like, as an alibi it sucks because nobody else can confirm it. The cops probably figure if he can't come up with anything better than that, he must of done it."

"If he wasn't out sleeping in the desert, Katie, where was he?"

She looked off toward the office, her eyes unfocused. "I don't know what to do. Luke told me not to tell anyone. Well, he told me not to tell the cops. I guess he didn't think anyone else would ask. But I feel like I gotta to do something. I'm not even sure why I'm talking to you about all this. It's not like you can help or anything." Her voice sounded shaky.

I sat down beside her under the tree and let the silence hang for a couple of minutes. "Katie," I said, "It's true that I have no legal jurisdiction whatsoever here, and you don't know me from Adam. But I've got to say, I think the whole case against Luke stinks. I don't know Luke personally, but I just can't see him murdering someone. I mean, why? What's to be gained? Luke's a smart guy. Plus, even if Luke were with ELF, that organization just doesn't kill people. The whole case against him doesn't add up, and I think the sheriff's department knows that. But the feds are determined to pin it on him so they can say they hung an eco-terrorist. Luke needs an out. And pretty damn quickly. I'm not sure what I can do for him, but I've gotten involved in the case, and I'll do whatever I can to see that justice is served."

"If I tell you, are you going to tell the cops?"

I thought about it. It might be the only way to get Lewis off. But if I said I would, Katie might go silent on me. "What if I promise not to take action before I talk to Luke? Maybe I can convince him that his loyalty will get him put away for life, where he can't do another thing for the environment."

Katie's expression brightened. "Yeah, that's what he needs to understand. Okay, I'll tell you." But she didn't. She just sat there. The dapples of sunlight filtering through the mesquite trees danced on her hair and face. I noticed the wind had picked up, tossing the branches overhead and pushing sheets of sand across the parking lot.

I decided that she needed prompting. "Is the person Luke is protecting involved in Cole's murder?"

"Oh no," she said. "Nothing like that. No, he didn't have anything to do with it. In fact, Luke and him weren't even in Desert Rock that night. They were in Martinville." She mentioned a tiny town up in the mountains by Lake Pont. Silence again.

I was now sweating and eager to get home to a cold glass of water and some lunch. I was ready to squeeze it out of her if I had to. "And?" I said.

Then it all came out in a torrent. "See, I overheard Luke talking on his cell phone that day. He was talking to John. John McGinnis. He's an old college friend of Luke's. They started protesting together when they were with EnviroPriorities, but they left that group because it was not going far enough. You know, to protect the Earth. So, John and Luke went to EarthOne. But John became more and more radical, way more than Luke, and John finally left to join ELF."

ELF? Shit, I wondered if ELF was involved in this after all.

She continued her story. "John's been trying to get Luke to join ELF. But Luke doesn't like their methods. That's what he says, 'their methods.' Torching houses and SUVs, costing people so much money and stuff like that. Luke's pretty intense, but he draws the line at hurting people, he's way too gentle. He hates violence. People at EarthOne say his ideas are getting more whacked all the time, like coming out here. But you can't talk to Luke about it. He's so driven and dedicated."

"But you don't see him changing in a violent direction?"

"No. That's exactly right."

This was taking forever! I ground my teeth. While all this history was fascinating, what I really wanted to know was where Luke was the night Cole was killed. "So, what about the night of the murder?" I said, my jaw clenched.

"John called him to beg Luke to join ELF again. When Luke hung up, he seemed kinda pissed off. He told me John had called, and he had agreed to meet him at his cabin in Martinville. I think Luke was going up there to tell John once and for all that he wasn't interested in joining ELF. It couldn't be that John had finally worn him down and Luke was going up to see what joining up involved. I just can't see Luke doing that. Anyway, he left right then and drove up there in my car."

That's what she assumed anyway, I thought. "What makes you think Luke was there all night?"

"I guess I don't know. But why would I think otherwise?"

"He could have driven up there and been back here in time to kill Cole. It's only a two-hour drive one way."

She stared at me, looking flustered. "Well, yeah, I suppose he could have."

I tried out another theory. "Or, maybe he met with John and then they both came back here to carry out Luke's first assignment for ELF."

"No way! You said yourself this isn't the kind of thing ELF does. As crazy as they are, they don't kill people. Look, I didn't follow Luke around with a mini-cam, all I can say is that he wasn't where he told the police he was. I'm saying he had an alibi and didn't use it. He's protecting John, like I said."

"I'm not sure I follow. Why wouldn't Luke just tell the deputies that he was up in Martinville with his friend?"

She looked at me like I was one evolutionary step above a paramecium. "Because of all the ELF stuff that came out the day after Mr. Mintock was killed. The minute his body was found, the cops came up with this theory about eco-terrorists killing him to stop the wind farm expansion. That was our fault, probably, for being out here protesting. If we hadn't been here, blaming environmentalists would be the last thing they'd think of probably. But we were here, and Luke has a history of getting arrested at protests. So they started harassing him. Because of all the anti-terrorism stuff these days, they were thinking ELF all the way. Even though Luke and I don't have anything to do with ELF, we have no way of proving that. Luke was afraid if he told the cops he met with John, he'd be putting John in danger. The FBI suspects John is with ELF—they've questioned him before—but they've never been able to pin anything on him. Getting him for murder would be, like, a feather in their cap or whatever."

"So Luke figured telling the detectives that he was in Martinville that night was essentially trading his life for John's."

"Exactly. So on the spur of the moment Luke made up that story about sleeping in the desert. I don't think he really thought they'd make a case against him. I mean, he isn't with ELF and he was nowhere near Desert Rock when it happened. He didn't kill the man. He stupidly thought his innocence would, like, make him immune, or whatever. But now look what's happening. I'm sure he never thought it would get this far. He's scared, but I can't get him to see reason. Telling the truth doesn't have to mean screwing John."

I worried that at this point it did. The authorities had their minds made up that this was an eco-crime. But they had not yet been able to make a case against Lewis, who, although a bit crazy, had no past history of violence and was not affiliated with any terrorist group, at least that they could prove. McGinnis was another matter. He was affiliated with ELF, and he had been involved in what the FBI considered domestic terrorist acts. McGinnis would be a bigger fish, and an easier one to land.

Katie broke into my thoughts with a plea. "Please talk to Luke. See if you can convince him to tell the truth. Make him see how serious it is."

I nodded and got to my feet. The wind nearly pushed me into the tree, and I grabbed its skinny trunk for support. "I'll talk to him. I don't know what good it will do, but I'll talk to him."

Walking back to my car, leaning forward into the wind so that I wouldn't be blown off my feet like a tumbleweed and rolled to the other side of town, I thought about Katie's story. If true, Lewis was an honorable man, willing to sacrifice himself to save a friend. It seemed in character somehow. He was a person who would sacrifice for his principles. Would Lewis make the ultimate sacrifice by giving his life so that McGinnis could be free?

On the other hand, the more cynical side of my brain said, Lewis could be a liar. What if he had sold Katie a bill of goods? The only way to find out was to talk to him. And to McGinnis. I felt excitement build inside me. I might be able to prove that Lewis was innocent after all.

My good feeling dissolved in an instant. As I climbed into the Corolla, the wind caught the door and slammed it right into my left kneecap. I pulled my wounded leg into the car and closed the door before giving vent to a plume of obscenities. It was cathartic, really, sitting in the baking car, my hands clenching the hot steering wheel, my face contorted and sweat pouring out of me.

But that wasn't the full extent of the reversal. When I got home, I found a message on my answering machine. I pushed the play button and heard a familiar voice, tight with fury: "I told you stay away from me and my family. I don't like to be disobeyed, Ms. Larkin, and I will not tolerate it. Consider this your last warning. If I hear that you talked to my wife or secretary again, or come near my house or business, you will be dealt with."

Well, well. Richard Sampson. What a blowhard, I thought. What was he going to do, break my ankles? I looked down at my throbbing knee. Man, but that would hurt.

Chapter Fifteen

Despite Sampson's threat—or maybe because of it—I sat down at my desk and worked on my book for five hours. I had just a little over a week before the project was due, and I hadn't even sent Vince an outline. I could sense his fury building over there on the coast, and I knew any day now he'd be calling me. I needed to get some writing done, and I wasn't going to let Sampson derail me. He wasn't going to get me to stop working on Cole's case either. No one, not even The Bald Giant, was going to frighten me. Solving the case now seemed bound to my work on the book. It was as if completing the project had no meaning as long as Cole's killer was at large. Long after the book was printed, I would think about Cole's body being stuffed in that turbine, his life's work mocked. I wanted to be able to look at that volume and know I did my best, not only to paint an accurate picture of wind power as Cole had hoped, but also to see that justice was done on his behalf.

When the doorbell rang at five o'clock, I had just turned off the computer.

"Eddie!" I said when I opened the door. He strolled into the foyer carrying a six-pack of Coronas. I noticed that his white-walls were already grown out, and his dark curls had softened the planes of his face. I caught a whiff of Irish Spring. It wasn't like Eddie to just drop by without calling first. He obviously wanted to surprise me, and I was more pleased than I should be.

He said, "Connor told me not to bring anything, but I didn't want to come empty handed."

"Connor?" I repeated. I didn't understand.

"Yeah, when he invited me to the barbecue." Eddie eyed me, his head cocked like a dog's trying to decipher a command. "Uh-oh. You don't know anything about this, do you?"

I felt my chest constrict and my face grow hot. What an imbecile I was. Of course Eddie hadn't stopped by to surprise me. He came over to see Connor. I was furious with myself for having read more into his appearance than was warranted. I wished that he would go, but I couldn't very well dis-invite him.

I attempted to smile as we walked into the kitchen, but I could feel disappointment and anger freeze my face. I plunked the beers one by one into the refrigerator with excessive force. "Connor didn't say a word to me about you coming over," I said like I didn't give a shit. "Where is he anyway?" Just like Connor to invite someone to dinner and then not be there when he arrives.

"He called me on his cell. He's at the store buying steaks." Eddie's voice was wary. He had picked up on my mood without understanding the reasons for it.

I limped to the kitchen table and sat down, taking the weight off my banged-up knee. Eddie noticed the limp. "What happened?"

"Wind slammed the car door on it."

"Ah."

We glanced around the room.

"How's the book coming?"

"Good. How's the shop?"

"Good."

We sat at the table and looked down at its shiny surface. Mom's wind chimes tinkled and clanked in the wind. Lacy's panting filled the kitchen, her breath wafting over us like pond fumes.

Then the front door squeaked, and Connor rambled in carrying grocery sacks. I never thought I'd be so glad to see him.

As it turned out, Connor had included me in his dinner plans. Three steaks, three potatoes, enough prepared coleslaw for ten people.

He'd also bought a watermelon the size of a baby rhino. While Connor barbecued the steaks, I brought the two of them up to speed on my investigation into Cole's murder. At this point, why should I care if Eddie disapproved? He must have sensed my indifference because he listened without comment. I'm sure he was dying to tell me to butt out of other people's business and write my damn book, but he knew I'd ignore his advice, so why bother. I ran out of stuff to say, and everyone got more cheerful when Connor finished cooking the steaks and the three of us sat down to eat.

Eddie and I avoided talking to each other. Instead, we peppered Connor with questions. My brother was stunned to find himself so fascinating. When I asked what he planned to do next (meaning a job), he answered, "I'm going to do an Ironman."

I nearly ejected the watermelon chunk I had forked into my mouth. "An Ironman? As in triathlon? Like that Hawaii thing?"

"Yeah! There's an Ironman in San Diego early next spring. If I start training now, I can be ready for it."

"But you don't know the first thing about triathlons!"

Eddie joined in. "Why start with an Ironman? Why not do some shorter races, like a few sprint or Olympic distance events?"

I had no clue what he was talking about, but I said, "Yeah, why not do shorter races?"

Connor laughed and waved us off. "You guys!" He popped a piece of watermelon about the size of a deck of cards into his mouth. "Where's your sense of adventure," he said, watermelon juice dribbling out of his mouth.

"Do you have a training schedule?" Eddie, a shameless sports addict, asked.

"Yeah, I just talked to a buddy of mine in Temecula whose going to train for the same race. He's done it before, and he's going to coach me."

Sensing his imminent departure, I said, "You're moving to Temecula?"

He shrugged. "I don't know. Jerry can coach me online. I can train anywhere."

"Have you ever done an endurance event?" Eddie asked.

"Are you going to get a job?" I wanted to know.

Connor stuffed more watermelon in his mouth. It was just like him to go off on some big adventure without the slightest bit of preparation and no plan. How would he earn money while he was training? Where would he live? How could he buy the running shoes and whatnot he'd need to do the race? Connor never bothered to think about these issues. Like the time he decided to go to Idaho and do some white water rafting. He didn't start out with a trip rated "1" for easy. No, of course not, he signed up for a class "6," the highest rating, and nearly got himself killed. Or the five-day hike in the Grand Canyon. He wore brand new sport sandals and wound up with so many blisters he could barely walk, and they almost had to get Life Flight to come take him out of there.

He said, "I've done a lot of multi-day hikes up in the Sierras. I know how to pace myself."

"And what about work?" I prompted.

"I don't know yet. Jerry said a lot of people train for Ironmans while working full-time. The training takes from two to five hours a day, so you'd definitely have time to put in eight hours on the job."

I looked at him as if he had sprouted a horn in the middle of his forehead. "Connor, I'm sorry to say it, but you seem overtaxed with just a job. How can you possibly think you can add all that training and still work?"

He took no offense. "I'm up for it. I already started training. This morning I ran six miles!"

Eddie asked, "Where are you going to swim? Are you going to buy a bike?"

Connor shrugged, a lopsided grin on his face. "I don't know yet. I'll figure something out."

Eddie and I glanced at each other across the table. I made a circling motion around the side of my head with my index finger.

"Well, come on Eddie," Connor said as he pushed out his chair. "Let's throw these dishes in the dishwasher and get down to The Hideaway for a pitcher and some pool."

Within five minutes they were out the door, leaving Lacy and me alone. The house smelled like baked potatoes and chives and Irish Spring. I poured a big glass of Glenlivet and limped out to the patio. My knee throbbed, and I felt tired. At seven-thirty, the wind had died down, and the heat had drained from the air. Peeps and murmurs from the trees indicated that the birds were settling down for the night. The clouds that had built up in the late afternoon were gone, but they had left the scent of rain behind. As I sat down on a patio chair, Lacy flopped down beside me, her legs splaying out in all directions like a rag doll. At nearly a year old, her body still retained that rubbery quality that makes puppies so endearing. I reached down and scratched her wide head. She moaned and looked up at me, her brown eyes bright with surprise at my touch. Her simple openness, her easy affection, made tears fill my eyes. I took a sip of scotch and savored the heat as it burned down my throat. The alcohol began to perform its magic, flooding my body with a sense of well-being. Happiness had been in short supply lately, and I was not opposed to shortcuts.

Chapter Sixteen

The reek of burning incense engulfed me as I entered Desert Designs on Saturday morning. The store felt warm and stuffy, and the incense seemed to suck the air out of the small space. The New Age CD playing in the background did not help. I suddenly couldn't breathe. Within seconds, the edges of my vision darkened, and I broke into a sweat. I stumbled forward looking for a place to sit, fearing I might drop face first onto Jillian's tile floor. But it was too late. I felt myself crumple, and all went black.

I gradually became aware of two strong hands grabbing me beneath the armpits and hoisting me to a sitting position. My head cleared, and I remembered where I was. Not good. Attempting to rise, I felt my legs buckle, and my damaged knee sent a jolt of pain up my leg. I felt an icy hand on my elbow lifting me up and guiding me toward a chair at the back of the store. My body was pressed into it and my head pushed toward my knees. Mortification set in.

"Feeling better?" Jillian asked, handing me a glass of water.

"Sorry," I said. "Lately I've developed a knack for grand entrances." The cool water washed away the last of the murkiness and enabled me to breathe normally. I blotted at my clammy face with a used tissue I found balled up in the pocket of my capris. The Kleenex probably left little balls of lint all over my damp face, but I didn't care. It was hard to believe my dignity could sink any lower. Gratefully, I realized I was the only customer in the store.

"Sit as long as you need to," Jillian said. "I'll make you some tea. Tea always makes me feel better, although I detest the stuff. I'm a black coffee drinker at heart." She busied herself with tea bags and coffee filters while I tried to regroup.

"You have a beautiful store," I said, as if I had not just made an ass of myself in it. She placed two mugs on the small round table by my chair and sat down. I noticed her mug was filled with coffee, and I suffered a pang of envy. But Jillian was right about the tea. While the flavor was what I imagined urine might taste like, as soon as the brew hit my stomach, I was certain I would live.

She asked. "Have you been ill?"

What she meant was, Why would a grown woman faint while walking into a store? Good question. I didn't have a good answer, so I just told the truth. She seemed the kind of person who disliked bullshit, so I refrained from practicing my newfound skills in that area. I said, "I have a little problem with closed spaces. It was so warm in here, and the incense . . ." My voice trailed off. I realized that saying something negative about the incense might offend her.

Jillian got up, walked over to where the incense was burning and snuffed it out. Then she went to the wall thermostat and lowered the temperature. I could hear the air conditioner click on, and by the time she had sat back down, cold air flowed down on me. I breathed in gratefully, if somewhat guiltily.

"I didn't mean for you to—" I started to say.

She cut me off with a wave of her hand. "Think nothing of it. I'm a fainter, too."

Jillian sipped her coffee and looked at me over the rim of her mug. I noted again how beautiful she was. She was thin as a credit card, but rather than make her look anorexic, the slenderness enhanced her delicacy and grace. Her movements were slow and deliberate, as if choreographed for artistic effect, yet they did not look studied. She kept her straight blonde hair longer than a woman nearing fifty would normally wear it, but the style suited her. My gaze settled on the odd necklace she wore. Unlike her other jewelry, which was southwestern in style, the necklace was a combination of diamonds and gold, silver and turquoise. She noticed me examining it.

"An interesting piece, isn't it? It's a mix of old and new. I got the diamonds and gold from the wedding rings given to me by my two ex-husbands. The silver and turquoise are symbols of my new life with Cole." She began to run her fingers over the necklace.

"I'm so sorry about your husband," I said, wanting to keep her unexpected openness going. At the CalWind office she had seemed aloof, chilly. Here, in her own milieu, her manner appeared to be merely circumspect. I found myself liking her and had to remind myself why I was there. I was investigating Cole's murder, and she was one of my prime suspects. I knew that the interview was going to be harder now. My fainting spell seemed to have created a sympathy between us, and I could feel my objectivity waver. On the positive side, our tiny connection might encourage her to open up more than she would have normally. I decided to try to strengthen the connection.

I said, "I'm not sure you're aware of this, but my mother and Cole worked together over the years on various committees to help the environment."

Jillian raised her eyebrows. "You aren't talking about Olivia Larkin?"

"Yes."

"You're Olivia's daughter?"

I nodded.

Her impassive face took on a look of tenderness. "Then I must offer my sincere condolences as well. Cole was distraught when he heard that your mother had died. I never met Olivia myself, but from listening to Cole, she was an amazing woman. He admired her."

"And she admired him."

For a moment, we were silent. I was thinking that just a few months ago, both Cole and my mother were alive, vibrant and active, doing good in the world. And now, both gone. From the drawn look on Jillian's face, I suspected she was thinking along similar lines.

I took a sip of tea and asked, "How are you holding up?"

She shrugged. "We were only married six months. But it's hard." For a while she said nothing more, and I just sat quietly, figuring if I kept silent, she'd continue in her own time. Eventually, she said, "He did so much for me. He made this store possible. I always dreamed of having my own shop, but I could never seem to get the money together. Let's face it, you'll never become a millionaire making art. But with the shop open, I'm making a profit, not a lot, but enough for me to live on. All I ever wanted was to be able to support myself with my art."

I was surprised that instead of talking about how much she missed Cole, she talked about how helpful his money had been to her. Interesting.

She seemed to read my mind. "You must think I'm a money grubber. What I meant, though, is that Cole believed in me. He didn't look at my art as just a hobby. That's what most people think. Truth is, most people think artists are flakes. Cole never did. Even though he was a practical, worldly man, he appreciated the need for art. I was never with a man who got what I was about until I met Cole."

"What will you do now that he's gone?" I said, zeroing in on what I wanted to know. "Did he leave you well enough off to continue with your shop?"

She didn't seem to mind the invasive nature of my question. "Oh yes. He left half his assets to me."

"And the other half to Brandon?"

Her face hardened like the surface of a pond on a cold day. I couldn't tell if it was my nosy interest into her financial affairs that had riled her or the mention of Brandon. I decided to plow on as if I hadn't noticed her irritation. I said, "I've spent some time with Brandon over the last few days. He seems surprisingly okay for having just lost his father."

Her steely look remained unchanged. She said, her voice tense, "Cole set up a trust for him. He'll have money coming to him every month for the rest of his life."

"A trust? How does that work? Who actually gets the wind farm?"

She said, almost dismissively, as if the financial details were beside the point, "Basically, the wind farm is in trust. We each get half of everything. But Cole named me trustee, so I'm responsible for maintaining the trust's assets and discharging its debts. Which means that I'm responsible for the wind farm."

"And Brandon gets a payment every month?"

Her eyes flash. "That's right. And so do I."

I couldn't figure out what was making her so angry. She seemed upset that Cole had established a trust for his son. Was she pissed that her plan to murder Cole and take all his money had been thwarted? Even with Jillian inheriting only half of the estate, it was still a huge chunk of change, especially for someone who made earrings for a living. Another possibility was that Jillian was just mad at me for being nosy. But I didn't think that was the case. I felt a rapport between us, and I sensed she trusted me because of my kinship with the great Olivia Larkin.

Trying to get a bead on her anger, I said, "You seem upset about the trust."

"Damn right I am. Kid treated Cole horribly. He doesn't deserve a single cent."

Whoa. That was harsh. I didn't want to come right out and tell Jillian she sounded like a bitter bitch, so I said instead, "I'm surprised to hear Brandon would treat his dad like that. I can't imagine a more wonderful man to be my father. My mother was always saying how caring he was. When I met him, he seemed so kind and gentle."

Jillian's hands gripped the coffee mug so hard I thought it might shatter. I could see emotion rippling through her facial muscles, but she held her body still. I had no doubt Jillian was always in control of herself.

She said, "Brandon would totally disagree with your assessment of his father. He's fond of saying that Cole was responsible for his mother's suicide. Which is ridiculous. Every last person I've talked to in this town—I'm not from Desert Rock—has said how devoted Cole was, how he stayed with his first wife no matter how bad she got. He got her the best help, but nothing made any difference. She was very sick, and living with her was hard on Cole. So was Brandon's uncontrollable behavior. Cole said Brandon treated him horribly. The kid was always mocking him and acting up just to be perverse. Brandon hates me, too, of course. When Cole and I got married, Brandon told everyone we'd had an affair before Anastasia died. But that's not true. As anyone will tell you, Cole and I didn't start seeing each other until after Anastasia died."

The only "anyone" who could confirm that was, of course, Cole, and he was dead. Her story had me confused. I had not heard anything about Cole's first wife having mental illness or committing suicide. I wasn't sure if I ought to feel more respect for Cole for sticking by his wife or less because of the questionable judgment he had used in remarrying so quickly after her death. One thing was for sure: Jillian saw Cole as a saint, enduring his wife's illness with unimpeachable grace and compassion. Jillian seemed to view Cole's wife strictly in terms of her adverse effect on Cole, as if the poor woman purposely made his life miserable. I knew from writing a book on mental illness that it is hardest on the one who is ill. Those struggling with schizophrenia, manic-depression, or any number of other horrific conditions do not set out to make others' lives unbearable. They do the best they can under circumstances the rest of us cannot even imagine.

But I could understand Jillian's point of view. Her way of looking at the situation probably made her and Cole's hasty marriage easier to justify to herself. The way Jillian probably looked at it, Anastasia made Cole's life hell, and her suicide provided Cole relief from an unendurable obligation. Who could blame Cole for wanting to forget all that misery as soon as possible and start life anew with someone else? I decided to forgo the judgments and just focus on obtaining information.

I said, "Does Brandon live with his grandmother because he doesn't want to live in the same house with you?"

"Yes. He refused to live with Cole and me. I grant you, from his point of view, our marriage must have seemed too soon, but Cole's marriage to Anastasia had been over for years. He only stayed because he didn't want to break up the family. He didn't want to turn her out when she had no way of taking care of herself. His sacrifice is one of the things I most admired about him."

She grew quiet then, looking blankly at her coffee cup. The store was quiet except for the hum of the air conditioner and the quiet strains of a pan flute emanating from invisible ceiling speakers. The acrid stench of the incense still clung to the air. I let the silence sit there, waiting to see if she'd say anything more.

After a moment, Jillian said, "I can't believe he's gone. I can't believe someone murdered him. It's too awful."

"Do you know if the police are close to charging anyone?"

She shook her head. "They keep hauling in that environmentalist. The police are idiots."

"You don't think Lewis did it?"

"Absolutely not," she said.

Now, that was interesting. Why was she so sure Lewis didn't do it? I thought if I expressed agreement, she might open up and reveal her reasons. "I don't think Lewis did it either," I said.

Her green eyes scrutinized my face. "And why is that?"

I sipped my tea. "I've written numerous books on environmental topics. I know that environmentalists don't make a habit out of killing people. It just doesn't happen."

"Oh," she said, sounding disappointed. But, why? Had she hoped I'd give another reason for thinking Lewis innocent? Perhaps she wished I harbored suspicions about someone else. If that were the case, she obviously didn't think I suspected *her*. Good. I could only get information from her if she trusted me.

I asked, "Why don't you think Lewis did it?"

"I'm no detective," was all she said.

"But you have an opinion."

"What does it matter?"

"Look," I began, my voice intense, "Someone murdered your husband. If the police are wrong about Lewis, and we both think they are, the killer goes free. Is that what you want?"

"Of course not," she snapped. Then she eyed me. "Why are you so interested in this?"

I wet my lips, thinking of how I wanted to play it. If Jillian did kill Cole, my telling her that I was investigating the murder would put her instantly on guard. I would learn nothing more useful from her, and I might even put myself at risk. On the other hand, if Jillian wasn't the killer, telling her of my interest in the case might encourage her to share vital information with me. I decided to take the risk.

I said, "The truth is, I've been doing a little investigating on my own. When I heard the feds were trying to nail Lewis, I felt that they were wrong. I know this is none of my business, but my mother and Cole were friends, and she would have been devastated to learn he was murdered. Even more so if she found out the killer was going to walk. I decided it wouldn't hurt anything if I just poked around to see what I could find out."

I sat back and watched the effect my words had on Jillian. She stared at me with narrowed eyes, and I saw her nibble the corner of her lip. She said, "But you said you're a writer. You're not a P.I. or a cop. What can you do?"

"I don't think I could be more inept than the feds at this point."

She smiled wryly. "I'll grant you that." Jillian looked around the room, then began studying me again. She sighed deeply.

"What is it?" I said.

"I don't know if I can trust you."

"You don't know you can't, either."

After staring at her coffee cup for a while, she said, "You have to promise me you won't repeat what I'm about to tell you to anyone. Least of all, the police."

"I can't promise if I don't know what it is."

She shook her head. "You don't understand what's at risk. You've got to promise."

I decided it didn't hurt to do it. If there were some good reason down the road to repeat it, then I'd just have to break my promise. "Okay," I said.

Jillian leaned toward me, and to my utter amazement, she said, "I think Brandon killed his father."

My body jerked away from her as if she had shocked me with a cattle prod. "Brandon?" was all I could say.

"Brandon," she said. "He's sick, and quite dangerous."

"Dangerous?" I said in disbelief. I knew I sounded like an idiot, sitting there parroting her, but I was thrown completely off by her accusation. I tried to square what she was saying with what I knew of Brandon. The teen was moody, even angry, but that seemed understandable considering what he'd been through. But sick and dangerous, a murderer? Jillian's accusations seemed absurd.

I managed to say, "Why don't you want the police to know what you suspect?"

"Because Brandon said that if I told anyone, he'd 'make me regret it.'"

"You told Brandon that you thought he killed his father?" All this went a long way toward explaining the hatred I had seen on each of their faces when they encountered one another that day at CalWind.

"We had an ugly scene the night of Cole's funeral. Let's just say I lost my head. It was incredibly stupid of me."

I felt myself reeling. How much stock should I put in an accusation made by one of my favorite suspects? If Jillian were being honest, her accusation exonerated her. After all, if she truly believed Brandon killed Cole, that meant she didn't do it. But I had no way to verify that, and I could see two good reasons why she would lie. The obvious reason was to deflect suspicion from her and place it on someone else. But if that were the case, why not tell the police? They were the ones with the authority to put Brandon away, not me. Another reason she might be lying was for money. If she managed to get Brandon convicted of the murder, the entire inheritance might become hers. Perhaps the trust was written is such a way that if Brandon misbehaved egregiously, he'd be cut as a beneficiary. Again, though, if that were Jillian's motivation, why not tell the police? The only reason I could think of was that she took Brandon's threat seriously.

"You're truly afraid of Brandon," I said.

She shoved her coffee cup away and nodded vigorously. "You don't know the half of it. I have no doubt he'd follow through on his threats. Obviously, if I think he killed his father I'd have every reason to think he'd kill me. Or someone else I care about."

"Such as?"

She tried to smile, but it came out looking like a grimace. "Let's just leave it at that, shall we?"

"Just one more question. Why tell me all this?"

She looked around her store again without appearing to see it. The shop was silent now, the new age CD apparently ended. "When you told me you were investigating Cole's murder, I felt a glimmer of hope. I said to myself, maybe I'm not as much under Brandon's control as I thought. He warned me not to tell the cops, but why would he care if I told you? I guess I'm hoping maybe you can do something about this. I'm desperate, and I can't think of any other way." Jillian looked down at her hands, and I saw her work to get her emotions under control. After a moment she stood up. "Now," she said, "If you're finished with your tea, let me show you some pieces that might be appropriate for your sister."

I'm sure my face registered complete incomprehension—I had forgotten my purported reason for being there. I now felt compelled to purchase a pendant, but I damn sure wasn't going to give it to Vanessa.

Moving through the store toward the display case felt surreal. How could I shop for a pendant just minutes after hearing that Jillian thought Brandon killed his father? The abrupt sifting of gears had me off balance, and I walked as if in a trance.

Jillian led the way to a glass case with pendants displayed against a carpet of fine sand. They were similar to the one I had seen Diana wear, only they were smaller, thank God—I didn't have a semi-truck to bring my purchase home in. Prices were written in hand on small scraps of paper placed beside each piece. I was relieved to observe that the prices weren't as high as I expected. I'm a freelance writer, after all—workers at McDonald's make about the same amount of money as I do. In the end I chose a reddish sandstone pendant about the size of a quarter. Instead of a Kokopeli, Jillian had sandblasted a mini-desert scene, complete with cactus and coyote and a tiny setting sun. I hated to admit it to myself, but it looked like a piece Vanessa might like. She so loved the desert. I asked Jillian to put it in a gift box for me, and I paid the thirty-five bucks.

As she handed the box over to me, I said, to ingratiate myself in case I needed to dig more information out of her, "Again, I'm really sorry about Cole. And I'm sorry I made you think of it."

She looked around the store in an unfocused way. "Actually, it helps to talk about it. I don't make friends easily. The only friend I have in Desert Rock is Diana Oliver. And I have my sister. She lives in San Diego, though, so I can't just pop by for a cup of coffee when I need to talk. Thank God I was with my sister when I got the call that Cole had been murdered. I don't know how I could have dealt with the news without her."

"Well," I said, "Thanks for the tea."

"Stop by any time," she said and ushered me to the door.

I promised that I would and headed out into the wind.

Chapter Seventeen

After I left Desert Designs, I decided to pay Trent Wise a visit at the sheriff's office. I wasn't sure if he'd be working on a Saturday, or whether he'd tell me anything about the Mintock case, but it was worth a shot. Trent used to have a crush on me, so he was obviously susceptible to my many charms, and I thought I could finagle at least some information out of him. I was eager to learn how advanced the case was against Lewis. Clearly, it was not going well, otherwise Lewis would be behind bars by now. Yet the detectives persisted in trying to make the case, ignoring other suspects who, to me, appeared to have greater motive. After talking with Jillian, I now had to add another suspect to my list: Brandon.

When I entered the Sheriff's office, I took a deep breath. I felt that familiar dread that law enforcement establishments have produced in me ever since my run-in with a rogue cop in college. The feeling is remarkably similar to the one I felt while trapped in the collapsed tunnel as a kid: terror.

Before the incident with the rogue cop, I never minded jails that much. I'd had my share of experiences staying in them, given my involvement in protests of all sorts, many of which got out of hand. Generally, the cops hold you a couple of hours, then release you on bail. No big deal.

Then came the rogue cop. Our paths crossed outside a nuclear weapons lab in New Mexico. I was there with a peace group protesting the construction of a new class of atomic arms. The police showed up, claiming we were on private property, and they ordered us to disperse. A few of us refused. The officers grabbed hold of us one by one and shoved us toward their police cars. The guy who grabbed me evidently thought that anyone against the building of more nuclear weapons was anti-American. He called me a traitor and said I was a threat to the country. This kind of thinking—or rather, this non-thinking—always sends me over the edge. It was stupid of me, but I couldn't help it, I told him he was an ignorant fuckhead (yeah, I know) who equated military might with moral superiority. He was less than pleased. Before delivering me to a female officer to be searched, he managed to get in a few good punches, most of which landed on my breasts. Not good. He must have had rank, too, because he arranged for me to cool my heels in a cell until six the next morning. My compatriots were long gone by then, released on bail within hours of our arrest.

Being trapped in that jail cell hour after hour took its toll on me. The place smelled like vomit and sweat, and as the walls closed in on me, I panicked. It became harder and harder to breathe in that place, and I honestly thought I would suffocate. Knowing I was there because of the whim of some asshole didn't help. The experience left me with a mistrust of people who wear badges, as irrational as that is. He was one cop, after all, not representative of law enforcement generally. But the impression stuck, and my hackles raise every time I have dealings with the men and women in blue.

Luckily, my meeting today was with an old high school acquaintance who just happened to be a sheriff deputy. I knew once I got into Trent's office, I'd be fine. As quickly as I could, I got directions from the desk clerk and made my way to his cubicle at the back of the small building.

I found Trent tapping away at a computer keyboard. A Styrofoam cup half filled with bitter smelling coffee, and a greasy maple bar sat on the edge of his desk.

"Hey, Trent," I said from the doorway.

"Sam! What a surprise! What brings you here?" He waved me to the visitor's chair across his desk, and I sat down.

"I was in the neighborhood and thought I'd drop by."

He stared at me, a worried look on his face. He probably thought that I wanted to jump his bones, even though he had told me about his wife and kids.

"Actually, the truth is, I was hoping to talk to you about the Mintock case."

He looked relieved, then confused. "The Mintock case? Why would you be interested in that? This have something to do with that book you're writing about the wind farm?"

I had to think how I wanted to play it. I could probably make something up he'd believe, such as saying I planned to write about the case in the book, but he was an old friend, and lying just didn't feel right. I decided I'd try the truth, or some semblance of it. "No, my curiosity about the case is strictly nonprofessional. I mean, I did meet Cole while researching my book, that's how I got interested in the first place. But now, well, I guess it's just curiosity. After spending so much time out there and meeting the people involved in the case, I find I just can't stop thinking about it. I did have a specific reason I came to see you. I've unearthed a disturbing inconsistency in what one person told me about where he was the night Cole was killed, and I thought you might want to know."

Trent got up and closed the door, his leather boots squeaking on the linoleum floor. Sitting back down, he stared at me over the cluttered desktop. He appeared pleased that I was there, intrigued that I might possess information relevant to the case, but also irritated that I had gotten my non-law enforcement ass involved. Curiosity won out. "Who?"

"Richard Sampson."

I thought he'd look more surprised, but instead he nodded as if what I told him was ancient news. He even looked a little angry. His brown eyes narrowed, and he swiped a hand over his buzz cut. "You're saying the alibi he gave is bogus."

"Looks that way to me. Sampson told the Sheriff's Department that he was working late the night Cole was murdered. I checked out the story with his secretary, who said he wasn't working late. In fact, she said he never works late. I also talked to his wife. She also dismissed the working late story. I got the idea that she believes he was out with one of his mistresses, which is why he lied about it. Please keep that one under your hat, Trent, as she would not want that to get around town."

"But, Sam, if Sampson was out with some mistress, he still has an alibi."

"But it makes one wonder why he'd lie. Maybe he's having a hard time keeping his story straight. Maybe in reality Sampson was in Desert Rock that night stuffing Cole into a turbine. I don't mean to offend or overstep my bounds, but if I were investigating the case, I'd check out his story. I'd double check the alibis of everyone close to Cole."

Trent picked up the Styrofoam cup, took a sniff of its contents, then plunked it back on the desk with enough force to eject a black plume onto his desk. He ran the tips of his fingers down the bridge of his sizeable nose and then over his cheeks, his palm rasping against stubble. Finally, he said, "Let me level with you. But what I say can't leave this room. Do you understand?"

I nodded. "Yes."

He stared at me, his eyes focused on my face. "The feds took over the case once it was known that Lewis was a suspect. They would love to get their hands on another ELF operative. Let's just say they are very motivated to send another eco-terrorist to prison. Let me tell you, Sam, their fixation on ELF is irrational. I know it's important to fight domestic terrorism so that we don't have another Oklahoma City Bombing, but these ELF characters just torch buildings, they don't kill people. I'm not even sure ELF should be called a terrorist group. Well, that's beside the point. What I'm saying is that the department doesn't agree with the feds on this case. We think other suspects ought to be looked at."

I nodded and let him continue.

"Look. You've got the wife, who stands to inherit a shitload of money—uh, pardon the French. Only been married to the victim for a few months. And the developer, he's been overheard threatening Cole on numerous occasions, he doesn't want the expansion to happen. Kill Cole, stop the expansion. If it were up to us, we'd be interrogating these people, checking out their stories. I'd interview other people in Cole's life: his accountant, his secretary, his son, his running buddy, anyone who knew him."

"But the feds aren't doing that."

"No, and they won't let us do it either. They say they're 'working in tandem with local law enforcement,' but that's a crock of shit—oops, sorry again."

"Trent," I said, "I am not a nun. You can curse all you like."

He grinned. "Sorry."

"Now you're apologizing for apologizing."

"Sorry! I mean, God, Sam! You haven't changed a bit since high school. Still as feisty as ever. You always did make me crazy."

"Because you're so easy, Trent. You're a sitting duck."

"Don't I know it."

We sat in silence, then. A phone rang somewhere down the hall, a copy machine clunked, air whooshed out of the air conditioner ducts. The place smelled like old coffee and paper. I said, "So Lewis is going to be it."

"Yep."

"That's fucked."

He laughed. "Sam Larkin! You are too much!" Trent studied me a moment, his laughter dying away. "I'm grateful that you're looking into this, Sam, because I think the feds are mucking it up. But I got to tell you, what you're doing is dangerous. I couldn't in good conscience let you walk out of here without telling you to stay away from the case. Course," he said, a twinkle in his eye, "if you just insist on persisting, what can I do about it?"

I smiled and stood up. "Thanks, Trent."

He came around the desk to follow me out. "Be careful. I mean it. Whoever killed Cole wouldn't think twice about killing you. I don't want to live with that on my conscience."

Chapter Eighteen

I got up Monday morning at six so I could be at Coffee Buzz before Sierra arrived for her daily caffeine purchase. I wondered if her heart was still in it now that Cole was dead. It was likely one of those habits people acquire and then continue out of sheer momentum. I guessed that it gave Sierra some comfort to keep up the tradition, as if Cole would walk in the office door every day as he had always done and she could surprise him with the latest concoction. I wondered if she ever guessed he didn't like fancy coffee much but drank it because he didn't want to hurt her feelings. Probably not. He was too kind to let it show.

Eddie hadn't arrived at the shop yet, so I had no one to pass the time with while I waited for Sierra to show. Bored, I sat down at a table and reviewed my plan. My ostensible excuse for being there was that I wanted to pay for her coffee as thanks for all the help she had given me. I had also promised Sierra that I'd buy her donuts, so I had a box of Desert Donuts selections with me. My main goal was to see what Sierra knew about Brandon's relationship with Jillian. Sierra talked to Brandon when he went in to deliver and pick up paperwork, and I had seen the friendly intimacy between them. Sometimes people will open up to those on the periphery of their lives even while finding it difficult to talk to close family and friends. I hoped Brandon had found in Sierra a confidante.

I also wanted to see if Sierra could get me in to see Diana. The myopic accountant didn't seem to like me very much (hard to imagine), so I wasn't sure she'd agree to see me. My excuse for wanting to meet with her was that I wanted her views on the economics of wind energy. What I really wanted was the goods on her friend Jillian. I wanted to know what story Diana would relay about where Jillian was the night of the murder. I also wanted her take on Jillian's and Brandon's relationship. Diana seemed to dislike Brandon even more than she did me. Since she and Jillian were friends, she likely knew about the problems between stepmother and son and would have an opinion on it. Whether she would talk to me about these matters, or at all for that matter, was highly uncertain.

I saw Sierra the minute she walked in at seven fifteen. Her wild red hair looked like a forest fire on top of her head. She wore a canary yellow dress that clashed with her hair color, but she sauntered in as though Christian Dior had personally outfitted her. I had to admire her élan.

I left my table and walked up to her as she was placing her order. I told her to put her wallet away. "This one's on me," I said like I was picking up a hundred dollar tab. I plunked down a twenty to cover the order and handed Sierra the box of donuts. "I didn't even drop it," I bragged.

She seemed bewildered by all this, and I concluded that she was not a morning person. Her gigantic bosoms attracted appreciative looks from the male patrons, but her brain still slept, and their leers were lost on her.

While we waited for the order to be filled, I interrogated her over the screech of the steamed milk machine. "How's Brandon doing these days?" I hollered.

"Brandon?" she repeated as if I'd mentioned someone she'd never heard of. "He's fine. I guess. Actually, he seems kinda weird lately. But then his dad just died."

"Weird in what way?"

"Oh, moody I guess. I mean, he's always moody, but lately even more. He doesn't joke around as much as he used to."

Meaning he didn't flirt with her as much as he used to. "You know what I've been thinking? I'm wondering if he feels guilty. He and his dad did not have a great relationship from what I've been told, and sometimes survivors in that situation feel a lot of guilt. Like they should have done more to make amends. Once a loved one dies, there's no longer any chance of mending fences." I realized with alarm that I was repeating what Vanessa had said about my reaction to our mother's death. Did I secretly believe that she was right? Thankfully, Sierra's voice broke into this disturbing thought.

"Could be guilt, I guess. Brandon did not like his dad. I never did get it. Cole is—was—such a sweet man."

"I happened to have a chat with Jillian Mintock," I said, as if I had not tracked her down like a bloodhound on a scent. "She said some pretty nasty things about Brandon. What's up with those two?"

Sierra shrugged. "The usual, probably. She married his dad. And pretty soon after his mom died, too. Lot's of people wouldn't like that."

"No, I suppose not. But Jillian painted a picture of Brandon as mentally unstable. Dangerous. That seems to go beyond the typical jealousies and whatnot that afflict blended families."

She seemed to wake up at that. "That bitch. No wonder Brandon can't stand her. And to think she may be my boss soon."

"You think she'll keep and run the wind farm?"

"God, I hope not. But it could happen, I guess."

"What don't you like about her?"

"How much time do you have? Basically, I think she married Cole for his money. She never even appeared to like the guy. She's an ice maiden. And she was against Brandon from the beginning. I think she tried to drive Brandon and his dad further apart. She's barely civil to me. What a cold bitch."

"She and Diana seem pretty chummy."

"Yeah. But Diana can be pretty bitchy, too. I mean, she's alright on the whole, I guess, but sometimes, like maybe its menopause or something, watch out."

Sierra's order was called and I went to retrieve it since she had her hands full with the donut box. I walked her out to her car. The parking lot was busy with sleepy workers pulling in to get their daily fix. "Sierra, would you do me a favor? Do you think you could get me in to see Diana? I'd like to get her views on the wind farm, and to tell the truth, I'm a little scared of her. She doesn't seem to like me."

She brightened, seeming to like the idea of tormenting Diana with my presence. "Yeah, I can get you in. No problem."

"Another thing. Do you happen to know Brandon's grandmother's name and address? I'd like to send a condolence card to the house."

"I don't know the address, but his grandma's last name is Brittel. Ruth Brittel. She's probably in the book."

"Ah, so she's Brandon's maternal grandmother."

"Yeah."

"One last thing, and I promise I'll let you get to work. Jillian said that Brandon was dangerous. Do you know why she'd think that?"

"Dangerous? No. Well, there was a thing last summer when Jillian's niece was visiting from San Diego. Jillian got all upset about something Brandon did—he was hanging out with the niece, although I can't imagine why. Kid wasn't going to win any beauty contests, let me tell you. There was some brouhaha, but I never did get the full scoop. Maybe the niece didn't like Brandon, you know, didn't appreciate him coming on to her. Anyway, Jillian flipped out and shipped the niece home."

"So you don't see Brandon as unstable or dangerous?"

"No way," she said, jingling her keys to remind me that she had to leave. "A little cruel, maybe, but not dangerous."

"Cruel?"

"Not toward people. Like, toward animals. Big difference."

"How is he cruel to animals?"

"Don't tell anyone, because it's like totally illegal, but he and his buddies go out shooting tortoises at night. In the preserve. He told me that's where he was the night his dad was killed, so he made up some story to tell the cops, said he was home sleeping, or something. He didn't want to get in trouble."

Shooting tortoises? Lying to the cops? I tried not to let the disgust I felt cloud my face. I wanted her to think I was on Brandon's side, but now I was having my doubts. I asked, my voice carefully neutral, "Why would he shoot tortoises?"

"Got me," she said and climbed into her red Volkswagen Bug, "but they get off on it. It's a guy thing. I think he's pissed that they made that land out there off limits to off-roading. He's always going on about the damned environmentalists. I'm like, all right already. I think he could kill that skinny guy we got protesting out at the wind farm one day."

She turned on the ignition and rolled down the window about an inch. I took this as my subtle clue to wrap it up. "Thanks, Sierra. As usual, you've been a tremendous help."

"See you later," she called, and sped off down the street.

When I got home from Coffee Buzz, I found the red light blinking on my answering machine. It was my editor, Vince, and I could tell by the tight way he said "call me as soon as possible" that I was in big trouble. Reluctantly, I called him back.

"Sam, what the hell is going on?" He bellowed into the phone. Two packs a day had made his voice raspy, but there was nothing wrong with its volume. I pulled the phone away from my ear several inches. I could just visualize him sitting hunched over the phone, punching his cluttered desk with his index finger. If he hadn't changed since I'd seen him six months ago, the nail hitting the desk would be overly long and filthy. Vince was a brilliant editor, and I loved my job, otherwise I'd have moved on years ago. I heard his voice growling in my ear: "Your book's due in a week and you haven't sent me a bloody thing! Zip! Nada!"

I had the urge to point out his redundancies but felt he would not be impressed. "Vince, let me just—"

"Sam, this is it! This is the last time I'm going to assign you a title. I've given you chance after chance and you never have met a deadline in your life. I wash my hands of you."

Washing his hands was a damn good idea, I thought. How many times had I heard his lament? You don't keep giving writers chances for ten years if you don't think it's worth it. Vince knows my books get excellent reviews and win awards and sell well. He was just blowing smoke. I said, "I'll mail out the outline and first chapter today."

The idea that he had browbeat me into getting the work done must have sent shivers of pleasure up and down his spine because he was nice as pie after that. Vince didn't have to know I had completed this phase of work anyway. Let him think it was his fearsome personality that got results. The big blowhard.

He said, "Well, that's all right then, that's fine, very good. So, how's the rest of the book coming?"

"Fine," I lied. "All the research is done, and I'm just putting the finishing touches on the remaining chapters." Right, like "finishing touches" equated to "start writing."

We signed off, Vince in a much cheerier mood. He was getting some work from me, and he could enjoy the thought that he'd pounded it out of me. Whatever made him happy.

I glanced over the outline and first chapter, stuffed them into a UPS envelope, and drove the package to the UPS office on Feldspar. I should have begun writing the second chapter, but instead I decided to spend a few hours checking on what Sierra had told me about Brandon's little shooting sprees. What Vince didn't know wouldn't hurt him.

I'm no great animal lover, but even less am I a fan of hunting. The idea of enjoying the act of killing is alien to me. My brain knew that Sierra was right: A lot of boys and men got into hunting, legally or illegally. Even Connor, the biggest softie on Earth, begged for a bb-gun one Christmas, telling our mother that he wanted to shoot old cans out at the rifle range. Once he got the gun, he graduated to shooting lizards and ground squirrels. Then one day, he just stopped. He sold the gun to a friend and he never owned a gun again. I always assumed there was some hunting gene in the male of our species, left over from all those centuries before the arrival of plastic-wrapped steaks. Then, if you wanted meat, you had to shoot it.

Although uncomfortable with the idea of shooting critters, I could live with the idea of men going out and shooting legal game to stock their freezers. But shooting small, helpless creatures just for fun disgusted me. Normal juvenile male behavior or not, phase or not, I was disappointed in Brandon, if Sierra's accusation was true. I liked the kid. And sympathized with him. His life had not been a happy one. A mentally ill mother who commits suicide. A new, hated step-mother. A father murdered. I imagined that such experiences so early in life would leave a lot of anger, even rage. That, I supposed, could be what drove him to shoot tortoises. But while I could understand what Brandon was doing, I could not approve of it.

I brought up a search engine and typed in "desert tortoise shooting." The very first hit told most of the story. The document was a Federal Register Notice issued by the Bureau of Land Management in 2003. Essentially a notice to the public, the document stated that the BLM now restricted firearm use in the Gypsum Mountain quadrant, located in the southeastern portion of the Ancho Desert. The restriction applies to the Desert Rock Preserve, which was set aside to protect threatened plant and animal species such as the desert tortoise. This is the place Sierra said Brandon and his pals went to shoot. From reading through the document, it was clear that what the boys were doing was illegal. The BLM explained that the desert tortoise, *Gopherus agassizii*, has been fully protected in California since 1961. Despite the creature's status as a threatened species, dead tortoises containing gunshot holes have been found throughout the Ancho Desert, the most found in the Gypsum Mountain quadrant. The number of tortoises dying in this location from gunshot wounds as compared with other causes of death was 28.7 percent, in contrast to other parts of the Ancho, which averaged 3.1 percent. The BLM attributed the greater number of deaths near Desert Rock to the higher number of human visitors and the greater off-road vehicle activity. Apparently, some people here liked to use desert tortoises for target practice.

Scanning another twenty entries, I discovered that the desert tortoise is California's and Nevada's state reptile. The average tortoise weighs between eight and fifteen pounds, with shells approximately nine to fifteen inches in length. They eat herbs, grasses, wildflowers, and some shrubs and cacti. An adult tortoise can go over a year without drinking water, and they have life spans of up to eighty years. Natural predators include coyotes, Gila monsters, and roadrunners. Ravens kill a disproportionate number of hatchlings, and an outbreak of upper respiratory disease has claimed many turtle lives.

I read that human encroachment into tortoise territory has had a devastating impact on the creatures. Tortoise Rescue reports that there has been a 90 percent decline in the numbers of desert tortoises since 1980. The organization claims that cattle grazing had the first impact on the tortoise population. The cattle trampled on the tortoise's burrows and consumed the grass that is one of the turtle's primary sources of food. Development in the desert also led to decreasing numbers, as desert towns expanded into tortoise territory. Some people take the tortoises out of the desert to be sold as pets. And with the increasing popularity of off-road vehicles, more land has had to be set aside baring vehicular traffic in order to protect the remaining tortoise population. Some people riding around on motorcycles, four-wheel drive trucks, and quads enjoy shooting the creatures, or even rolling the tortoises over on their backs and leaving them to die. Brandon was one of those people.

I turned off the computer and thought about what I'd learned. The most upsetting part of my tortoise research was all the photos of the beasts. Round, honeycombed shells, flipper-like front legs, back appendages that look like miniature elephants' legs. Their eyes look less reptilian than snake or lizard eyes, and combined with their downward turned mouths, make the creatures appear serious and determined, as if they have somewhere to be. They are quiet, gentle creatures, their only protection a fast retreat into their shells. Not a great defense against bullets.

I made a quick call to the ranger station out at the preserve. The ranger I talked to confirmed the information I had found online. But she added one thing: Tortoise shootings in the preserve had increased of late, and the rangers had stepped up their investigation into the shootings. They were getting out into the field more, retrieving dead tortoises in order to measure the scope of the problem and hoping to catch shooters in the act. Ranger Caven also said they had scheduled more night shifts, as a lot of the shooters liked to operate in the dark, using spotlights to locate and blind their prey. She told me that she had an idea of the identity of some of the boys who were doing this, but of course she didn't share those details with me. I thanked her and rang off.

Staring at my desk top, I tried to take comfort in the knowledge that Brandon was part of a wide circle of desert dwellers that took pleasure in killing the original desert residents. I tried to explain away his behavior as a natural release of anger at all the shitty things that had happened to him. I tried to look at his actions as normal boy behavior, a phase he'd grow out of. The problem was that I knew most people living in Desert Rock were not out shooting tortoises. I knew that lots of angry people never shot anything in their lives. I knew lots of boys—Eddie was one—who never got into guns.

My mind sifted through all that I had heard about Brandon in the last couple of days. He was cruel. He was unbalanced. He was dangerous. He hated his father. I wasn't sure what to make of it. So the boy shoots turtles. Connor liked shooting squirrels for a while and he grew up fine (well, sort of). So Brandon's stepmother mistrusts and resents him. Such reactions must be common as water in blended families. So he was moody. How many people on this Earth are happy twenty-four-seven? I had the sense that engaging in bad feelings about Brandon was in essence blaming the victim. It felt traitorous and unkind. After all, the boy just lost his mother and father. Go ahead, Sam, hit the boy while he's down.

Still, the bad feeling persisted. I looked up Brandon's grandmother's name in the phone directory and dialed the number. An answering machine came on, and I left a message asking Brandon to call me. I said I wanted to take him out to dinner when he had time. I had a few more questions for him.

That done, I went looking for Connor. I was in the mood to play Monopoly or Gin Rummy, maybe barbecue some back ribs, drink a couple of beers. Instead of my brother, I found a note saying he had gone to the gym to use the pool. Rats. Just when I needed a playmate he decides to become an Ironman.

Chapter Nineteen

Diana Oliver examined me across her desk. The quarter inch thick glasses she wore made her eyes appear owlish. I felt like a small rodent scurrying through an open patch of desert under a full moon. True to her word, Sierra had gotten me an appointment to see the accountant just a day after we had talked at Coffee Buzz. I had prepared questions regarding the economics of wind energy that I hoped to pose as evidence of my professional reason for wanting to meet with Diana. Then I hoped to steer the conversation to the more pressing topic, Jillian Mintock.

Under her steady gaze, I asked my first question: "My research indicates that a lot of the criticism of wind energy concerns government subsidies. Critics scoff at the idea that wind energy is now competitive with electricity from traditional sources. They say the only way wind energy can compete is with the help of generous tax breaks and other subsidies. That, in essence, taxpayers foot the bill for wind industry development. What's your take on that?"

She seemed less hostile to me now that I asked for her opinion. After smoothing her wiry, graying hair, she answered my question readily. "Please understand that I'm no expert on the economics of wind energy. But as the bookkeeper here, I can say that CalWind has never received a government tax break. A wind farm has to be quite large to amass the amount of taxable income required to be eligible for such subsidies. Even without the extra help, CalWind makes electricity for four cents a kilowatt-hour, which is competitive with other energy sources. It wasn't always that way. In 1982, when the wind farm opened, the cost was thirty cents."

"What accounts for the reduction?"

"New technology. The newer turbines are much more efficient."

I scribbled on my notepad, even though I already had this information and much more in the stacks of documents I had printed off the Web. When I had finished writing, I asked, "A lot of the critics talk about the 'hidden costs' of wind energy. For example, they say that because wind energy is intermittent, localities must have back up services such as a gas-fired plant in order to provide consumers with electricity when the wind isn't blowing. Can you comment on that?"

She took her glasses off and polished them with the hem of her white cotton blouse. Without the magnification, the predator image vanished. Her gray eyes were now proportionate with her round face. She said, "What you said is true, strictly speaking. Desert Rock does have a small gas fired plant that is used when the wind dies down. But, you live here, how often is there no wind out by the pass? It blows at the plant over 90 percent of the time. So, sure, initially there was a greater outlay because two electricity generation systems had to be built, but both systems have more than recouped initial installation expenses." She put her glasses back on. The owl was back.

I wondered how many more questions I had to ask before I could get to the good stuff. If she suspected my real motives, I was raptor food. "Another question. Wind farm opponents claim that the industry exaggerates the benefit to local economies in terms of jobs. They argue that the number of lasting jobs is small, and that they pay poorly. Do you agree with that assessment?"

"Well, again, I'm no expert, but just looking at how many people work over at Mill Maintenance, CalWind created over a hundred fulltime jobs. I don't know what their salaries are, but I think windsmiths make over thirty thousand a year, and engineers would certainly make much more than that. A hundred jobs doesn't sound like very much, but in a community the size of Desert Rock, it's significant."

I nodded and wrote everything down. "So, in general, what are your thoughts on the merits of wind energy?"

She rubbed the palms of her hands together. I noticed she wore no rings, and her nails were short and jagged. She was probably a gardener. Desert Rock's hard soil—if the nutrient-starved organic concrete we have here can be called soil—can destroy fingernails, not to mention axes and shovels, in mere minutes. Diana said, "Well, look, we seem to have two big problems. One, we're running out of fossil fuels. Whether sooner or later, we will dig every piece of coal out of the ground and suck out every liter of gas. And then where will we be? Two, burning fossil fuels pollutes the environment, causes global warming. People say it could kill us off. The way I look at it, why wouldn't you want to develop renewable energy sources now, before the major trouble starts? Sure, wind energy isn't perfect. People object to the towers blocking their view, they don't like the noise of the blades, they don't like to see birds killed, but what are you going to do? No energy source will ever be without problems. It seems to me if you start working on the technologies sooner rather than later, you can work out the kinks. Wind energy costs have gone way down in just twenty years. It stands to reason the technology will only get better. Maybe work on wind turbines will spark ideas for other kinds of energy technologies. I don't know. Cole knew way, way more about all this than I do, but I wouldn't work at a company I didn't believe in. To me it makes perfect sense."

"So you don't sympathize with Richard Sampson's position that the expansion should be stopped to avoid spoiling his view?"

She let out a long sigh. "Actually, I can see where he's coming from. I mean, if I had the money to build a house like his up on the hill, I wouldn't be too excited to lose my view either. But, that's life. He's got the money to build somewhere else. The irony, when you think about it, is that all those rich cats up there use three times as much electricity as the rest of us do. They're more reliant on energy than anyone. You'd think they'd support the expansion."

"And what about the protestors? See any merit in their complaints?"

"They're strange birds. They seem to think they can stop progress by standing out in front of a remote wind farm office with tag board signs. Nobody wants to give up their TVs and air conditioners to return to the dark ages. Those two just aren't dealing with reality."

I changed course. "So, will the daily operations around here change much now that Jillian will be taking over?"

Diana shook her head emphatically. "No. Jillian understands the business. She's been somewhat involved in it, coming in to sign checks and make decisions when Cole's away on travel. Most of the work involved with keeping us going really occurs out at Mill Maintenance anyway. We have a lot of decisions to make out of this office, of course, and we have the ultimate authority concerning what gets done, but Jillian will know what Cole would have wanted."

"Decisions such as the expansion?"

"Sure."

"Think it will happen now?"

"Probably. It's what Cole wanted."

I nodded and glanced down at my pad. Then I looked up at her. "I'm curious. Who do you think killed Cole?"

The question surprised her, which I expected it to. "I don't have an opinion on that," she said.

"Do you think the police are right in fingering Lewis?"

She sat up straighter in her chair. "I really couldn't say. I haven't looked at the evidence."

I got the idea she did have a strong opinion about it. I began fumbling around in the dark to see if I could get a line on her thinking. "The Sheriff's Department is also looking at Sampson and Jillian."

When I said the last name, she looked as if someone had stunned her with a whack to the head. "You're kidding. Jillian? Are you serious?"

I tried to beat a hasty retreat. The last thing I wanted was for her to call the Sheriff's office demanding to know why Jillian was on their suspect list. Trent had asked me to keep his and the other sheriffs' suspicions under my hat, and I had promised I would. Now I had just opened my big fat mouth. I didn't want to get Trent in trouble. I said, "Of course, the police always cast the widest net possible. I don't know whether Jillian and Sampson are serious suspects or not."

She took a deep breath, relaxed a jot. "I guess that sounds reasonable. Still, Jillian? It's absurd."

I ventured forth again. "I suppose they're just looking at her because she inherits. Anyone with a motive, especially a profit motive, would be immediately suspect."

"Jillian isn't the only person to inherit," she said, her voice pinched with emotion. "Cole's son gets money, too. And the boy hated his father. Pretty good motive, I'd say."

Ah, another person implicating Brandon. Interesting. Diana had made it clear she won't make any guesses about who killed Cole, but a minute later is presenting Brandon as a prime suspect. I said, "Jillian seems none too keen on the kid."

"You talked to Jillian?" She asked, surprised.

"After seeing your pendant, I went to her shop to buy one for my sister. I fainted, actually, and while Jillian revived me with a vile tasting tea, we chatted about this and that." I hoped my casual tone conveyed a scene of womanly camaraderie and innocent gossip.

Diana seemed to buy it. "Oh."

"Jillian seems upset over the way Brandon treated his father." I didn't say anything about Jillian's suspicion that Brandon *killed* his father—I had promised I wouldn't. "She also said something about Brandon bothering her niece." Actually, Sierra had told me that, but who was checking?

"Yes," Diana said. "Last summer Jillian's thirteen-year-old niece, Ann, stayed with her here in Desert Rock. Brandon took an immediate interest in her—she's a pretty girl. Ann didn't feel the same way about Brandon, though. For one, she's a couple years younger, and I think the attentions of an older boy quite intimidated her. She's a shy, quiet girl. Anyway, Jillian told Brandon to leave the girl alone, but of course he wouldn't. He hates to be told what to do by anyone, especially Jillian or Cole. I think he bothered the girl more and more just to irritate his step mom. Jillian finally sent Ann home. Not that that would stop a boy like Brandon." Diana's voice had sounded angrier the longer she talked. She now seemed to radiate enough energy to power Los Angeles.

I wanted to learn more about the situation between Brandon and Ann, but I sensed she had said as much as she was going to on that subject. I decided to steer the conversation to the night Cole was murdered. Here it got pretty dicey. "I can tell by your reaction that you care about Jillian a lot. She seems grateful to have you as a friend. She told me she doesn't make friends easily. At least Jillian was with her sister when she heard the news that Cole had been murdered. Not news you want to hear alone."

Diana looked confused, concerned even. "But she wasn't. She wasn't in San Diego. She was with a friend in Phoenix. Where did you get the idea that Jillian was in San Diego?"

Phoenix? Now what was this about? "Well," I said, confused. "I thought that's what she said. I must have misheard her. I wasn't feeling very well, as I said." But I wasn't that out of it.

Diana continued to look worried, and her mind seemed to drift. She looked at the phone. "Well, if there are no more questions, I've got to get back to work."

I stared at her, reluctant to leave, wanting to ask more questions, but I knew my time was up. Diana had given me all she was going to. I nodded and gathered up my purse and notebook. As I walked out of her office, I glanced back and saw her hand reach out and pick up the phone.

Driving back into Desert Rock, I thought about my interviews with Jillian and Diana. One of them, or both, lied about where Jillian was the night of the murder. But why? In both scenarios, Jillian was out of town and therefore safe from suspicion. If Jillian was indeed in San Diego with her sister as she claimed, why was Diana claiming otherwise? Had Jillian told Diana to say that? But why? Or, if Diana spoke the truth, and Jillian was in Phoenix, why had Jillian lied to me and said she was in San Diego? No matter how I looked at it, I couldn't come up with any theories to explain the inconsistency. I stopped when my head began to throb. It was like Sampson's lie all over again. Both had alibis; the problem was, they had too many. What was going on?

When I got home from the interview with Diana, I found Lacy sound asleep on my bed, drool puddling on my pillowcase. Some watchdog! The nerve of her! I clapped my hands and shouted "Get down!" and she bounded from the bed and tore out of the room, tail between her legs. I looked at the puddle of drool and the brown and black hairs strewn over the sheets. I thought, how did my mother put up with this beast? And then, Why should I? Something had to give or I was going to call Brandon and have him come over and dispatch the dog forthwith. As far as I knew, Rottweilers were not on the endangered species list. Not that Brandon would care, apparently.

Chapter Twenty

I had made a pact with myself that the next time I saw Eddie, I'd confine my feelings for him to friendly ones. I would not let my mind (or any other part of my anatomy) dwell on how good he smelled or how sexy his dimple was. We had been friends a long time, and I had come to depend on him always being there. Making our relationship into more than it was would put at risk the one thing that seemed stable and good in my life. Besides, as was obvious the night he came over for Connor's barbecue, he viewed me as just another friend, nothing more. Eddie had always been more sensible than I.

I have since come to mistrust pacts you make with yourself. I hadn't been with Eddie twenty minutes before I broke all the rules I had set down for myself. He had called the afternoon I met with Diana to ask me if I wanted to go down to The Hideaway for a burger. I asked him if he'd take a drive with me instead, have a picnic out at Pioneer's Hill. He seemed mystified, but agreed. After throwing together a rather odd picnic dinner with the food scraps I had in the house, I swung by his place, and we drove out to Sampson's upscale community. The entire hillside had pretty much been built out, a home every five acres, but a few empty lots remained to be sold. It was on one of these pads that we set up our picnic. I hoped that Sampson wouldn't happen by on his way home and see me there eating carrot sticks in close proximity to his precious wife and kids.

Looking out over the desert from where we sat, I felt my first twinge of sympathy for Sampson's position. From our vantage point, we had a 180 degree view of Rock Valley and the town of Desert Rock. At the western edge of the city, I could make out the wind farm, rows of white turbines with their flashing blades fading from view in the evening light. Mt. Barton and Smyth Peak rose from the desert floor, their eastern flanks forming a near vertical wall. From our vantage point I could just make out the terminus of Thomas Pass, through which flowed the high winds that made the wind farm possible. Much of the western valley belonged to Cole—well, now to Jillian and Brandon. This was the future sight of the wind farm expansion. I tried to visualize the empty desert populated with hundreds of two hundred foot towers, the waning light reflecting on thousands of whirling blades. Sampson's complaint no longer seemed frivolous to me. Thinking of those white rows cross-hatching the expanse seemed tragic, like the loss of something precious. I hated the thought of the gorgeous open space being despoiled. I was fairly certain I wouldn't want to look out at those turbines every day of my life, especially if I had paid a cool million for the view.

As Eddie and I unwrapped the foodstuffs and placed them onto the big wool blanket I had spread over the sand, I found my mind drifting from Sampson's view to more personal issues. I started, to my horror, to share with Eddie my feelings about all that seemed wrong with my life. The end result of this disgorgement could be tears (mortifying enough) and deep, humiliating confidences I would never live down. I heard myself saying, as though the words came out of someone else's mouth, "I'm not even sure what I feel anymore."

Ack! Such a chick thing to say. To Eddie's credit, he didn't flee. Then my mouth opened again and I said, "Vanessa and Connor and I fight all the time. Lacy's driving me nuts. Vince laid into me yesterday about being late on my book—I know, don't say it. And if things keep going like they have been, you'll have to come visit me in the hospital next time we meet. I mean, look at me." I showed him the long pink swaths on my elbows and knees where the abrasions from my Iditarod accident were healing, and my still swollen and purple knee, which I had slammed in the car door.

"You've been preoccupied," Eddie said. "Mind not focused on what you're doing. What's this?" Eddie held up what appeared to be a white French fry.

"Jicama. Come on, you must have had it before. It's used in Mexican salads."

He shook his head with certainty. "Nope." He started to put it back into the plastic bag.

"Try it."

"Nope."

"Come on."

"Alright." He took a tiny nibble of one end. "Tastes like water."

"Jicama."

"Interesting picnic," he said and bit into a tuna burrito.

I nodded. "Last minute. No food in the house." Why did I always talk like Eddie when I was with him? It was as though we talked via telegram.

"What else?" He asked.

When I just stared at him, he added, "What else has you down?"

"Promise me you won't lecture."

"You're still working on the wind farm murder."

I nodded.

He said, "Go on."

So I told him how I found that just about everyone in Cole's life had lied about where they were the night that he was murdered. Jillian said she was in San Diego, but her best friend Diana told me she was in Phoenix. Sampson said he'd been working late, but his assistant and his wife contradicted that claim. Even Lewis, who I was convinced was innocent, lied to the cops about his whereabouts. He said he was out sleeping in the desert that night, but Katie told me he was actually in Martinville meeting his ELF pal John McGinnis And then there was Brandon. He told the Sheriff's Department that he was at his grandmother's house sleeping, but he told Sierra he was out shooting tortoises in the preserve.

I then explained to Eddie how the case also frustrated me because my opinions of all the players kept changing. I told him that I had liked Brandon from the first moment I met him because he was funny and charming and seemed brave in the face of tragedy. Later I heard claims that he shoots helpless creatures, torments teenage girls, and may have homicidal tendencies. Jillian appeared calculating and unfeeling when I first met her, an opinion shared by many who knew her. But on closer acquaintance, I found her genuine, almost warm. Sampson, who initially appeared to be an irrational brute, now seemed to have a legitimate complaint about the wind farm expansion. Still, he was probably a philanderer, not to mention a bully. To illustrate this last point, I told Eddie that he had threatened me.

"He threatened you!" Eddie dropped his burrito on the blanket. His body went rigid.

Oops. "He just left a message on my machine, told me not to pry into his business. It's not like he sent hired goons after me."

"But the threat was implied."

"I guess."

"Sam."

"What?"

He rubbed his eyes with enough force to pop them out onto the blanket. Eddie didn't seem to know what to say, or rather, he knew what to say, he was just trying to figure out the best way to say it so I wouldn't get defensive.

I bailed him out. "I know what you're about to say. I'm too involved. It's making me crazy. Its dangerous."

"About sums it up."

"But don't you see? The feds don't care who killed Cole, they just wants to nail ELF. It isn't right"

"You're a writer, Sam. You're out of your league."

"I disagree. I'm the only one asking the right questions. The Sheriff's Department's hands are tied. If I don't do it, nobody will."

"I just don't want anything to happen to you." He looked at me, blinked once, then grabbed his burrito off the blanket and took a bite. He extracted a bottle of iced tea out of the cooler and gulped half of it down.

I felt my face heat up, and confusion washed through my brain. I watched him as he made a great show of wiping his goatee with a napkin. Why was he so embarrassed? Was it possible that Eddie cared more about me than I thought? No, I was letting my imagination run away with me. With great resolve, I changed course, ignoring his comment. "Look, the one person I still feel the same about is Cole. He was a visionary. He didn't just espouse ideals, he lived them. I can't just walk away and let his killer go free."

"You can. You can acknowledge that you are not responsible for what happened to him. Or for finding his killer."

"No one else is taking responsibility for it."

"Sam, let sleeping dogs lie."

I looked out over the desert. Twilight had pitched the rocks and gullies into darkness. Stars were now visible in the sky, except in patches, where the last of the afternoon's cumulus clouds blotted them out. The wind had died down, and I felt a faint expectation of rain. The air actually felt cool. "I can't let it go," I said. "I really can't."

He examined me. "I wonder if the case is serving as a distraction from the one thing you refuse to talk about."

My heart pounded. He couldn't know about my confused feelings for him, could he? I wasn't up for this discussion. I said coyly, "I don't know what you mean."

"I think you do."

I shrugged, looking as bewildered and uninterested as I could.

Eddie said, "Your mom."

"My mom!" I said. Air escaped my lungs in a whoosh. I wasn't sure if I was relieved or annoyed. "You're wrong. I'm fine about that."

"Uh-huh."

"Really."

"Some day you'll need to talk about it, Sam."

Looking at Eddie, a bolt of energy shot through my body from the top of my head down to my toes. I wanted him at that moment. But it wasn't just sex I needed—was that what I needed?—I had the urge to throw myself into his arms, lay my head on his shoulder, and sob until morning. I wanted to say how much I missed my mom, how I dreamed about her nearly every night, how the house was such a comfort and such a torture all at the same time, how I hated Vanessa and Connor because they had lived and she had not. How I lied when

I said everything was all right between us when she died. I wanted Eddie to know these things about my life. And I didn't.

"Did you know that vanilla wafers have less fat than other cookies?" I said instead, watching him bite into one, the stale cookie exploding apart on contact with his straight white teeth.

Chapter Twenty-One

Brandon returned my call, and we agreed to meet for dinner on Wednesday evening. I thought it would feel strange seeing him, after learning such negative things about him. My opinion of the teen shifted daily. Sometimes I felt empathy. Brandon and I shared the unfortunate circumstance of having lost both our parents, and one quite recently. I felt admiration for the stoic way he was dealing with his father's death. And I liked the boy—he was witty and liked to laugh. On the other hand, I loathed his harassment of Jillian's niece and his using tortoises for target practice. If true, they revealed a boy with a cruel streak, someone who uses—even harms—others for his own amusement. The information also made Jillian's accusation that Brandon killed his father seem less absurd, though I was far from accepting it as truth.

I tried to keep in mind that everyone has a dark side that we keep hidden away. I had done many things in my life I hoped like hell would never see the light of day. How would I feel if someone were investigating me and found out about certain episodes in my life? Wouldn't it seem unfair to judge me now in terms of my past mistakes? We all behave in ways we're ashamed of from time to time, but hopefully we grow out of them, can one day put all that behind us. I was meeting Brandon during the middle of his darkest hour, perhaps, and I felt a kind of duty to be tolerant, to try not to judge too much.

Still. Despite my effort to reassure myself, two facts had me worried. One, Jillian and Diana had intimated that Brandon was dangerous. They both had suggested he could have killed his father. Two, Brandon had lied about where he was the night of his father's murder. Was he at his Grandmother's house, as he had told the Sheriff's Department, or was he in the Desert Rock Preserve, the story he gave Sierra? Or, was he somewhere else? I felt compelled to check out his alibi as thoroughly as I planned to check everyone else's. There was an epidemic of lying occurring amongst the people in Cole's life, and Brandon was infected as well. I found I just couldn't rationalize away the teen's behavior so simply, at least not yet. I needed to learn more.

My mission for dinner was to assess Brandon in light of the new information I had about him. Perhaps I had been too blinded by empathy to judge his character accurately. Admittedly, I had another goal as well: I hoped to dissuade Brandon from killing any more tortoises. If I accomplished nothing else in my investigation into Cole's murder, at least I could say a few more tortoises lived because of me.

Despite my resolve, I can't say I looked forward to my interview with the kid. He was not likely to appreciate my interrogation. My discomfort at the idea of questioning him, however, paled in comparison to my distress at having to eat at Burger Mania, Brandon's choice of eatery. The company's disgusting commercials depicting greasy-looking people practically having orgasms while burger grease and ketchup dripped from their faces had put me off the fast food chain forever.

I met the teen outside the restaurant. He was dressed in baggy khaki shorts and a stained white tank top, which accentuated the muscles in his arms. A blue Dodger's cap clamped low on his head obscured the top half of his face. With the cap hiding the distinctive blonde spikes, I may not have recognized the teen except for those arms, the well-defined musculature and the thick covering of blonde hair. After greeting one another, we went through the double doors of the restaurant. I paid for our order, and we settled into a booth by the window overlooking the parking lot. I could see that Brandon had parked beside my Corolla. His big Ford truck dwarfed my little import. I'd hate to get into a head-on collision with him, I thought idly as we waited. When our number was called, Brandon went to get our order and returned bearing trays heaped with food, most of it his. He dug right in, barely stopping for air. I eyed my cheeseburger without enthusiasm and began picking at the greasy fries.

When he finally showed signs of flagging, I said, "I wanted to thank you for showing me the ropes the other day. And for not making too much fun of me for being a chicken."

"No worries," he said around a chunk of hamburger in his cheek. "I thought it was hilarious."

I ate a few more fries and sipped my iced tea. I didn't know where to start, so I decided to just be direct. Maybe if I got him off balance he would reveal more of himself. "You know, I never did ask you. And please tell me if it's too painful to talk about. Who do you think killed your father?"

He stared at me and sucked on his soda straw, his expression unchanged. He looked at ease, his attention focused on the heap of food he was consuming. Without hesitation, he said, "That environmentalist freak. He threatened my dad every morning he came into the office. I wanted to rough him up so he'd go away, but my dad said to leave him be. Right," he said, then snorted. "That was good advice."

"I get the sense you don't like environmentalists."

He shook his head while sucking on his soda straw. "They want to turn every square inch of dirt in this town into an animal sanctuary or something. As if animals are more important than people. It's public land, and I've got a right to use it, too."

Interesting that Brandon said "I've got a right to use it" as opposed to "everybody has the right to use it." He seemed to view his own rights and desires as the only things that mattered. I said, "You want to use the land for off-roading."

"Yeah."

"And for shooting tortoises."

He stopped chewing the chunk of burger stuck in his cheek. His expression changed abruptly from merriment to nonchalance to anger. He glared at me. "What are you talking about?"

Speaking quietly so the whole restaurant wouldn't hear, I said, "I've been doing a little investigating into your dad's murder, and I learned that your truck was seen out at the preserve the night he was killed. Which surprised me, because you told the Sheriff Department you were home sleeping."

He was having problems digesting that, as if I spoke in a foreign tongue. He said, his voice hissing, "Why are you involved in my dad's murder case? I thought you were writing a book." He held his hands mid-air, as if he still held a burger preparatory to taking a bite. Except that his fingers had clenched into fists.

"I'm just a writer who got interested in the case. Seems to me the detectives are doing a poor job of investigating it, so I thought I'd see what I could find out."

He snorted. "You know better than the FBI who killed my dad?"

"Like I said, I'm just looking into it. If I called your grandmother, would she confirm that you were home sleeping the night of the murder?"

"You got a lot of nerve," he said, his voice rising in volume. "Where do you get off checking up on me?"

"I just want to know where you were. Were you out at the preserve or were you at home sleeping, or were you somewhere else?"

"I don't have to answer to you," he said. He pushed back his tray with so much force it rammed into my cup, overturning the tea. "Fuck this." He stood up and turned to leave. I threw a stack of napkins on the puddle of tea spreading across the table and stood too. "Brandon, I've got someone who puts you in the preserve that night. That's an alibi. Isn't it better that the truth about where you were come out now rather than later? Isn't it better to be caught shooting tortoises than to be accused of something worse?"

"Worse? What are you talking about?"

"Don't you see? If the cops find out you're lying about where you were that night, they're going to suspect everything you told them. You'll be a suspect."

"A suspect? What the—? You mean they'll think I killed my own father."

"All I'm saying is that they'll start to wonder about it. They're investigating a murder, Brandon. This is serious."

I noticed he now held his clenched fists at his sides, his knuckles white. Would he hit me? Great, that's all I needed, more injuries. But he didn't, he just stood frozen by the table, staring unseeing out the window. Finally, he said, his voice suddenly calm, "Okay, yeah, I was out in the preserve that night. With Garrett Toverson. I lied to the cops because I didn't want them to know we were shooting illegally."

"You need to tell the Sheriff's Department, Brandon. Go talk to Trent Wise. Tell him that I sent you."

He shrugged. "I just didn't want to get in trouble."

"I know."

He stared at me for a beat, then stalked out of the restaurant without another word. How rude. He didn't even thank me for dinner.

It was darker outside the restaurant than I expected it to be for the hour. I looked up. No stars. The rain clouds that had built up that afternoon still blanketed the sky. The clouds were building in size and staying around longer each day, teasing the thirsty desert. I wasn't fooled. I had lived in Desert Rock too long to believe in a cloud's every promise. By morning, those suckers would be gone, leaving the desert as hot and dusty as ever.

I started up my car and rolled down the windows, letting the warm air swirl in. I pulled my hair back into a ponytail so I wouldn't have to untangle a hundred knots later. I remembered as a kid sitting for what seemed hours while my mom worked out the tangles in my long hair. Eventually, she got wise to the inadvisability of girls having long hair in a desert where it blows nearly every day, and she cut off Vanessa's and my thick chestnut manes. I had hated those painful untangling sessions, but once they were over for good, I found I missed Mom's gentle fingers in my hair and the little things we'd talk about. When I got old enough to take care of my hair properly on my own, I grew it back, but it was never the same.

As I drove, I thought about the evening. I wasn't sure how I felt about what had happened with Brandon. Obviously, he was pissed at me and would probably never speak to me again. I couldn't blame him. I was nosing into his life, and he clearly resented it. But there was more in his reaction than understandable resentment. Something bothered me, but I couldn't get a handle on it. He just seemed so, what? Disingenuous. His confession about being in the preserve that night seemed to have been given too easily, as if he was simply giving me what I wanted. At this point, I still wasn't sure where the teen was the night his dad was killed. Maybe I had blown it by telling him I already knew where he was (which was a lie, of course). It had been easy for him to just confirm what I said and get me off his back. I suddenly knew he would not go talk to Trent. So, where did this leave me? At the same place I'd started, unfortunately. I decided that it might be helpful to talk to the Toverson kid, Brandon's shooting buddy. Maybe he could shed some light on Brandon's activities that night.

I woke from my ruminations with that start you always feel when you arrive at a destination with no recollection of how you got there. I noticed I had driven clear across town on autopilot. Gratefully, I turned off busy McKinley Street into my quiet neighborhood. While making the turn, I noticed that the vehicle behind me turned too. It then sped up and closed the space between us. The high, bright headlights identified the vehicle as a truck or SUV. I thought I had left aggressive drivers behind when I moved from San Diego.

I had a few streets to go before I turned down my street, and I was tired of the tailgater's headlights blinding me. Hell, if the jerk was in such a hurry, let him pass. I pulled over to the curb. But the vehicle did not pass, it slowed abruptly and pulled in behind me. Its lights continued to strike my rearview mirror, which reflected the bright beams into my eyes, making them squint and water. Nobody got out of the vehicle, the truck just sat back there, idling. Shit. What was going on?

Chapter Twenty-Two

I pulled back into the street, my hands sweaty and trembling. The truck pulled out, too, following even closer than it had been before, practically driving up over my bumper. I was less than four blocks from home, but I didn't dare drive there now. No way did I want the lunatic finding out where I lived. Speeding up and rounding the next corner at Sage, I drove away from my house and began fumbling around in my purse for my cell phone.

My fingers couldn't find the device amidst the pound of junk in the bag. As I drove with one hand, I walked the fingers of the other through all the crap inside the bag: I-Pod, lipstick, chewing gum, wallet. No phone. The truck behind me was now so close its headlights had vanished, obstructed by my car's rear seats. In the sudden darkness, I looked into the rearview mirror, hoping to catch a look at the driver, but it was too dark. All I saw was a figure at the wheel illuminated red from my taillights. I thought the truck was white and the driver male, but I couldn't be sure.

Then I remembered. The last time I searched in my purse for my phone I swore never to drop it into those endless depths again. I now carried it in the pocket of my capris. I extended my left leg as far as I could and pushed my foot against the floorboard, humping my butt up off the car seat. Steering with my right hand, I dug in the pocket with my left. It was there. As I extracted the phone, my elbow hit the shoulder harness and the phone flew out of my hand and landed on the floor.

I had seen too many of those teenybopper horror movies depicting women as imbeciles to be amused by my own klutziness. I pushed my flip-flop off my left foot and felt around for the phone with my toes. My foot connected with it after what seemed an hour, and I shoved it toward me across the gritty floor mat. Reaching down, I grabbed it and held on tight. My fingers sweating and clumsy, I dialed 911 and stuck the phone to my ear.

That was when the driver behind me turned off. The truck screeched down a side street and the taillights vanished. At first I didn't believe it. I drove, looking right and left, ahead and behind, scanning for it. I turned down one street and then another, waiting for the headlights to reappear. Nothing. I pulled over to the curb, my hands sweating so profusely I almost dropped the phone. Why was no one coming on? I brought the phone down where I could see the illuminated display. 913. I had dialed 913 for the love of Christ!

Then I laughed, the sounds coming out of me in happy explosions. Relief coursed through me. After wiping my hands on my capris, I slipped the phone back into my pocket and steered the car back out into the street. It was then I realized I didn't know where I was—I had driven blindly without paying attention to street signs, and I didn't know the area as well as I once had. After meandering around the streets for a minute or two, I determined my location and headed home.

Over and over I thought, who the hell drove that truck? I couldn't ignore the fact that I had just been with Brandon, the owner of a white Ford truck, and I had certainly angered him. On the other hand, I also recalled Sampson's threats all too well. Sampson, I remembered, had access to a white truck, too—I had seen a fleet of them parked in the R. Sampson building parking lot. Come to think of it, Mill Maintenance had a fleet of white trucks as well. It dawned on me unhelpfully that white trucks must be as common as flies—Eddie drove one, for God's sake. While identifying the owner of the truck that had followed me would prove to be impossible, of one thing I was sure: I would call Trent Wise in the morning and tell him everything.

Chapter Twenty-Three

I was just concluding a phone conversation with Trent when my sister sped through the front door, seeking me out like a guided missile. In tow were Vanessa's two daughters, Molly, 9, and Kaylee, 7. What a way to begin my day. I rung off, thanking Trent profusely. He said he'd have deputies drive by my house as often as possible to keep an eye on things. He also gave me his cell phone number so that I could call him any time I needed to. Trent had been troubled by my account of being tailed the night before, concluding, as I had, that someone out there was getting nervous about all the questions I'd been asking. I felt better knowing Trent and the other deputies would be looking out for me.

"Where's Connor?" Vanessa asked the minute I hung up, helping herself to a cup of coffee. She had corralled Molly and Kaylee into the family room and turned on the TV. Cartoons blared, but the girls seemed more interested in Lacy, who was trying to escape their grasping fingers, eyes wide. In Vanessa's house, there is always a hoard of rescued animals shedding hair all over her Ethan Allan furniture, tearing up the designer draperies, and peeing on the hardwood floors, but my sister doesn't mind. She can rehabilitate a half-dead bird or earn an abused dog's trust like nobody's business. Her offspring lack her humane touch, however. When Vanessa's daughters enter a room, all sentient beings (including people) not too sick or injured flee. Lacy finally escaped Molly's clutches and bolted over to Vanessa, hiding between her legs. Without the dog to torment, Molly started to hit Kaylee over the head with her purse, a pint-sized version of Vanessa's Louis Vuitton. Neither girl deigned to greet me, the little aunt with the big mouth, who didn't seem to like them very much.

Seeing my sister and her brood at any time is a frightening experience, but before nine o'clock in the morning, it was intolerable. I flopped down at the kitchen table and held my head in my hands. "Connor's out running," I said drearily.

"Running! Good grief, what for?"

"Like, maybe he saw your car pull up?"

"Ha ha." She glared at me, not willing to let me derail her question with my witty jibes.

Seeing that an explosion was inevitable, and kind of relishing it, I answered, "He's training for an Ironman."

"An Ironman!" Her voice was so shrill, Lacy shot out from between her legs and bolted down the hall to the back of the house. It was good to know I had such a fearless beast to protect me should Sampson show up with a tire iron.

"Yeah, that was my reaction, too," I said. "This is just another one of his adventures. It will pass."

"I assume he's doing this ridiculous Ironman thing instead of working."

"He claims he can do both."

She guffawed, a noise totally at odds with her image. "Like he doesn't have a hard enough time just working."

"I mentioned something like that to him, too."

"You tried to talk him out of it?" She seemed to approve of me for the first time in her life.

"Yes, but in vain."

"Humph."

By examining the muscles jumping around on her face, I could tell she was already strategizing how to talk Connor out of this latest nonsense. Poor guy. "So, what brings you here so early?" I asked, fairly sure I didn't want to know.

The muscles in her face stopped writhing and grew still. She looked at me as though I were a repulsive insect whose bite causes worldwide plagues. "I talked with Abby Sampson yesterday, at the library fund raiser. She told me what you've been up to, Sam. I could not believe my ears when she said you were interrogating her about that awful murder. I thought she must have had you confused with someone else, but she said, no, it was Sam Larkin alright, my sister. Abby's husband is furious that you've been accosting his family. As a courtesy to me, Abby let me know what's going on so I could talk you into minding your own business. What are you thinking of, Sam? I had hoped you'd outgrown this need to stick your nose into issues that don't concern you. For the life of me I cannot fathom why you are involved in that business at the wind farm at all. You cannot imagine how mortifying it is to me."

She had temporarily wound down and obviously expected some response from me. It didn't matter what I said, she was already thinking about the next thing she was going to say. I decided to change the trajectory of the conversation. "How well do you know the Sampsons?"

It worked. Her pride in belonging to the same set as the rich Sampsons blinded her to my decoy-setting tactics. "Thomas and I run in the same social circle as the Sampson's, so I know them fairly well." With a supercilious sniff, she added, "Thomas plays golf with Richard, and Abby and I work together on the annual book fair." She sat up as straight as she could, shoulders back, chest (what there was of it—as I said, we look alike) puffed out. I watched her tap at her hairdo with sharp red nails to make sure every strand was lacquered into place.

"What do you think of the Sampsons?" I asked.

"Abby's a sweetie. A very nice woman, good to the community. She runs the literacy program at the library and volunteers to help shelve books and whatever else the staff needs. She also works on the Women's Health Committee, and I think she still sits on the hospital board. And unlike some snooty people in this town, she treats everybody the same whether they have 2 million or two hundred dollars."

I felt like putting my finger in my ear and routing it out. Vanessa throwing stones at others for being snooty? Ha! That was rich. "What about Richard?" I asked.

She sat back, her puffed up body leaking air as she considered how to answer. I guessed she didn't think Richard was "a sweetie." She tapped her fingers on the table top, putting in grave jeopardy the red nail polish. "Richard is, well, Richard. He's loaded, of course. He's the biggest developer in this part of the desert, you know. He donates a lot of time and money to community projects. But he's, well, what's the word? Unrefined."

"Unrefined. What do you mean?" I could tell she was trying to be generous, not wanting to badmouth someone in her social circle, someone who represented wealth and influence in this town. As small as Desert Rock is, such condemnations had a way of traveling back to the subject. Vanessa's arrival at my house this morning was clear evidence of the efficiency of the Desert Rock rumor mill. While I could understand her reticence, it was growing tiresome. I said, "I found Sampson to be aggressive. He actually threatened me."

Her eyes grew wide and she stopped that infernal tapping. "Threatened you? How?"

"He left an angry message on my machine. Told me to stay out of his business or else."

"Or else, what?"

I shrugged. "That's kind of why I'm asking for your opinion of him. I mean, should I take his threats seriously?"

"Well, now, I don't like this at all," she said. Did I hear protectiveness in her voice? "He has no right to threaten you. If he has a problem with what you're doing, he should discuss it with you in a civilized manner. That said, I can understand his concern. He's protecting his family. The best thing I can say about the man is that he's a good father. He goes to every single game his kids play. He watches their school plays and band recitals. He would certainly take a dim view of anything he perceived as a threat to his family."

"Ever hear talk that he cheats on his wife?"

Her brown eyes bulged out. Was she surprised to hear this gossip about Sampson or simply that I knew it? She bit her lip and sighed, not eager to admit that someone of her set acted so boorishly. "I've heard talk," is all she was willing to give me.

"If he's so concerned about his family, why doesn't he keep his dick in his pants?"

"Sam, honestly," Vanessa said, glancing at Molly and Kaylee. They were too absorbed in a commercial for some sugar-laced breakfast cereal to notice my remark.

"Well, it's a valid question."

She sighed again. "I agree with you. If Thomas cheated on me I'd take the girls and leave in a heartbeat. But some women will put up with it. I guess they think it's better than being alone."

"So Richard is hurting his family, whether he wants to admit it or not."

Vanessa spread her hands, palm up, conceding the point.

"So," I said, "In my mind, he's not as concerned about his family's welfare as he claims to be. I'm just wondering if his threats are motivated by something more than family concern."

"Like what? What do you mean?"

"Like maybe he killed Cole Mintock and doesn't want me sniffing around."

"Bah!" She flapped a hand. But she began biting her lip again. I wondered what that expensive lipstick she wore tasted like. Blood, pretty soon, by the looks of it.

"I'm serious. He had a motive: He wants the wind farm expansion stopped to protect his view. And Cole said he'd like to buy the property and develop it. Plus, I've heard he and Cole had an acrimonious relationship. Why, nobody seems to know."

"What you're suggesting is preposterous."

"Why? You don't think he's capable of killing someone?"

That seemed to stump her. A blank look came over her face like a curtain, her mind remembering or processing something.

"What is it?" I asked.

She didn't want to tell me, but I could see she was getting interested in my theory. "I heard something a long time ago about Richard being accused of murder when he was young. Like, early twenties or something like that. The jury acquitted him. If I recall right, the police department mishandled the evidence or botched the case in some way. The end result is he got off."

"Well, now that's interesting," I said. Of course, I had already read about the case during my research into Sampson, but I didn't want to put a damper on Vanessa's unusual cooperative mood by saying so.

"There's another thing," she said. "A few years ago, Richard hit one of the city council members in the nose during a city council meeting. He didn't agree with the guy about some zoning ordinance or other. I was there, I saw it happen. Richard looked like he wanted to do more than pop the guy in the nose, but he stopped himself. I mean, you should have seen him. He looked like an angry bear, ready to tear the man's head off. You'd need a lot of self control with a temper like that."

"I've seen that self-control at work. At one point, I thought he wanted to tear my head off, too, but he didn't. I wonder what it would take for him to lose it."

"I wouldn't want to find out."

I nodded. "So far he's verbally threatened me to my face, he's left a nasty message on my phone machine, and he's asked Abby to talk to you about me. I suppose one would say these are fairly innocuous methods of lodging a complaint. But here's the thing. Someone followed me when I drove home last night. They only turned off when they saw me calling on my cell phone. Who knows what they intended to do. Is this something Richard would do? It seems so childish."

Vanessa's eyes registered shock and concern. She leaned toward me. "Sam, this is serious. You've got to stop whatever you're doing. I don't like this at all."

"I don't either, and that's why I'm not going to let some bully like Richard Sampson make me back down."

"That's just crazy. What do you have to gain by persisting in this?"

"Vanessa, did you ever meet Cole Mintock?"

"Sure. I knew Cole. We served on a couple committees together with Mom. But Thomas is the one who really knew him. They used to hang out at the club, play tennis and golf, drink in the bar."

"Then you must have some feelings about his murder."

"Of course I do. It's a tragedy. But that doesn't mean I'm going to risk my neck trying to find out who killed him. That's what the police are for."

"The feds are messing up the case. I think they're going to string up the wrong guy. Then the real killer walks. Free. In Desert Rock."

That got her. She glanced over at Molly and Kaylee. Though she pretends to view them as insufferable brats (they are), in reality she loves them fiercely. She said, "You really think Cole's killer will go free?"

"I do."

"And you think Richard Sampson killed him?"

"He's one possibility. There are others."

"But you could get hurt. It's too dangerous."

"All I'm doing is asking questions."

She blew enough air out her regal nose to fill up a gallon milk jug. "I know you too well, Sam. There's nothing I can say to change your mind. You're the most stubborn person I know."

I thought I heard a little respect buried in the aggravation. "I'll be careful. I'm not stupid."

She got up, walked over to the sink, and rinsed out her coffee cup. Placing it in the dishwasher, she said, "Let me know if there's anything I can do. I don't like our family threatened."

"Thanks. I do have one more question for you. Ever hear talk of Cole having an affair while still married to his first wife?"

She rolled her eyes and sighed. "Here we go again."

I attempted to placate her. "I know you don't like gossiping about people in your set—which is very commendable—but I wouldn't ask if it weren't important."

She sighed again, but after a moment, said, "It's just that you're so on the mark with all this. Sure, I've heard talk about Cole having an affair."

"What do you think? Was he?"

Vanessa screwed her mouth up as if to keep herself from speaking. Finally, she answered. "It's not a matter of what I think. I know he was."

Her words jolted me. "How do you know?"

"Cole told Thomas about it over drinks one night at the club. And Thomas told me."

So, it appeared that Jillian had lied about the affair. That wasn't so unusual—few people take out an ad in the local paper advertising their indiscretions. However, if she lied about that, what else had she lied to me about? Just when I was beginning to entertain the idea that her accusation concerning Brandon may have merit, her veracity had become questionable.

"Well," Vanessa said. "I've got to go. Tell Connor to call me. I want to have a little chat with him about this Ironman business."

I smiled, glad I wasn't the one Vanessa was gunning for, for once. On impulse, I said, "Vanessa, wait. Before you go, I want to give you something." I walked back to my bedroom and retrieved the pendant I had bought at Desert Designs. Returning to the kitchen, I handed her the box.

"What's this?" she asked, eyes wide.

"It's no big thing. Just thought you might like it." I didn't tell her I had bought it in order to pry information out of Jillian.

My sister took the lid off the box and exclaimed, "It's beautiful. I can't believe you bought this for me. Why?" She was staring at me as if she'd never seen me before in her life.

"No reason. Thanks for the info about Sampson and Cole. I really appreciate it."

She placed the lid back on the box and placed it in her handbag. With supreme awkwardness, she reached out and gave me a hug, during which our bodies touched for a nanosecond, and I think she kissed the air by my cheek. Then she walked into the family room and turned off the television set, evoking shrieks from the girls, who protested this interruption in their viewing pleasure. Vanessa grabbed each girl by an arm and dragged them through the house and out the front door.

In the sudden quiet, I poured another cup of coffee and sat at the kitchen table, studying Mom's garden through the patio window. Lacy slunk into the kitchen, sniffing the air for signs of tiny humans. Relieved to discover none, she sighed and heaved herself onto my right foot. I was surprised at how much I had confided to my sister. I never did that. And I was confused by her protectiveness. Once she had realized that I had been threatened, her strong motherly instincts had taken over. I saw for the first time that her fierce family loyalty perhaps extended beyond Thomas and the girls to encompass Connor and me. Maybe what I always construed as bossy meddling was just her way of trying to look out for us. Maybe with Mom gone, she thought it was her job now to protect the brood.

How horrifying to entertain the idea that Vanessa might not be as bad as I thought. And, strangely, how comforting.

Chapter Twenty-Four

After Vanessa and the girls left, I made a decision: I would put my book on hold indefinitely and concentrate on solving Cole's murder. Seeing my sister's reaction to the threats I had received made me realize that the case had become personal. I felt as though I were engaged in a battle of wits with an opponent determined to silence me. Instead of scaring me off, the threat motivated me. I refused to be defeated.

With renewed resolve, I drove out to the wind farm to talk to Lewis. I was in luck. He stood under the mesquite tree with Katie, his protest sign held high above his head. As I approached the pair, I noticed that Lewis's eyes were bloodshot and his sun bleached hair dirty. If possible, he was thinner. Being accused of murdering someone had left him as stringy and dehydrated as beef jerky.

I got right to the point. I told Lewis that I knew where he had been the night of the murder. As I talked, his pupils expanded, darkening his green eyes until they were almost black. He turned a malevolent stare on Katie, his thick eyebrows drawn low over his eyes. I hated to admit it, but he looked unhinged. Katie held up well under his scrutiny, though, explaining to him that she was only trying to protect him.

"I didn't know what else to do," she said. "You're so damned stubborn, you'd go to prison for no good reason."

"I have good reasons!" He glared at me.

"Which are?" I asked.

"Isn't it obvious? If I tell the police I was with John, he'll be arrested. At least this way he doesn't get involved. You two are acting like I'm going to prison. They haven't arrested me yet, have they?"

I said, "Not yet, but they will. And then what? Can you afford a good lawyer?"

He shook his head as if to clear his ears of water. He stared out at the wind farm, his face hard. While following his line of sight, I caught a glimpse of Sierra, watching us out the office window. How did she ever get any work done? No wonder Diana was cranky.

"If you go to prison, who will fight the good fight?" I said to Lewis. "If your values are worth fighting for, why are you giving up so easily?"

"I'm not giving up! I'm protecting John."

"Have you ever asked John if he wants protecting? At the cost of your life?"

He took stock of that. Dropping his sign onto the sand, he looked up at me briefly, his face registering uncertainty for the first time. His shoulders slumped.

"Luke," I said, "Why don't we go see John and tell him what's going on. Just see what he says."

Lewis shook his head. His long, brittle curls swirled around his head like a dog's coat when it shakes off water. "No. He'll say I should tell the cops the truth. He'll put himself at risk to protect me."

"And what's wrong with that? Isn't that what you're doing for him? You seem to forget that neither one of you killed Cole Mintock. You were together that night, in Martinville. If you tell the truth, you provide each other with an alibi."

"So what? Why would they believe two crazy environmentalists when they won't even believe one?"

"Was anyone else with you at the time? Anyone who can put you both in Martinville at the time of the murder?"

He rubbed his lined face. I could hear the stubble on his jaw rasp against his palm. "John's wife and kids. But I don't want to involve them in this. Besides, who would believe John's wife anyway? The feds will think she's suspect because she's married to him." He paused, thinking hard about something, then said, "Wait. We went out that night. To a local beer joint. Someone there might remember." His eyes had cleared, and he looked hopeful.

"Why don't we go talk to John and his wife. Let them decide how involved they want to be."

He stood for a moment and looked out at the turbines. Finally, he said to Katie, "Call it a day." To me he said, "You'll have to drive. Katie will need her car."

Lewis was silent during the trip to Martinville. I tried to engage him in conversation, but he grunted monosyllabic answers, clearly not wanting to talk to me. About an hour into the drive, I thought, here I am, driving alone in the middle of the desert with a murder suspect. The thought made the blood flood my veins with such force I thought it might explode out the top of my head. My ears began to ring, and I had to wipe my nose. But when I looked over at my traveling companion, at his ratty t-shirt stretched over his angular shoulder blades, I just didn't feel afraid of him. Yes, he was intense. Yes, he was unstable, probably getting more extreme as the years went on and he saw that every effort he made to save the planet failed. I could feel desperation in the energy that forced his fingers to thrum on his legs, the dashboard, the passenger side window. He smelled like he hadn't bathed in days, indicating a surrender of dignity. I understood that desperation could make people dangerous, but all I felt was sympathy for him, and anger that he wasn't trying to help himself. I gave up trying to talk to him and let him contemplate his demons in silence.

We arrived in Martinville around six. Lewis gave me directions to McGinnis's house, and we wound our way past the lake and out of town, turning east onto a steep asphalt road that petered out into a gravel tract. McGinnis's cabin, a tiny wood structure with an asphalt roof punctured by a stovepipe, stood alone in a grove of pine trees about a mile from the main road. When we emerged from the car, a cool breeze swept over me, bringing the scent of pine trees and dry weeds. The only sound was the wind in the trees and the ticking of my car cooling down. As I looked toward the cabin, I saw a face appear at the window, then vanish. Nobody came out onto the porch, no dogs barked. I felt my blood pressure rise again, the adrenaline making my nose run and my ears ring. I tried to remember the calm assurance I had felt in the car on the way up. Lewis was not a killer, I reminded myself. He wouldn't have friends who were killers. But I couldn't shake the feeling that I was at Ruby Ridge and soon the bullets would start flying, leaving me a mass of mutilated tissue.

A hawk cried out and I jumped as though I had been shot. With shaky legs, I followed Lewis up the splintery wood stairs to the porch. I stood behind him as he knocked on the door, feeling vulnerable and tiny. My five-foot-two frame felt no more substantial than a sack of cotton.

"John, it's Luke," he called.

I half expected the door to burst open and a rifle to be shoved in my face, but for a second or two, nothing happened. Then I heard voices coming from within the cabin, and the door creaked open. "Luke! What brings you all the way out here?" A good-looking, dark-haired man came out onto the porch and shook Lewis's hand. He glanced at me, his blue eyes curious, suspicious.

"I need to talk to you," Lewis said. "It's important."

"Who's she?" McGinnis nodded at me.

"A friend. You can trust her."

McGinnis said nothing, but he stepped aside to let us pass.

Lewis entered the cabin, and I forced myself to follow on his heels. I expected the interior of the place to be dark and dirty and draped in cobwebs, but in fact the small room we entered was flooded with light from a picture window that faced west onto a small clearing. The place smelled like Murphy's Oil Soap, all the furniture gleamed, and woven rugs brightened the wood floor. An attractive, tall woman of about twenty-five entered the room from what must be the kitchen, an infant suckling at her breast. She hadn't thrown a towel over her breast or anything, she just let it all hang out. Good for her. A girl, about three or four, stood behind her mother in the doorway.

"Hello, Luke," the woman said.

"Hello, Mariah. This is Sam Larkin."

I saw McGinnis and his wife shoot each other a look. I couldn't tell what they had communicated, but it was something negative about me. Probably wondering what kitchen implement to use to dismember me. Or worse, wondering if Lewis and I were an item.

"So what's up, buddy?" McGinnis asked. Neither he nor his wife asked us to sit down.

"Have you heard anything about a murder down in Desert Rock, out at the wind farm?" Lewis asked.

The couple shook their heads. Mariah said, "We've been holed away up here for weeks. Haven't even gone into town for supplies."

Lewis explained. "The FBI thinks an eco-terrorist killed the owner of the wind farm. I've been out there protesting, as you know. They think I murdered the guy."

For a moment, the cabin was silent. The two stared at Lewis, then glanced at one another. The little girl's eyes grew big. McGinnis said, "You've got to be kidding."

I said, "He's not kidding. And I convinced him to come up here and ask you to go talk to the police. Tell them that Luke was here with you the night of the murder." I watched McGinnis's face, then Mariah's, for any evidence of confusion or surprise or denial. I didn't see any.

Mariah said, "Do you mean the man was killed the night you stayed with us?"

Lewis nodded.

I said, "If you tell the Sheriff's Department he was here, he'll have a verifiable alibi. If you don't, he may well go to prison."

Lewis looked miserable. He stared down at the floor, refused to meet his friends' eyes.

"But that was over three weeks ago," McGinnis said. "Why didn't you come to us sooner?"

Lewis kept silent, so I said, "Because he wanted to protect you. He felt if he said anything about being here that night, he'd be turning the FBI on you. He feared that because of your affiliation with ELF, they'd choose you over him."

"Sit," Mariah said and waved us toward the couch and chairs, which were grouped around a wood-burning stove, now cold. Homemade throws covered the battered upholstery. I sank down into a corner of the couch, feeling the soft knitted afghan against the backs of my bare legs. The others also sat, Lewis beside me on the couch, McGinnis and Mariah (the baby still nursing) in the chairs. The little girl flounced into the room twirling her dress and plopped down beside her mother's feet. She gazed up at her little brother as he suckled, then stared at Lewis and me. She looked like her father, dark-haired and blue-eyed.

McGinnis said, "For Christ's sake, Luke, you should have come to us immediately. I can't believe you put yourself through this."

"I didn't want to get you and Mariah in trouble. I just figured they'd never make a case against me, so it didn't matter what I said."

Mariah said to me, "Thank God you talked some sense into him. We planned on staying here the whole summer. By the time we'd have heard about it, it might have been too late."

"I appreciate what you tried to do, buddy," McGinnis said. "But it was a dumbshit thing to do. I'd have been royally pissed to learn you wouldn't come to me for help. I feel like taking you out back and beating the shit out of you."

The little girl was picking up a nice vocabulary, I noted.

Lewis's eyes showed a mixture of relief—could it really be over this easily?—and confusion—I am being laid on the carpet for sacrificing myself for a friend?

"Mariah and I'll drive down tomorrow and talk to whatever morons are in charge and get this settled."

I said, "Luke also mentioned that you went out to a bar that night. Think there's anyone there who could confirm your story?"

Mariah said, "Ruth Polenski. She owns the place. She knows us, and she'd remember because we brought Luke. We usually go alone, just the two of us, when we can get someone to watch the kids. We'll talk to Ruth tomorrow. I'm sure she'll be willing to help. In the meantime, stay for dinner. I'm making fried chicken and potatoes."

The little girl jumped up and said "Wheee!" I took it that this meal met with her approval. The baby appeared to have fallen asleep, his tiny mouth clamped onto his mother's nipple like a limpet.

Lewis glanced at me. I wasn't sure if his eyes were asking whether or not we should stay for dinner or if he was imploring me to say something to McGinnis to change his mind. "We'd love to stay," I said, standing up. "What can we do to help?" I hoped she wouldn't ask me to hold the baby. Babies scare me.

Lewis slumped deeper into the couch. Air escaped his nose as if he'd sprung a leak. He was a man of conviction, a zealot who saw the world in black and white. He had been so clear on what his moral obligation was: protect McGinnis. It never occurred to him that McGinnis might not appreciate his sacrifice, that it would leave his friend with a moral debt he could never repay. Lewis couldn't see that perhaps the sacrifice was unnecessary. The two men were innocent. They'd have to entrust their lives to the system, hope that the truth would vindicate them. I would do everything possible to make sure it did. In the morning, we would tell Trent everything about that night, and hopefully it would be over. For Lewis, anyway.

"Come on," McGinnis said to his friend and slapped him on the side of the head. "You need to eat. You look like a freakin' skeleton."

Lewis decided to stay overnight with the McGinnis's, and then catch a ride with them into Desert Rock in the morning. I had called Trent on my cell and arranged a meeting with him at eleven. The McGinnis's asked me to stay the night as well, to save me the drive back to Desert Rock at dusk, but I declined. As refreshing as I found the cool mountain air, I was eager to get home, pour a glass of scotch, and call Eddie. I couldn't wait to tell him that I'd been right about Lewis's innocence. Maybe now he would have to acknowledge the depths of my investigational talents.

As I drove down from Martinville to the desert, the clouds that had threatened us all week let loose. Approaching Desert Rock, I hit pockets of rain, huge drops hitting the windshield and the top of my car with such a clamor I could barely hear the hum of the engine. Lightening tore bright rends in the darkening sky, the flashes illuminating vast sections of desert across the dry valley. Rolling down the driver's side window, I breathed in the welcome scent of wet asphalt. Beads of cold water collected on the side of my face where the rain blew in.

I was eager to get home so I could enjoy the storm without having to drive in it. In the desert, storms generate flashfloods that roar down dry streambeds and take out twenty-foot sections of road in minutes. Desert highways are peppered with signs warning drivers that roads wash out during storms. The highway engineers are not kidding. There is one section of Highway 9 just past Sidell ghost town that has been washed out and repaved hundreds of times. Every now and then some doubting RVer disregards the warning signs and drives right into a flooded dip in the road only to be capsized and swept downstream. I pushed the gas pedal harder than usual despite the rain, not wanting to end up on the wrong side of a flooded roadway.

When I arrived home around ten, I found Lacy in a state of panic. Her eyes rolled around in her head as though the macular muscles had detached. She panted, sides heaving, tongue lolling out of her mouth. Saliva oozed out in elastic strings that swung as she jerked her head left and right. My first thought was that she had been poisoned. Then a flash of lightening lit up the backyard, followed by a thunderous boom. Lacy levitated about eight inches off the floor, gave a spine-chilling howl, then tore around the house as though her tail were on fire. Poor beast! Alone in a thunder storm. Where the hell was Connor?

I tried to calm Lacy and get her to drink some water. That was when I saw the note on the kitchen counter. It was from my brother. After glancing at Lacy, who lapped from her bowl, her body trembling, I scanned the note. Connor had packed up and left, heading to Temecula after all to train with his buddy. He thanked me for my hospitality and apologized for any inconvenience he might have caused. He even promised to call next time instead of just showing up unannounced.

I wasn't surprised. Just this morning I had given him the message that Vanessa wanted to talk to him, which was enough to make anyone flee the area. But, also, that was just Connor's way. He swoops in and out of my life as the whim takes him, when I fit into one of his adventures (or he needs something). I had always found his free form, freeloading behavior vexing, so I had thought I'd be flooded with relief when he finally left. But I wasn't. To my astonishment, I felt lonely. Leaning against the kitchen counter, Connor's note in my hand, I felt my legs go weak. My chest cavity felt strangely hollow. I already missed his goofy smile, his boyish pleadings to play Monopoly, his spontaneous barbecues. I'd miss having another body here in the house, filling the vast emptiness left when our mother died.

Another flash filled the sky, and I lunged for Lacy's collar. But I was too late, the lightening was so close, the thunder followed a mere second behind the flash. Lacy repeated her levitation and howl routine, then sped around the family room and heaved herself under the coffee table. I went over and sat down next to her, running my hand over her square head and down her slick back. I scratched her ears. We stayed liked that for a minute or two, and her trembling subsided. Then the lights went out.

The interior of the house plunged into darkness, and all the sounds of the storm grew louder, the clamor filling the air like sand, choking me. The darkness and noise and humidity pressed in, and I became that little girl again, back in the collapsed tunnel, buried alive. I felt myself fight for breath, sucking in the air in irregular, raspy breaths, choking on my saliva. A sudden flash lit up the room and I reached for Lacy. I pulled her warm body toward mine and held on. The thunder exploded, and I felt her shiver and jump under my hands, but she remained where she was, leaning into me.

After another minute or two, I got my breathing under control and forced myself to limp to the kitchen for a flashlight. I noticed that all the neighbors' lights were off as well, throwing the whole neighborhood into darkness. I cracked my sore knee on the corner of the coffee table and cursed. Lacy whined. Pulling open the junk drawer, I felt around and located a flashlight. The minute I turned it on, the shaft of light carved out a path of light, and the walls began to retreat. I started to laugh. Here we were, a grown woman and an eighty-pound dog, scared of a little storm. I shone the light on Lacy's face and saw her looking up at me, her ears perked up.

By the time the next thunderclap hit, we were ready. I held Lacy's collar and she leaned into me. Her skin rippled, but she did not whine or bolt. I patted her head and told her she was good girl. Between thunderclaps I went out to the garage for the Coleman lantern, Lacy attached to my leg as though we were in one of those three-legged races they hold at country fairs. I brought the lantern back inside and within minutes had it lit, creating a broad circle of light that pushed the darkness back. The rain continued to pour down, water cascading over the eaves like a waterfall, but the thunder and lightening had begun to subside. I poured a glass of scotch for myself and fed some leftover steak scraps to Lacy.

I sat down at the kitchen table to sip my drink, and Lacy plopped down beside me. While listening to the rain drum on the roof and rush over the eaves, I reached into my pocket for my cell and checked the time. It was only ten-thirty. Good. Eddie would still be up. I found his number on my contacts list and hit the call button.

"Hey," I said when he answered.

"Wicked storm, huh?"

"I found out Lacy's not too keen on thunder."

"Typical. She in the house?"

"Yeah."

"Lucky. If she'd been outside, she'd be in Tijuana by now."

I sipped some scotch. "I got confirmation tonight that Lewis could not have killed Cole. I talked to two people, friends of his, who confirmed he was with them in Martinville the entire night."

"Friends lie for friends. How does this clear him?"

I smiled to myself. He gave me no credit. "They went out to a bar that night. The owner of the place can verify that all three were there until closing time. Lewis could not have gotten back to Desert Rock in time to kill Cole. The coroner puts the time of death at early evening."

Eddie was silent for a moment. I enjoyed visualizing his face soured in grudging acknowledgement that my involvement in the case was netting rewards. "Why didn't the FBI find this out?" he asked, postponing the moment when he'd have to congratulate me.

"Lewis never told them he was in Martinville. He lied, said he was out sleeping in the desert. He didn't want the feds going up there talking to his friends. They're associated with ELF."

"Ah."

"He was protecting them."

"But you convinced him to tell the truth."

"Well, I convinced him to go to Martinville to talk to his friends. They talked him into telling the truth. They're all going to talk to Trent in the morning."

"Nice job," Eddie said, sounding impressed despite his efforts to seem disinterested. "What next?"

"I pretty much always figured Lewis was innocent, but now that I've confirmed it, I can turn my attention to the other suspects. Tomorrow I want to talk to Jillian. To be honest, I don't think she did it. But she did lie to me—or Diana did—and I want to find out why. I guess at this point it's a process of elimination."

"What will the Feds do now?"

"Take ten weeks confirming Lewis's alibi. Then they'll spend another ten weeks trying to pin it on Lewis's friend. After that, maybe they'll look at other suspects. Maybe."

"So you're narrowing it down for them."

"Yeah. I think—" I stopped talking and listened. The rain was letting up and in the ensuing quiet I thought I heard a noise at the back of the house. It was a click, metal hitting metal. The hair follicles on my arms tingled. Lacy raised her head and growled. The fur at the nape of her neck rose up.

"Sam?" Eddie said into my ear.

My heart pounded. I took the cell away from my head and listened as hard as I could. Nothing. Putting the phone to my ear again, I said, "I thought I heard something. Lacy growled."

"What was it?" His voice was tight.

"A chinking sound, toward the back of the house. Like—" I heard it again. This time there was no doubt. It sounded like someone was prying out an aluminum screen on one of the back windows. Did I leave a window open? Think, Sam. Yes, this morning, after my shower, I had cracked the bathroom window like I always do. Half the time I forget to close it when the air conditioning comes on, wasting all that electricity to "cool the great outdoors" as my mother used to say. Lacy stood now, her body rigid. A growl emanated from deep in her chest. I realized I gripped her collar, keeping her close to me. Should I let her go? She strained against my hand, pulling in the direction of the sound.

"Sam!" I heard Eddie's tiny voice coming from the cell phone, which I had pulled away from my ear again.

"Someone's breaking in," I said, my voice shaky and high. "Call 911. I'm letting Lacy go."

Chapter Twenty-Five

I released my hand and Lacy shot toward the back of the house, barking and growling. I heard her slam into a wall, her body thudding against the drywall. A towel bar crashed to the tile floor, and she was barking, barking, barking. I stood up and pushed my back flat against the kitchen wall, an instinctive gesture to protect my flank. I looked down. The cell phone was still in my hand. I looked at it, wondering why I held it, what it was for. The barking echoed in my head, making it impossible to think. What was I supposed to do? What was happening? My nose dripped. Sweat rolled down my face. Lacy barked and barked. I stared at the phone, trying to think. It felt like the barking went on and on. How much time had passed? Was someone coming to help me? Was someone coming down the hall?

I eased away from the wall, dropped the phone on the kitchen counter, and began rummaging through drawers. In the drawer next to the sink, I felt my hand close around the handle of a big, heavy knife. The one Connor used to cut back ribs apart. I extracted it, grabbed the flashlight from the kitchen table, then moved to the hallway, facing the back of the house where all the commotion was. Should I just stand there and wait, wait until whoever it was came to me? Or should I go toward them? Trying to make up my mind, straining to hear what was happening down the hall, I waited, knife in one hand, flashlight in the other.

Every nerve in my body jumped as if attached to an electrode, and I knew I had to do something. I began to move down the hall. The flashlight drilled a bright hole down the middle of the passage, but the walls and ceiling remained black, making it feel that I moved through a subterranean wormhole. The sensation squeezed the breath out of me, and I began to fight for air. Feeling myself suffocate, I waved the flashlight around in desperation, illuminating one wall, then the other, then the ceiling, pushing them back, widening the passageway. Breathing more normally, I eased forward toward the master bathroom, where Lacy had taken her stand against the intruder. Her barks clanged in my head, sounding like pots and pans in a clothes dryer. I kept walking, moving toward the noise with the big knife, flashlight held out like a drill reaming out space.

Then I heard pounding. "Sheriff's Department!" A voice bellowed outside the front door. "Sam, it's Trent!" I jumped, almost dropping the knife and flashlight. Lacy bounded up the hall past me and rounded the corner into the foyer, her claws losing traction on the tiled entryway. She scrambled to gain purchase, and her body slammed into the hall table, knocking over the vase my mom had bought in China. It broke into pieces on the floor. Lacy barked and growled at the front door.

My legs trembled as I moved up the hall into the foyer. I grabbed Lacy's collar, flipped the deadbolt, and opened the door. Trent's face, lit by my flashlight, looked ghoulish. Another deputy stood behind him, flashlight pointed at my face, rainwater dripping from the eaves into his collar. And then Eddie pushed forward, entering the house, kneeing past Lacy. The minute she smelled him, she stopped barking and began wagging her tail. I let go of her collar. She wiggled forward, saying hello to everyone.

"You alright?" Eddie said, staring down at the knife in my hands. I looked at it, too, surprised to see it there. Would I have used it? Would it have been taken from me, used against me? Eddie looked so concerned, I felt an overwhelming urge to laugh. I stared at him, silent and grinning.

"She's in shock," Trent said.

Eddie took my arm and gave it a quick shake. "Sam!"

"I'm alright," I said. "Lacy scared them away." I looked down at her, amazed.

When Trent and the other deputy had inspected the window and verified that the intruder had left, they departed. I made sure the window was locked, and then Eddie and I retired to the kitchen for a much-needed scotch. Eddie insisted on staying the night in case whoever it was who tried to break in came back. I said I was certain the intruder would never come back so long as Lacy was in the house, but Eddie was unmoved by my arguments. He insisted. We fought about it. I said I wasn't a helpless female in need of a man. He said I was worse, a stubborn jerk in need of a brain. In the end, he stayed. We sat up talking until one, listening to Lacy's rumbling snores and the periodic drum of rain on the roof. The electricity was still off when Eddie tossed himself onto the family room couch, pulling a throw over his feet. I took the Coleman down the hall with me and climbed into bed. When Lacy jumped up to join me, I didn't complain. I lay there thinking, Eddie is here in my house. Eddie is sleeping on my couch. I'm in bed with the dog. An empty feeling swelled inside me. But I was too tired for regrets.

Chapter Twenty-Six

Despite the late night, Lacy and I awoke before dawn, eager to get outside and move. I noticed with relief that the electricity was back on. Eddie woke up when Lacy's kibbles clattered into her stainless steel bowel (I held the bag as high up as I could). He gave us a sleepy and somewhat grouchy greeting, saying he'd be gone by the time we got back from our run. I asked him to join us, but he declined, claiming he needed to get into the coffee shop early. That was bull. I knew full well he was going to go home, crawl into bed, and sleep until nine.

For once, Lacy and I were in tune. Vibrating with energy pent up from the night's events, we ran at a fast clip. My stride was awkward at first as I worked out the pain and stiffness in my sore knee, but once it warmed up, I felt fine. The sun was still below the horizon, but a pink glow illuminated the eastern sky. Not a single cloud remained from last night's storm, but water still ran in the streets.

As we ran, early-rising neighbors smiled and waved, calling out, "How're you doing, Sam?" and "Some storm last night, eh?" Some of the neighbors had noted the activity at my house the night before and had no qualms inquiring about what had happened. In a city like San Diego, if neighbors happen to notice—and care—that cops showed up at your house in the middle of the night, they certainly wouldn't be so rude as to ask you about it. But in Desert Rock, your business is everyone's business. The intimacy of smaller communities is both a blessing and a curse. On the one hand, the lack of privacy can be distressing, and once things are known about you, your reputation is sealed forever, for better or worse. On the other hand, people know and care about you, forming a net you can fall into when the chips are down. That morning, I was grateful for the safety net.

While Lacy and I ran, I tried not to think about what had happened last night. I needed to recharge, clear my head, before I let myself reflect on the fact that someone had tried to break into my house, perhaps to kill me. Possibly, the intruder was just a burglar, seeing the blackout as an opportunity to snare some cash. I just couldn't make myself believe it. My gut told me that the intruder was the same individual who had followed me Wednesday night. The same person who had killed Cole. No, I would not dwell on all this now. I needed some downtime to think about other things.

So I started to ruminate about the fact that I needed to do laundry, rake the yard, go to the market. My nails needed serious attention, and it was time to get my hair cut. Those chores would have to wait, however, because I had a busy day ahead of me. At eleven, I was meeting Lewis and the McGinnis couple at Trent's office. After that, I'd grab a quick lunch and head over to Desert Designs. It was time to get the truth out of Jillian concerning her whereabouts the night of Cole's murder. Was she in San Diego or Phoenix? And why was she—or Diana—lying? I also wanted to ask her why she lied to me about the affair.

It amazed me to think that just a few weeks ago I had made my first visit to the wind farm. A few days after that, Eddie told me that Cole had been killed. Before those fateful events, I had been researching my book, trying to cope with my mother's death, and hoping to meet a deadline for the first time in my life. I thought at that moment I had more than I could handle. And now, here I was in the middle of a murder case. What the hell had happened?

Well, Cole had happened. His desire to make a positive difference in the world had moved me, and his death had affected me deeply. Brandon had happened. I related to his tragedy. And Lewis had happened. The innocent accused of murder. The man whose passions and ideals made him the object of scorn. If Cole was a practical idealist, Lewis had become an extremist, no longer able to embrace practical solutions or hold to workable ideas.

Lewis had decided to expend all his energies protesting energy producers. But instead of stationing himself in front of a polluting oil refinery in Los Angeles, he had chosen Cole's remote wind farm. His gesture was symbolic, and futile. Generally, people will support the preservation of beautiful lands and furry, adorable creatures but scoff at similar attempts to protect swamplands and deserts, insects and weeds. That these less endearing features of the natural environment are just as important to the health of the planet as the breathtaking and cute seems a concept lost on most people. Humans are not subtle thinkers in this way. Lewis's ultimate point—that wind power is bad because it helps maintain the illusion that modern life is sustainable—just wasn't going to resonate with most people.

As Lacy and I jogged along, I wondered, Was Lewis right? Were Americans just burying their heads in the sand, as he accused, hoping by some technological miracle to develop clean, renewable energy sources that would enable their comfortable lifestyles to continue?

Lewis fought an uphill battle. Few people want to go back to the time before modern conveniences. Most people want the next great thing, like the automobile that runs on water. Technology is a juggernaut, its evolution cannot be stopped. For good or ill, human ingenuity strives to find ways to make living more comfortable. Lewis's vision of a world without automobiles and central air conditioning runs counter to human evolution. Societies embrace technology, depend upon and even honor it. Sure, I could see the lure of Lewis's thinking: Return to a simpler time, and the problems of modern society would be solved. But life is dynamic, and societies progress or die.

Lacy and I made our final turn toward home. My skin was drenched in sweat, and my heart pounded, but the sweaty fatigue left me feeling cheerful for the first time in weeks. As we neared the house, I saw Hattie standing in her driveway, hand on her walker. I smiled. It was Friday, not our regular day to walk, but I wasn't surprised to see her there. She'd want to know what all the ruckus was about last night. Living right next door to me, she was bound to have heard Lacy's barking and seen the lights from the Sheriff's vehicle. I didn't resent Hattie's curiosity. Quite the opposite. I took it to mean she cared about me.

Hattie got right to the point. "What in the world happened last night? Are you all right?"

"I'm fine. It was just a burglar trying to break in during the blackout."

"My goodness, Samantha. 'Just a burglar,' indeed. As if it's the most common thing in the world."

Hattie couldn't know that an attempted burglary was far better than what I thought had happened—an attempted murder. I said, "Nothing came of it. Lacy scared the guy off."

Hattie clapped her withered hands together. "Well, see, there you have it. And you were wondering why your mother loved that dog so much. And where was Connor during all this? I didn't see his car out front when I looked out last night."

"He left for Temecula yesterday. I was home alone." I pointed to Hattie's athletic shoes. "You look ready for walking. Want to go, even though it's not our usual day?"

She flapped a hand at me. "Oh no, you have things to do. I don't want to keep you."

I could tell she wanted to walk with us in the biggest way so she could drill me with more questions. I said, "I'd enjoy it. Come on."

As expected, while we walked she peppered me with polite queries about the previous night's events. I answered them as best I could, sticking with the facts where I could, bending the truth when I felt it might alarm her. I told her about the knife, for example, but left out my suspicions about the intruder's real motives.

After I had satisfied her curiosity, Hattie said, "Your mother was always saying how brave you are. She would have been proud of what you did last night. I'm not sure even Olivia would have handled that as calmly as you did."

Brave? Proud? I said, "I would have characterized my mother's opinion of me as impetuous and willful."

Hattie shook her head dismissively. "Well, of course, you are that, Sam. But she admired you for it. She was always telling stories about you, like when you beat up that boy, what's his name, you know, the Myers kid, who was always tormenting Bobby Green."

Bobby Green had some kind of degenerative muscle disease and used crutches throughout grade school. Willard Myers was the worst kind of bully, throwing rocks at neighborhood cats, calling the Hispanic kids "spics," and his favorite occupation, tormenting anyone different such as Bobby Green. One day in the fourth grade, while walking home from school, I saw Willard kick one of Bobby's crutches out from under him, sending Bobby sprawling on the pavement. I rushed at Willard, knocked him down and began pummeling his face. I only stopped when Bobby told me to. He said he didn't want me to kill the boy. That evening, Willard's mother called my mother and pitched a hissy fit about what I'd done. My mom lectured me on the futility of dealing with problems through violence, and grounded me for a week.

Now Hattie was saying my mother was proud of me for that incident. I told Hattie I didn't believe her.

She laughed. "Sam, you really are too much. What was your mother supposed to do? She had to punish you, it was the right thing to do. Besides, a child like you needs a firm hand. She knew that. But out of your hearing she went on and on about what you did, saying she was glad she had a child who stuck up for the underdog."

"How come I never knew how she felt?"

Hattie stopped walking and looked at me. "You were so convinced she disapproved of you that you were never open to any other interpretation."

I felt confused. Hattie was suggesting that my mother admired me, when all I had ever felt was her disapproval. "But I'm sure I was right. I always got into trouble. She used to ask why I couldn't behave like Connor and Vanessa."

"Parents always say that. She probably told them she wished they could be like you. Then there was your father."

"My father? What does he have to do with it?"

"Everything," she said. "I don't know how much you remember of him—he died when you were very young—but he was such a passionate man, especially about animals. That's how he and your mom met, they both belonged to the same environmental group. When your father began teaching at the community college here, he worked tirelessly to get his biology students interested in protecting nature. He formed an environmental organization on campus and was constantly organizing letter writing campaigns to legislators and that kind of thing. During summer breaks, he'd take any students interested to whatever protests were occurring in the state. He didn't stop at anything, and he managed to get himself—and his students—arrested on more than one occasion. He once got into it with an off-roader, and the guy punched your dad in the face. Broke his nose and busted a couple of teeth. "

I found myself gawking at Hattie. My mother had never told me any of this. Maybe she found it too painful to talk about my dad. Still, I felt a surge of anger. She should have at least told me what he was like. I felt that I was learning who he was for the first time. I said, "Why didn't my mother ever tell me about him?"

Hattie sighed. "Your mother was devastated when he died. And angry. She blamed him."

"Blamed him? What, she thought the man chose to have a heart attack?"

Hattie looked at me and said as if she were speaking to a nitwit, "Olivia thought he pushed himself too hard. On top of teaching a full class load every semester, he went to the ends of the earth to tackle every environmental catastrophe within a radius of a thousand miles. All that was time and energy he could have spent on you and Connor and Vanessa."

"Or time he could have spent on Mom," I said, beginning to get it. "She was mad at him for neglecting his family."

She shook her head. "It wasn't quite that simple, I don't think. Olivia admired your father—that's why she loved him. She always said how noble and compassionate he was. But he was also headstrong and single-minded. When he was on some tear, he gave it everything he had. It wound up affecting his health."

"So Mom thought he had the heart attack because he was stressed out."

"He left her a widow in her early thirties, with three young children. It was very difficult."

Sure, but it didn't seem fair to blame him for dying. I said, "He might have had the heart attack anyway. Maybe he just had a bad ticker."

"Maybe. But when you suffer a great loss like that, sometimes rational thought goes out the window."

I stopped walking and looked over at Hattie. She stopped, too, and looked back at me. The bright sun illuminated every line of her withered face. She looked impossibly old. "So, why are you telling me all this?" I asked.

Hattie reached down to pet Lacy, who stood as close to the woman as was possible without actually being in her space. Then my mom's old friend looked at me, narrowing her eyes. "As if you haven't figured it out."

"Figured what out?"

"Sam, does your father remind you of anyone you know?"

A quick study, I said, "You mean me."

"Olivia always said you were a chip off the old block. And she worried about you the same way she had worried about him."

I shook my head as if I could scramble my thoughts into a more logical alignment. "She thought I would have a heart attack, too? At age six, or twelve, or twenty-two?" I snorted. It was absurd.

Hattie laughed. "Sam, for as bright as you are, you can be so obtuse. She just worried that something bad would happen to you because you were just like him. She thought one day you'd go too far. She didn't want to lose you as she had him."

"But it wasn't fair," I said. "I wasn't my father. She never gave me a chance."

"Maybe not fair, but understandable, don't you think. She loved you."

This was too much to absorb. Perhaps if I'd known about Mom's feelings about my father, I might have understood why she treated me like she did. I might have acted differently, to ease her mind. Or maybe I'd have been able to convince her that just because I had my father's personality didn't mean I would die young, as he had. Who knows what our relationship might have been had I known.

Tears welled up, and my mind went back to the day before my mother died. I was alone in the room with her, taking my shift so that Connor and Vanessa could sleep. She had been in what the hospice nurse called a coma for several days, but suddenly, my mother opened her eyes and said, "You know I love you." I thought at the time that she was confusing me with Vanessa. After all, she had been pretty out of it, and Vanessa and I do look a lot alike.

I didn't say anything to my mom, not wanting my voice to give me away. If it gave her comfort to think I was Vanessa, so be it. I remember just stroking her hand to let her know she had been heard.

With a force that almost buckled my knees, regret washed through me. Maybe my mother *had* known it was me.

I wanted the moment back. I would have said, "I love you, too."

Chapter Twenty-Seven

When I entered Desert Designs, I checked my vital signs. If I felt any dizziness, I would turn around and walk back out. No way did I want to begin this interview from a point of vulnerability. I was determined to find out why Jillian—or Diana—had lied, and I was pretty sure I couldn't do that lying prostrate on the floor. When I closed the door, Jillian glanced over from where she was standing beside a plump woman wearing a purple muumuu and a fluorescent orange baseball cap. One might be taken aback at seeing such a get up worn by a gallery customer in Los Angeles, but in Desert Rock such attire is common. The only dress code here is that your private parts have to be covered. While Jillian relayed the price of every art piece the customer pointed to, I loitered at the back of the shop, eyeing the coffee pot. It exuded the heavenly odor of a wicked brew. My veins shivered in anticipation of my next dose.

While I waited, I thought about my earlier appointment with Trent, Lewis, and the McGinnis's. Ruth Polenski, the tavern owner, had showed up as anticipated, and Trent seemed to accept her assertion that Lewis and the others were in her establishment the night of the murder. She even mentioned other patrons who would corroborate her story, if needed. I felt good about how the meeting had gone. Lewis and McGinnis both were off the hook, it seemed.

Finally, Jillian's customer left, and she came over to where I stood at the back of the store. She saw me covet the coffee and asked if I'd like a cup. I said "yes, please" so forcefully she jumped.

"In the market for another birthday present?" she asked, raising an eyebrow. She knew what was coming. I thought of Diana's hand on the phone at the conclusion of my interview. Jillian handed me a mug and sat down at the table. She waved me to a chair.

I took a seat and slugged back some coffee. It oozed down my esophagus like hot engine oil, scorching membranes every inch of the way. I was in heaven. "I wanted to ask you to clarify something for me."

"And what would that be?" she said, her green eyes wary as a cat's.

"You told me you were with your sister in San Diego when you heard the news that Cole died. Who called to let you know?" It could not have been the Sheriff's Department—they had been told she was in Phoenix.

"I'm not sure why that is relevant," she said. Her gorgeous body remained still, but her eyes shifted around, scanning everything in the store but me.

"Would you just answer the question?" I said.

"Why should I?"

"Because you lied to the police about where you were the night your husband was murdered. And I plan to tell them about it unless you give me a good reason why I shouldn't."

She didn't move. She kept her eyes trained on me, and I saw a glimmer of something in their cold, green depths. Fear? Anger? I waited as she sorted through whatever it was, deciding what course of action to take with me. I sipped my coffee as if we were just chatting about the price of pendants. It got boring looking at her struggle, so I let my gaze wander around the store, falling on a painting the size of a garage door. I wondered how a person would get that sucker home in an automobile. After a while I studied my nails, which I noticed were in about as good of shape as the house and yard. If I stayed on the case much longer, nobody would want to be seen with me.

When she finally spoke, her voice startled me, it had been so long since she said anything.

"I told you the truth. I was in San Diego. When I left town, I told Cole I was going to Phoenix, to visit a friend. Only Diana knew the truth. When Cole was killed, no one knew where I was but Diana. When she learned what had happened, she called me at my sister's. I told her to tell the police I was in Phoenix. And that's what I told them later."

I believed her, but I couldn't figure why all the subterfuge. "Why lie?"

She bit her lip, just a nibble, showing an uncharacteristic crack in her inscrutable exterior. "For that, we'll need a refill." She rose and poured more coffee in our cups. She turned the coffee maker off and sat back down. "It's a long story."

The story was not that long after all, but I could tell it cost her to tell it. She maintained her feline composure throughout the narration, but I saw fear and exhaustion in the careful effort she made to remain placid. She was in San Diego, she said, to discuss with her sister what to do about Brandon. Brandon, according to her, had stalked her niece since the day Jillian sent her home last summer. When I asked what had occurred that summer to cause so much consternation, she admitted that neither she nor her sister was sure. But they suspected that Brandon had tried to force himself on Ann, and when Ann refused, he began to tease and torment her. He'd come around and call even though she made it clear she wasn't interested. Jillian said that Ann was so upset about it that she asked to go home. So Jillian drove her back to San Diego. But that didn't stop Brandon's behavior. Ever since then, Brandon had written and called Ann, and he drove over to the coast to try to see her numerous times.

Jillian told me that whenever she would complain to Cole about Brandon's behavior, Cole would go talk to the kid, and then the teen's stalking would intensify, get weirder. Ann gave Jillian's sister the letters, which the sister found increasingly bizarre. From smarmy sonnets decrying Brandon's love for Ann, they turned into veiled threats about what would befall the girl if she didn't talk to him. The family got calls in the middle of the night, sometimes several times a night, but when they picked up, no one was ever there. Graphic "love notes" were left in the screen door and underneath the wiper blades of the family car. Jillian told me that she had finally decided that enough was enough. So, the weekend Cole was killed, she drove to San Diego to talk to her sister about the possibility of telling the police there what was going on.

"Why didn't you just tell them when it first started happening?" I asked.

"You don't know Brandon. Every time we've intervened, he acts out more. I sometimes wonder, if I hadn't sent Ann home, would he have just tired of her and then left her alone? But I took her back to San Diego, and I asked Cole to talk to Brandon about the whole mess. I'm positive that is why he started harassing Ann. He was doing it to hurt Cole and me. And, to tell the truth, he seemed to enjoy it, like it was an amusing game. After a while, I stopped telling Cole what Brandon was doing. Every time I had talked to my husband about it, he'd get so angry he'd drive over to Brandon's grandmother's house and scream at the kid. Then the letters and calls to Ann would get worse. That's why I lied to Cole about where I was going that weekend. If he knew I was going to San Diego, he'd suspect it had something to do with Ann and Brandon."

"So, did you and your sister decide to tell the police?"

"We were still discussing it when Diana called. You must think we're idiots. But, look, I'm afraid of what will happen to Ann, to my sister, to me if we call Brandon out. He threatened to harm me if I told the police what I suspected. Why would he hesitate to harm Ann or my sister?"

I supposed that Jillian hadn't mentioned the Ann business to me before, even though it would have bolstered her theory that Brandon killed his dad, because she was trying to keep Ann out of it, to protect her. I studied my empty cup, thinking about what she had told me. "So, if I were to call your sister, she would verify you were there."

Jillian sighed and got up. She walked to the small office at the rear of the store and came back with a piece of paper. "That's my sister's phone number. She and her husband and daughter will tell you I was there. Diana will tell you I was there."

I took the slip of paper, feeling like a heel. "You should tell the Sheriff's Department. I have every reason to think they're going to stop trying to hang Luke Lewis and start looking at other people who had the motive and means to kill Cole."

"Such as me."

"You inherited. You had access to the wind farm keys through Cole. You're possibly strong enough to drag an unconscious man out of a car and into a turbine."

She raised her eyebrows, then nodded. "You've thought of everything."

"And hopefully now the police will."

"So I might have to tell the detectives about Brandon after all."

"Probably."

"Then God help us," she said.

"There's another thing," I said quickly, hoping to catch her off guard. "Why did you lie to me about your affair with Cole?"

Her body tensed. "What are you talking about?"

"I have it on good authority that you and Cole were sleeping together before his wife died."

"Who said that?" she asked before I barely got the words out of my mouth.

"That doesn't matter. I just want to know why you lied to me."

She seemed to wrestle with several thoughts at once, her usually placid face rippling with stress. After a moment, she said with a shrug, "So I lied. I didn't want you to think the worst of me."

"You've got to be kidding."

She shrugged. "Don't get me wrong, it's not like I care about your personal views of my morality. I just figured if I said I had an affair with Cole, you'd question my character. You'd be less inclined to believe what I said about Brandon. I wouldn't blame you."

"Your lying about it has made me question your claims more," I informed her. "I can't believe anything you've told me."

She stared down at her coffee cup, her body still. Then she looked over at me. "I'm not lying about Brandon."

I stood up, grabbed my purse, and left.

Chapter Twenty-Eight

I doubted that I'd ever use the number Jillian gave me for her sister. I believed her. I could understand why she lied about the affair. And both Sierra and Diana had mentioned the same unpleasant business concerning Brandon and Ann last summer. However, even if I believed her, I still found myself resisting her theory about Brandon. It didn't seem to fit the Brandon I knew, or, as was increasingly clear, the Brandon I had dreamed up. I realized that I had so identified with him, I hadn't seen him clearly at all. I felt so sorry for him that I thought of him only in terms of the grief I was sure he felt. I told myself, Brandon missed his father just as I missed my mother, and he felt guilty for never having made amends to his dad just as I regretted never making peace with my mom. My empathy had clouded my judgment. What I had initially seen as moodiness brought on by grief appeared to me now as a sign of instability. The sympathy and understanding I had felt for him was giving way to disapproval, even fear.

I had tentatively removed Jillian from my list of suspects. Now it was time to follow up on Brandon's ever-shifting alibi. I needed to talk to the teen's hunting buddy. I looked up Garrett Toverson's parent's address in the phone book and then worked out a plan.

I didn't want the kid's parents to overhear me raking him over the coals, so I decided just ringing the doorbell was out. So, at nine o'clock Saturday morning, I parked my car in front of the Toverson's house and waited for Garrett to come out. A white Chevy Silverado and a Pontiac mini-van were parked in the driveway, and a refurbished electric blue Mustang sat at the curb. It looked like all the Toverson's were home. I would have to hope that the senior Toversons would leave the house to run Saturday morning errands, and that Garrett would have some reason to leave the house before they returned. It was a long shot, I knew, but it was the best I could come up with.

I wanted to know whether Brandon really was out shooting tortoises in the preserve the night his father was murdered. If Garrett confirmed the story—and if I believed him—then I could put to rest the unease that had been building for several days. To get the truth out of the teen, I had come in uniform: Hair tied back and braided, khaki shorts and top, hiking boots, and a fake badge I had purchased at Wal-Mart the night before. Hopefully the kid would be so intimidated by my look of authority he wouldn't examine the badge too closely. I had also brought along a clipboard and pen, and an official-looking manila folder stuffed with scrap paper. Completing my look was a pair of aviator sunglasses. I looked like a bad ass—in my mind, anyway.

At nine-fifty-seven a chunky woman emerged from the house and waddled toward the mini-van. I turned away, pretending I was checking a street map (the one I was holding was for San Francisco). She clambered into the van, backed out, and drove away. About fifteen minutes later a young man with a similar plump physique emerged from the house and stumbled over the dry lawn toward the Mustang. Damn. Garrett had come out while his father was still in the house. Oh well, I thought, I'd just have to take my chances. I jumped out of my car and intercepted the teen, clipboard and folder in hand. I hoped his father wouldn't glance out the window and see me.

"Garrett Toverson?" I asked in an official voice, placing my person between him and the Mustang. The boy had a mop of brown hair that looked like it hadn't seen a comb this morning—or ever.

He kept walking toward the Mustang, but his pace faltered, his sleepy brain trying to process my unexpected presence. Taking in my "uniform," he seemed to be deciding whether I was a Sheriff's deputy or a meter reader. His main reaction seemed to be confusion, then irritation. He attempted to scoot around me and jump into his car before I could say whatever I had come to say, but I stepped to the left, putting myself in his path again. "Garrett, I'm Ranger Zahn, from the Desert Rock Preserve. I need to talk to you." I had no idea if rangers went out talking to the public about anything, but luckily he was as ignorant as I was. He stopped in his tracks, his eyes wide and defensive.

"Talk to me about what? I got to get to work," he said. He glared at my uniform. I could see how fond he was of authority figures.

"I want to talk to you about illegal shootings in the preserve," I said. "I have witnesses that say you were in the preserve shooting tortoises on July 19th. Can you verify your whereabouts on that night, Mr. Toverson?" I wondered if law enforcement officers really talked that way or if I had just been watching too much TV.

Garrett glanced at the house, either hoping his father would save him or hoping like hell the old man didn't come out there and hear what he'd been up to. He repeated sullenly, "I got to get to work."

"What you need is to answer my question, Mr. Toverson. Were you in the preserve on the 19th?"

He weighed what to say. I wasn't sure what the struggle was all about, but it made his facial muscles twitch as though he were being electrocuted. He glanced again at my "badge" and at his car. The kid in him probably believed that if he could just reach his vehicle and drive away, I'd miraculously disappear from his life forever. The young adult took over and he said, "I wasn't anywhere near the preserve that night."

"Brandon Mintock claims you were. He says you were both there on the 19th shooting tortoises."

His eyes flashed. "Brandon said that? You talked to Brandon?"

I nodded. "One of you is lying to me. Are you lying, Mr. Toverson?" I was going to have to stop with the Mr. Toverson bit—it was getting on my nerves.

He tugged at his facial hair, which was little more than a couple of patches of reddish-brown fuzz. "What would happen to me if I said I was there?"

Well, good question. I hadn't the foggiest idea. Time to bullshit. "If I can prove you were shooting in the preserve illegally, you'll be sent to juvenile hall for a year. But, if you cooperate with me, I'll go easy on you. Maybe you can avoid juvie entirely."

"Juvenile hall?" His eyes widened so much I could see the whites all the way around his irises. "Look, like I said, I wasn't anywhere near the preserve. Brandon told me to lie about it if anyone asked, but I'm not going to hang my ass for him."

That took me by surprise. I hid my confusion by reaching up and rubbing at my nose. I realized that the aviator glasses, which weighed about two pounds, were rubbing raw patches on both sides of the bridge. "Brandon asked you to lie and say you were out shooting tortoises in the preserve that night?"

"That's what I said."

"Why would he do that? Why would he want you to say something that would get you both in trouble?"

"I don't know, lady, he just asked me to do it, that's all. I said I would 'cuz I didn't think anyone would ever ask me about it. But I'm not going to juvie for something I didn't do."

"Just so I'm clear, Garrett. You were not in the preserve that night?"

"You got wax in your ear, lady? Want me to say it a third time?"

"Can anyone verify where you were that night?"

He huffed. "Jesus Christ. Yeah, my girlfriend. I was with her most of the night."

"What's her name?"

"Jennifer Hardin."

I scribbled the name down on my pad. "Anyone else see the two of you together that night?"

"Sure. Lot's of people. We were at Mindy's Pizza Parlor till about eleven. Lot of our friends were there. Then some of us went out by the gravel pit and had a bonfire."

"Was Brandon there?"

"At the bonfire?"

"At Mindy's, the bonfire, any place. Were you with him any part of the night?"

He looked down at his shoes, regretting that he needed to rat out his friend. "No. I have no idea where he was that night. All I'm saying is that I wasn't in the preserve. You can ask anyone."

"Garrett, did Brandon tell you why he wanted you to lie?"

He shook his head, his ratty hair falling into his eyes. "Like I said, if you'd been listening, no, he just asked me to do it."

"Didn't you wonder about it?"

"Like, yeah, of course I did. You think I'm some idiot? But like I said, I didn't think anyone would ever ask about it, so I agreed to do it."

I put the cap back on my pen and slipped it under the clipboard's metal clasp. "I'm glad you told the truth, Garrett. You did the right thing."

"Does this mean I'm off the hook?"

"I'll tell you what I think. I think you do go out shooting tortoises with Brandon. I also think that you're too smart to do it again now that we've had our little talk. What do you think about my theory?"

"I think you got it right," he said, relieved. "Brandon's off the hook, too, right?"

"Oh, I don't know about that," I said, thinking that Brandon was anything but. "Well, Mr. Toverson, it's time you got to work."

As Garrett drove away, I got back into my Corolla and sat for a few minutes, the engine running, air conditioner cranked to three. So Brandon had tried to set up an alibi for himself for the night Cole was murdered. Not only had he had asked a friend to lie for him, but the lie he wanted told would get the friend in serious trouble. That didn't say much for Brandon's brand of friendship. The lie would also get Brandon in serious trouble. Why do it? The only answer, of course, was that he thought saying he was at home sleeping might not be enough to clear him. And, more important, that the thing he was really doing that night was infinitely worse than shooting tortoises.

Chapter Twenty-Nine

After interrogating Garrett Toverson, I ran errands. My life had gone to pot since I had become involved in Cole's case. I hadn't been to the grocery store in two weeks, the nasal spray I use to control my hay fever had run dry, leaving me wracked with sneezes that threatened to eject my nasal passages, and I had seven overdue library books. Still clad in my attractive ranger outfit, aviator glasses on top of my head, I pushed a cart up and down the aisles at Albertson's, attracting not the slightest bit of notice. Had I worn nothing but polka dotted boxer shorts and duct tape over my boobs, the reception would have been about the same.

My weeks of eating canned soup and breakfast cereal for dinner had thrown me into survival mode. I had an overpowering desire for fresh fruits and vegetables, yogurt and orange juice, and whole grain bread. I wasn't so transformed, however, that I could walk past the liquor section without snagging a fresh bottle of Glenlivet and two six packs of Coronas. I also found myself unable to resist throwing into the cart the most enormous bag of sour cream and onion potato chips I had ever seen. It would last me a day or two, at least. Getting through the line at the check out stand was the usual excruciating experience, involving lots of chat between the checker and the customers in front of me. The talk ran to how hot it was (like the heat was something unusual), how the high school football team might fare this fall (poorly), and (sigh) the size of the onions.

It was only after I had loaded all the groceries in the trunk of my car that I realized I should have grocery shopped last. With visions of rotting chicken and curdling milk spurring me on, I completed the rest of my errands in record time. I was in and out of the drug store in seven minutes, and although I nearly had an apoplectic fit in the library—the late fee came to $12.25—I finished up there in less than five minutes. Such efficiency was unprecedented in Desert Rock. When I got home, I shoved the perishables into the refrigerator, leaving out the eggs, which I needed to make a batch of brownies. I wanted something to take to Brandon's grandmother's house in the event that she agreed to see me.

I called her before I went to all the trouble of mixing up the brownies and dumping them into a pan to bake. I said that I was a friend of the family and would like to stop by to offer my condolences and drop off a homemade dessert (believe me, lying becomes contagious once you start doing it). In a cracking soprano voice that almost shattered my eardrum, she invited me to come by any time.

While the brownies baked, I shed the ranger outfit and donned a pair of denim capris and a yellow tank top. I didn't wait long enough for the brownies to cool before I cut them, the result looking like a miniature field of brown crops plowed by a drunken farmer. I shrugged and covered the dish with plastic wrap, hoping it would not fuse to the top of the warm dessert. With any luck Brandon's grandmother would be of a philosophical turn and would think that it's the thought that counts.

Ruth Brittel lived about a mile from my house, but the drive took over seven minutes because I had to get through two stoplights. While I waited for each light to turn green, thrumming on the steering wheel and glaring down at the digital clock, I noticed other drivers sitting behind the wheel placidly, looking as if they enjoyed the little break a red light could offer in an otherwise busy day.

Her house was one of the older homes built when Desert Rock was no more than a stop along Highway 9. Though old, it was in superb condition. The asphalt roof looked new, and the paint—white base and blue trim—looked fresh. But it was the yard that impressed me most. Done in the English cottage style, it consisted of trimmed hedges, a small patch of green turf, and scores of healthy rose bushes blooming in colors ranging from lavender to scarlet. A short brick path terminated at a small fountain in the middle of the yard. While a style at odds with the surrounding desert, one had to admire its orchestrated beauty.

After I rang the doorbell, I had a moment to enjoy the burbling water and the heady scent of hundreds of roses. If it hadn't been over a hundred degrees already at eleven o'clock, I'd have set up a lawn chair in Ruth Brittel's yard under the shade of the ash tree and read a book.

When Ruth opened the door, she shouted, "You must be Pam Barkin—come in, come in!" Her voice came at me like the blast following an explosion, nearly blowing me off the stoop.

"My name is Sam. Samantha Larkin," I corrected.

"What?" she said, cupping a hand around her ear.

"I'm Sam Larkin!"

"Yes, yes, Pam Barkin, you called just a little bit ago. Come in out of that heat." She stepped aside so I could enter.

The inside of the house was as impeccable as the outside. It smelled like lemon floor wax and window cleaner. The surfaces of the cherry furniture gleamed, in grim contrast to the furniture in my house, which had been transformed from mahogany to blonde by a quarter inch layer of dust. Ruth took the brownies from me without a glance and invited me to sit down in the living room while she fixed tea for us. While I waited, a black cat streaked through the room as if it were being chased by a pack of dogs. It dove under the sofa across from my chair, and I had the distinct impression that it glared at me from below the fringe. My ankles prickled as I imagined the beast darting out and shredding my skin with its sharp claws.

Other than the cat, the only thing marring the comfort of the house was its lack of air conditioning. Most old desert homes were built with evaporative coolers, and some people never bothered to install AC. Usually the coolers work fine in the dry desert air, but when it is humid, as it had been for the last couple of weeks, they don't cool the air to a comfortable temperature. I could feel sweat roll down between my breasts.

Ruth came back with a silver tray on which she had placed a small silver teapot, two china cups, and a plate of Pepperidge farm cookies and a couple of my ragged brownies. I felt like I was in a Jane Austen novel. Except that Ruth didn't look real eighteenth century. She wore a purple t-shirt with the words "flower power" on it, and her feet were clad in enormous white tennis shoes with lime green laces. Her straight gray hair was cut in what I supposed to be a pageboy, although I had no clue about what that cut looked like. While she sat down in the chair opposite me and began pouring the tea, I received additional troubling vibes from underneath the sofa. I was certain the cat planned to launch itself at my ankles. I transferred several cookies to a plate and avoided the brownies.

Just as I was taking my first sip of tea, Ruth bellowed, "So, how do you know the family?" I nearly dropped the cup. I set it back on the coffee table in anticipation of further discourse.

"I knew Cole through the wind farm," I shouted. "And through Cole, I got to know Brandon and Jillian." Of course, my relationship with the Mintocks spanned just under four weeks, but my preposterous answer made it seem as though we'd been dear friends for decades. Ruth wasn't a stickler for specifics and seemed untroubled by the fact that she had never heard of me. I added, just to head off any uncomfortable follow-up questions, "I was so sorry to hear about Cole. How are you handling everything?"

She yelled, "Well, I'm okay, honey. It's Brandon I'm worried about. He's taking it hard. It was so soon after his mother's death." She stopped talking and looked down at her cup. When she glanced back at me, her eyes were full of tears. "Brandon's mother was my only child. A parent should never outlive her children."

"You've been through so much," I muttered. I knew firsthand the futility of condolences, but I also knew that attempts to comfort mattered, and somehow, in the end, they made it all a little easier. That someone cared enough to wade into the dark waters of your grief made you feel less isolated, the grief less hideous to bear. What I really came here for was to learn whether Ruth knew where her grandson was the night of the murder. But even I could not be mercenary enough to exploit Ruth without at least honestly engaging her sorrow. Besides (the little shit that had taken up residence inside my head noted), by asking about Ruth daughter's death, I might learn something revealing about the Mintock family dynamics that could bear fruit. I said, hoping I sounded circumspect and sensitive, "I know the circumstances surrounding your daughter's death were especially difficult."

She nodded and placed her teacup on the table. "Oh yes. The taking of your own life. I will never understand it. But Anastasia had been unhappy for so long. At least she is no longer suffering."

I thought that "unhappy" was a rather mild adjective to describe a woman who by all accounts had been mentally ill. Had Ruth seen her daughter as ill, I wondered? Or had she denied the evidence before her very eyes, as loved ones often do when they do not want to accept the truth. "You were not surprised when Anastasia took her own life?"

Ruth sank into her chair. She stared out the picture window at the back yard. I noticed the garden there was even more lush than the one out front. From our vantage point, I could see several small birdhouses in the trees, and a hummingbird feeder. Below the feeder was some kind of flowering shrub, the tubular red flowers profuse. "Anastasia was always a moody child," Ruth began. "She took after her father that way. He killed himself, too, you know. Anyway, she took everything so seriously, I think she found life hard. When she married Cole, I was ecstatic. He was such a nice young man, so full of fun and going places. When she was with him, she seemed happy. Then they had Brandon, and she just bloomed. She loved being a mother, and she and Brandon were very close, especially when he was little. I always felt a little sad for Cole because he seemed left out. But then Anastasia fell back into her old ways, getting the blues for days on end. I don't think Cole knew what to do, so he just buried himself in his work. He always took care of his family financially, mind you, but I don't think he was there for Anastasia emotionally. It distressed her terribly."

Her assessment differed from the other versions I had heard, especially Jillian's. Jillian had portrayed Cole as virtuous, sacrificing his happiness in order to care for his ill wife. Of course, I later learned that he hadn't denied himself all of life's pleasures. I wondered if Ruth knew about the affair. Of course, Ruth didn't need to know about that in order to feel that Cole had not been the perfect husband. After all, Anastasia was her daughter, her only child. Accepting that she was mentally ill would be difficult, and perhaps it had been easier to blame others, especially Cole, for her daughter's problems.

While I found the information about Anastasia interesting, I had come to find out about Brandon. I asked Ruth, "How did Brandon take his mother's death? That must have been so hard on him."

She cupped her hand in front of her ear. "What did you say, honey?"

"How has Brandon held up through all of this?" I shouted.

She shook her head. "Not so good, I think. He tries to seem happy, but then he remembers, and he gets sad. His mother's death devastated him, you know. They were very close."

Ruth was being surprisingly open, and I concluded that she would put up with just about anything I said no matter how violating or insensitive. So I commented, "I always had the impression that Brandon kind of blamed his father for what happened to Anastasia."

"Well, that's understandable, don't you think? His mother died and his father lived."

I nodded in agreement, but I didn't understand what she meant. Attempting to clarify, I said, "It is natural to blame others when someone dies. There is always so much anger. But eventually the anger subsides, and people stop blaming. I hope Brandon was able to do that. I hope he and his dad came to enjoy a better relationship."

She shook her head. "No, there was no time. Cole died, what, just five or six months after Anastasia. Poor child. He has lost both his parents. I'm too old to raise a teenager, but he needs someone to take care of him. He needs a home."

"He didn't want to live with his father after his mother died?"

"Oh no, honey, Brandon and Cole never did get along. And when Anastasia died, well, Brandon was just so angry at his dad. Then Cole married that woman, that Jill person, so soon after my daughter's death. It was too much for Brandon."

Her voice had gotten tight and hard at the mention of Jillian. Either Ruth knew about the affair, or she simply blamed Jillian for Cole's quick marriage after Anastasia's death. It certainly would have galled Ruth to think that Cole could get over her daughter so quickly. I brought the conversation back to Brandon. "How has Brandon reacted to Cole's death?" I asked.

At that moment, the black cat shot out from under the couch and leaped onto the top of the bookshelf behind Ruth's chair. I watched as the white-whiskered beast glared at me with disgust and slapped a small, white urn off onto the floor with its front paw. The urn hit the rug with a loud thud, and the cat flew out of the room. Ruth didn't hear a thing.

"I am worried about the boy," she said. "Of course, he doesn't say anything to me about his troubles."

"Was Brandon home the night Cole was killed," I asked. I hoped she wouldn't notice the non sequitur.

"Oh yes, he went to bed early like he often does. Especially in the summer when he has to get up so early for work."

Ruth had stopped drinking her tea. She sat in her chair, shoulders slumped forward, hands clasped together in her lap. I felt a wave of emotion break over me. Here Ruth was, in her late seventies, her husband and daughter dead, and the responsibility of caring for a teenager thrust upon her. I felt lousy just then for coming to her house under false pretenses and making her think about all these painful events. But not bad enough to abandon my mission. "Well," I said, placing my empty cookie plate on the coffee table. "I don't want to keep you. But before I go, I do have a small favor to ask. Please say no if you're not up to it. It's just that I admired your front garden on my way in, and I'd love to see the back."

Her gray eyes lit up, and she bounced to her feet. "Why, of course, I'd love to show you around. Are you a gardener yourself, Pam?"

I choked back a laugh. She should see the sand pit that was once my mother's garden. "I'm afraid not. But I enjoy looking at gardens, especially ones as lovely as your own. Do you do the work yourself?"

Her eyes sparkled. "Yes, I sure do. Well, except for the lawn. Brandon mows that for me if I badger him long enough about it. When the time comes when I can't work in the garden anymore, it's time to give up the ship."

I marveled that a woman her age could keep up such a yard. I blushed to think of my own meager efforts to keep up Mom's garden. I got overwhelmed raking for five minutes.

Ruth led me out the patio door, barking at me to close it so the cat wouldn't escape. Like the front yard, the back was done in

English style, with lots of trimmed shrubberies and flower borders. I shuddered to think of her water bill. While I pretended to look at the small koi pond she pointed to, I inspected the rear windows. Just as I expected, the screen on one bedroom window was bent, the result of being repeatedly pried out and replaced. The window ledge was smudged with dirt, and the stucco beneath the window scuffed. I almost jumped out of my skin when the black cat appeared in the pane and glared at me. Then I realized he actually looked past me, toward the pond, where the orange fish swam in lazy circles under the calm surface. I smiled, enjoying the image of the cat sitting on that windowsill day after day, staring at the koi pond, seeing lunch forever out of reach.

After the tour, I followed Ruth back inside and retrieved my purse. I thanked her for the tea and reiterated my sympathies, then made my way outside into the wind. Once I got into my car and cranked up the AC, I sat for a moment, thinking about Ruth. The old lady was deaf as a rock. Brandon could chop up his bedroom furniture with a chain saw and she wouldn't hear it. He had established a long habit of "going to bed early" and exiting through his bedroom window in the middle of the night to go shoot tortoises, harass Ann, and whatever else a disturbed teenage boy might think up to do. Ruth remained blissfully ignorant. She said he was in bed sleeping the night Cole was murdered. Her statement was worthless, and Brandon knew it.

Chapter Thirty

"I have some information you may find useful," Vanessa said when I answered the phone. "About Richard Sampson."

I had just got home from Ruth Brittel's house and was assembling a killer sandwich: Fresh hoagie roll, thinly-sliced ham, Swiss cheese, lettuce, onion, and tomato, and lots of spicy mustard. I had been stuffing my mouth with sour cream and onion potato chips when the phone rang, so I was having a little trouble answering my sister.

I said, "Grrth, whuth dith yuth llurn (Good, what did you learn)?"

But instead of telling me, she just breathed in my ear. I took the opportunity to finish chewing and swallowed.

"Vanessa?"

"Yeah, I'm here." More silence.

"Well?" I prompted. "Come on, Van, what is it?" I thought my use of the hated nickname would trigger some response, but she didn't seem to notice. I waited, listened to more of her breathing.

After a tedious interval, during which I had a chance to observe an enormous cobweb running from a kitchen cupboard to the ceiling, she said, "It really upset me that Sampson threatened you. Now, granted, I don't like you getting involved in a murder investigation, but I can appreciate that you're trying to do some good. I don't like

Sampson trying to stop you. So I decided to do a little sniffing around myself, see if I could find out anything that might help you."

I was too shocked to comment.

Since all she got was silence, my sister continued. "You know how you were saying that everybody in Desert Rock knows that Richard sleeps around? Well, you were right. I made some polite inquiries here and there and it seems to be common knowledge."

I wondered what kind of polite inquiries she was talking about. Did she ask the mayor, "Excuse me, sir, pardon me, but have you by chance heard a rumor that Richard Sampson enjoys sex with people he isn't married to?" Vanessa is so big on propriety, I could imagine how hard it was for her to ask questions about other people's sex lives.

After another excruciating pause, she said, "I asked Thomas about it."

"And?" I spotted another cobweb, this one hanging above the refrigerator. I eyed my sandwich-in-progress, wondering how stale the bread would get before my sister finally got to the point. The tomato slices on the cutting board filled the kitchen with the smell of summer. My mouth watered.

"Sam," I heard Vanessa say, "Thomas says that Richard sleeps with other men."

Whoa, I didn't expect that. Richard Sampson sleeping with guys? "Are you kidding me?" I said.

"No, Thomas said it was true."

"How does he know it's true?" I hoped he hadn't found out firsthand.

Vanessa gave no indication of that being the case. "I guess it's pretty common knowledge among some of the men here. He sleeps with some of them. Others despise him for it."

This was too much to absorb. I began to rub my temples, trying to massage my brain like medics do a stopped heart, hoping to bring it back to life. Of course it was stupid to think that a big, athletic man would not be gay. It angered me to think that I, the vocal proponent of rational thinking, had allowed myself to lapse into stereotypes. I did wonder how common it was that gay men married and had families. Was Sampson even gay? Was he bi? Was he straight but just liked to get off with other men? I was confused. And then there was the matter of what this meant for the case. Was it significant? It did provide a more plausible explanation for why he would have lied to the police about where he was the night Cole was murdered. If he were in bed with some guy, he'd be loath to tell anyone, even to provide himself with an alibi. Did Abby not know his affairs were with men? Then I wondered if this had anything to do with the animosity between Sampson and Cole.

"Did Richard ever sleep with Cole?" I asked.

"I know what you're getting at, and I had the same thought. I asked Thomas, and he thought no."

"Did Cole dislike Sampson because he was gay?" I asked, although I could hardly see someone as liberal as Cole having a problem with it.

"I doubt it," Vanessa said, echoing my thoughts. "Cole was way too compassionate."

"So who does Richard sleep around with?" I inquired.

"Sam," she said as though I had asked her to donate her left kidney. "I can't name names, it isn't right. Thomas told me in the strictest confidence. If their names got out, it could get them in a lot of trouble. You know how conservative this town is."

"But it sounds like their names are already out. The rumor mill has been very efficient."

"People know he sleeps around. Few know about the men. Look, I don't even know if this relates to the case at all. I just heard about it and thought I'd pass it on."

"I appreciate it. It could be relevant. But how can I know if you won't name names? At least tell me this: Was Richard involved with anyone connected to the wind farm or Cole?"

She didn't say anything right away, and I could hear her exhale through her nose. The exhalation went on so long I was worried her lungs might not be able to re-inflate. "Donald Van Dorn," she said finally.

I shook my head in disbelief. Van Dorn, the gruff Mill Maintenance foreman? With Sampson? Unbidden, an image of the two big men going at it in a room at the Super 8 popped into my brain. I laughed at the incongruity of it. But if it was true, what did it mean?

Vanessa asked, "Do you think it's significant?"

"I don't know. I don't see how." And then it hit me. Donald, the foreman, the guy with the master turbine key. A question that had been bothering me since the beginning of my involvement in the case was now answered. I had always wondered how Sampson could have gotten into the turbine where Cole's body was found. Now I had a possible answer.

I thanked Vanessa and hung up. I could feel the various strings of the case pulling together at last. I knew it was finally time to sew it up.

Chapter Thirty-One

After a long night, during which I spent more time mulling over the case than I had sleeping, I thought I had a pretty good idea who had murdered Cole. Still, I wanted to clarify a few more things before I went to Trent with my theory. I didn't want him to waste his time pursuing the wrong suspect, nor did I want to look like a fool. By morning, I had worked out a plan to test my hypothesis.

I decided to start with Van Dorn, who seemed less dangerous than Sampson. I had seen Van Dorn's temper, but he was out of shape whereas Sampson looked like a well-conditioned killing machine. This line of reasoning was specious, of course, as either man could crush me like a bug in three seconds flat. Eventually, I'd have to talk to Sampson, but after his threats, I wanted to delay that interview. Sampson was already on to me, but I hoped I could take Van Dorn by surprise.

After eating a bowl of oatmeal with brown sugar and raisins, and downing two cups of strong coffee, I called Mill Maintenance when the office officially opened at seven. The guys had been out working in the field for a couple of hours already, but the receptionist would just be getting in. When she picked up, I told her that I needed to talk to Van Dorn as soon as possible. She reported that he was in the field, and she volunteered to call him with my request and get back to me. Within five minutes she phoned to say that Van Dorn would be happy to see me when he got back to the office around nine. Two hours to go.

I spent the time reviewing the questions I wanted to ask him. To calm myself, I brushed Lacy, the first time I had attempted such an enterprise. I had no idea that a dog would enjoy being brushed. She moaned as the bristles moved through her short hair, and she rolled over and exposed her belly (and other body parts) to make sure I didn't neglect any portion of her anatomy. It was quite obscene, and I thought the least she could do was blush. The pile of hairs left when she got up to shake filled a plastic grocery sack. Clearly, I needed to groom the beast more regularly. No wonder the carpets and furniture looked as if they were evolving into primitive mammals.

At eight-thirty I threw Lacy a couple of biscuits, grabbed my handbag, and headed out the door for Mill Maintenance. I felt keyed up. Sweat began to dampen the fabric under my arms, and my stomach felt like I had drunk a quart of battery acid. It wasn't just the weight of an investigation reaching its critical point that had me so wired. How do you tell a two hundred and fifty pound man with a temper that you know he sleeps with other men? I was not looking forward to the prospect, but I needed to turn up the heat, see what he might say once he became aware that I knew of his relationship with Sampson. I'd remind Van Dorn that whoever killed Cole had needed a turbine key, and that Sampson could have easily obtained one from him. How Van Dorn would react to all this I hated to think about, but I needed to see that reaction. Perhaps it would give me the confirmation I needed.

I arrived at the maintenance yard at a quarter till nine and decided to wait for Van Dorn in the air-conditioned office. Why get my clothes more drenched than they already were? As I got out of the car, I noticed the temperature had to be in the nineties, and the wind had not yet come up to help cool things off. The thunderclouds that had hung around for weeks were nowhere in evidence.

When I entered the office, I found Brandon sitting in one of the two wooden chairs in the lobby, talking into a cell phone. His presence gave me a jolt.

After he hung up, Brandon said pleasantly, "That was Van Dorn. He's stuck out in the field. He asked me to drive you out there since he can't get away."

The kid was acting as if we had not had the run-in at Burger Mania, when I had called him a liar and suggested he made a good murder suspect. I had not expected to see him this morning, nor would I have guessed he'd be so friendly if I had. Buying time so I could orient myself to the situation, I asked, "What's the problem out there?"

Brandon shrugged. "Don't know. He said something about a row going down."

"He must be in a bad mood, then," I noted, my mind thinking up ridiculous things to say to postpone making a decision.

The receptionist and Brandon looked at each other and grinned, obviously appreciating my take on Van Dorn. Brandon slipped the cell phone in his pants pocket and extracted a set of keys. "Come on," he said and headed for the door.

I looked back at the receptionist, but she had returned to her work, her fingers tapping out columns of numbers on the ten-key. As hard as I tried to think what I should do, all I came up with was passive acceptance. The deviation from my plan seemed to carry me forward as if I were a piece of flotsam in a flash flood. I followed Brandon out to his truck, trying to shake it off. I'd be damned if I'd let this derail me. I'd just go with the flow, see what transpired. After all, what could happen to me in broad daylight in the middle of a wind farm? Van Dorn had asked Brandon to drive me to him, so what was the harm?

Brandon was silent as we rumbled over the dirt road, the truck's tires making alarming popping noises as they jolted over sharp stones embedded in the sand. I looked out the passenger side mirror as the maintenance yard and Desert Rock receded. I was nervous, and the drive seemed endless. The teen's silence seemed to fill the cab, pressing against me on all sides.

"Where are we going?" I asked, voice cracking. My throat felt tight, and my words were barely audible over the roar of the truck engine.

"Not far," he mumbled. He seemed different now, his mood had altered from cheerful to sullen. I glanced over at him. His handsome face looked hard as granite.

"Are there a lot of workers out in the field today?" I asked. What a moron. There would be the same number of workers as there always were, spread out over hundreds of acres. Brandon didn't bother to answer. His strong hands gripped the steering wheel, forcing the muscles in his forearms to bulge. He smelled of sweat and Juicy Fruit gum, which he chomped on with alarming vigor. He kept stuffing fresh pieces into his mouth, adding to what must be an already unmanageable lump. I felt myself gag, thinking about that wad in my own mouth, shutting off my air supply. Except for the mastication, his face was strangely still and his body rigid, as if he were one of those mannequins at the Hollywood Wax Museum that had scared me silly as a kid. They looked human, but no animation softened their blank gazes. Their lifelessness creeped me out. Brandon was having the same effect on me now.

I scanned the horizon. Turbines dotted the landscape as far as I could see. Nowhere did I see a congregation of trucks at the foot of one, denoting maintenance work in progress. It alarmed me to realize how big the wind farm was, how a hundred workers could be laboring away and never find themselves in sight of one another. In the desert, distances can mislead. An outcropping of rock can appear to be five hundred feet ahead, but in reality be five miles away. Hikers get lost all the time out here, misjudging distances and following trails that peter out into the desert sands. Some hikers die, disoriented and dehydrated, only a gully away from their vehicles.

Looking in the direction Brandon and I were headed, I caught sight of several bodies of water flooding the road, which disappeared as we came up on them: mirages, shimmering like lakes under the desert sun. Sometimes an entire row of turbines seemed to waver, nearly disappearing from view. Then, they'd come back into focus, their outlines sharp against the blue sky. The truck rocked and shimmied over the sun-washed sand, scaring a rattler sunning itself on the side of the road. The sidewinder snaked into a clump of cholla as we rattled by.

"How much farther?" I asked, my heart thumping.

Without warning, Brandon braked, and dust engulfed the truck. We slid to a stop at the base of a large turbine marked 311. When the dust cleared, I looked around. The place was desolate. No Van Dorn. No maintenance workers. No one. Shit, I was in a lot of trouble.

Chapter Thirty-Two

I stared out the windshield as if a site of bustling activity would appear if I just wished for it hard enough. The reek of Brandon's sweat and the stench of Juicy Fruit filled the cab, gagging me. I didn't look at him, but I could feel his attention on me, every cell in his body attuned to my body. I felt like prey, a small, helpless animal in the sights of a carnivore.

I reacted. I shoved open the passenger side door and burst out of the truck like a projectile during an explosion. With no thought at all but to run, I scrambled away from the truck and pumped over the sand and rocks toward civilization, a wavering dark sea in the distance. Behind me, I heard the driver's door open and the gravel crunch as he leapt from the truck and ran after me. I hadn't gone a hundred feet when he caught me. He grabbed my left arm behind my back and yanked it hard. I yipped, spun, tried to keep running. He pulled harder, forcing me to stop. Then he held both my arms fast behind me, giving them angry jerks that sent pain shooting through my shoulders.

"What the fuck, Brandon?" I said, feeling anger replace fear. I struggled to wrench away from him, tried to stomp on his feet, but he jerked my arms back, nearly dislocating my shoulders. The pain caused me to gasp. Sweat rolled down my face.

"Nosy bitch," he growled. He jerked me around and shoved me before him toward the turbine.

I knew that words were futile, but talking was all I had standing between me and oblivion. "Why are you doing this?" I asked. "You're sinking yourself. The receptionist knows you drove me out here. When I don't turn up, they'll come after you."

Brandon's only answer was a low growl. This was not good. His refusal to talk to me could mean that he had retreated into some alternate reality. I wondered if he had become something subhuman, a beast, angry and dangerous. One does not reason with an animal, but I found myself trying anyway.

"Why did you do it?"

He stopped pushing me toward the turbine and emitted a strangled howl. I could feel him lean in behind me, the front of his body pressing against my back, his hot breath in my ear. My skin shrank from him, the hair on my arms stood up.

He snarled. "My father was a bastard. He killed my mother."

I took a deep breath. "Your father didn't kill anyone. Your mother killed herself," I said. I knew that contradicting his version of the truth would enrage him further, but at that point, I didn't care. I would escape or I would die, but I would not participate in his delusion.

He yanked my elbows together, and I emitted a yelp against my will. My suffering seemed to empower and excite him. He pulled me up against him, thrust his groin into me. He began to snarl words into my ear, his voice low and menacing at times, at others, shrill. The pitch went up and down, and his cadence was erratic. He said, "My mother was pitiful, always sniveling about how sad she was. Whah whah whah, just like a little baby. I could get her to do anything I wanted if I just listened to her crap like I actually cared. And my dad, Jesus Christ, what a sucker. Sticking by my mother year after year like a fucking pussy. Until he started fucking that whore."

"Jillian said you threatened to kill her," I said just to keep him talking. The longer he talked, the longer I lived.

"That bitch! I told her I'd kill her, all right. How dare she fuck with me!"

"So why did you kill your dad, Brandon?"

The teen snarled and yanked my arms. "He didn't deserve to live."

I said, knowing I was baiting him and not caring, "You basically killed your mother, too, only you didn't have to get your hands dirty on that one. What did you do, Brandon? Tell her that your dad was cheating on her? Tell her about all your nasty pastimes, like stalking Jillian's niece? Or how you liked to blow tortoises to bits? Did you tell her you thought she was a pathetic excuse for a human being? What else did you have to say to push her over the edge?"

"Fucking cunt!" he yelled and yanked my arms. My shoulder muscles began to spasm, every jerk he gave me increasingly painful. He now tugged at my arms insistently, and I realized he was trying to get a good grip on me with one hand while he used the other to flip through the keys on his key ring. I could hear the keys banging together, the metallic clinks filling the air. I listened to the sound, my eyes now focused on the door at the base of the turbine. Sweat broke out all over my body and my knees felt like they were dissolving. He had one hand on me now. Just one. It was now or never.

I spun away from his grip, the momentum nearly throwing me to the ground. Scrambling to my feet, I ran, blindly, away from the turbine, down the slope toward town. The towers swirled at the edges of my vision, and I could hear my footfalls pounding on the sand. I pumped my legs as fast as they would go. Despite my conditioning, my lungs burned as I sucked in the dry desert air. As if in a nightmare, I felt like I was running in place, every lift of my leg painfully slow, forward momentum negligible. I could feel Brandon's presence behind me, tracking me like a predator.

I ran two hundred yards past half-dead creosote bushes and shimmering rocks and sprawling chollas before Brandon caught up with me and took me down. I speared face first onto the hot sand and sharp rocks, his body landing on top of mine, slamming the air from my lungs. As I struggled to breathe, my vision narrowing, he started pounding on my shoulders, my back, my head. He rolled me over and straddled me, his fists now connecting with my face. I heard a horrid crack and felt a surge of intense pain. Hot liquid streamed from my nose. The pain triggered something in me. I braced my back against the ground and shoved the animal off me. I kicked out, hoping to connect with his groin. I went for his face, my fingers clawing at his eyes. I felt saliva run out of my mouth. Blood covered Brandon's t-shirt but I wasn't sure if it was mine or his.

Like two pit bulls fighting to the death, we rolled over one another, clawing and biting. The hot sand scorched my arms and legs, caked my skin where the blood flowed. He was a bigger, stronger, younger dog than I, and I could feel my strength draining away. I continued to fight, but I was on the receiving end of everything now. His blows kept thudding into my skull, my breasts, my ribs. I didn't feel pain anymore, just anger, an intense red rage. Then I felt nothing, and the blinding sun and the blue sky faded to gray, then went black.

Chapter Thirty-Three

I woke in the dark. I did not know where I was. My body was a sack of pain. My broken nose sent stabbing pulses through my head and across my face. My shoulders ached, the ligaments ripped and ragged, and my ribs hurt every time I breathed. I could feel my hands and knees burn where the skin had been scraped away. Worse than all those miseries combined was the heat. It was so hot I could barely breathe. Sweat pooled on my skin as my body tried to cool itself. The heat and the dark of the place closed in on me, and panic rose. I needed to move, stand up, breathe. But when I tried to rise, I almost lost consciousness. Slowly, I rolled over onto my belly and raised myself onto hands and knees. Pain shot through my head, my nose throbbed, tears streamed down my face. I moaned and heard my voice echo metallically. I now knew where I was.

Realization brought more panic, and I began to hyperventilate. A tingling in my head warned of an imminent loss of consciousness. I forced myself to breath out, then in, then out, until my head cleared. I focused on the pain emanating from my nose and ribs and shoulders, beginning to remember how I had received each injury, how Brandon had jerked my arms behind me, how he had tackled me, driving me into the ground, how he had smashed at my face and head. I recalled his body straddling mine, his weight pinning me to the ground. I felt fury build, replacing the confusion. When I thought of Brandon dragging my unconscious body into the wind turbine and locking the door, the anger exploded. I yelled "No!" until I thought I'd eject my lungs, my shout echoing in the hollow chamber. With an intensity of desire I never felt before, I wanted to pummel Brandon's face until it was nothing but blood and tissue and bone.

Staggering to my feet, controlling my breathing with effort, I began to move. I couldn't see a thing, and I knew the first thing I had to do was to find light. I hadn't seen how Brandon turned on the lights that day I watched him work, but I knew there had to be a switch of some kind near the door. But where was the door? I thought, the turbines are roughly twenty feet in diameter, so I shouldn't have far to walk until I came to a wall, if a cylindrical object could be said to have walls. I put my hands out in front of me as though I were warding off an attacker, and within five short steps they came in contact with the wall. I kept my torn hands on the wall and began to move to my right. Eventually, I knew, I'd find the outlines of the door. It was fruitless to hope that it would not be locked, but I found myself propelled forward by some inner volition, made up of hope and desperation.

After ten steps, my right wrist banged against some object. Feeling around, I discovered that it was the steel ladder that the windsmiths climb to perform their maintenance work at the top of the turbine. To the ladder's right, I felt the bundle of cables running alongside it, the sheathing slick under my fingertips. I edged around the ladder and cables and continued my loop. A few more steps and my fingers found the door. I ran my hands over its surface, my fingers encountering what felt like a doorknob and several levers. I tried the knob. It didn't budge. I pulled and turned and yanked, but it was no good, the door was locked. I felt again for the levers. Wouldn't engineers have built in safety latches that could open the door in case it blew shut with someone locked inside? The levers did not open the door, though, no matter how I manipulated them. If they were safety hardware, Brandon had disabled them. My hope faded.

As the hope went out of me, the walls began to close in again, and I started struggling for air. Breathe, Sam, in and out, in and out. I forced my mind into focus, threw out all thoughts except those concerned with figuring out a way to escape. Don't give in to panic, I told myself, just keep thinking and moving. Just keep doing something.

After taking three deep breaths, I felt around the perimeter of the door for the light switch. Would it be the common variety, just a simple toggle, the kind found in every home? I pictured a slender lever protruding from a flat plate, and that's what my fingers searched for. After a few moments, with my heart beating faster and faster, I found it. The switch was just as I had envisioned it. With a flick of my finger, a bluish white light flooded the chamber, and my breathing instantly calmed. I saw the familiar outlines of the tower's innards, the curved walls, the access ladder, the thick cables running alongside. On the wall opposite the ladder, I saw the control panel, its metal doors closed. The space was well-lighted, clean, and surprisingly quiet but for the faint pulsing sound of the blades high above. I looked around the sterile space, despairing that I could find in it anything that would help me get out.

Think, Sam, I told myself, just reason it out. Maybe I could find a piece of metal or a tool that someone had left behind to pry the door open or break the lock. I walked around the perimeter of the tube again, mapping the interior just to feel that I was accomplishing something, to feel that I was in control. There was the ladder and cables, over there the door, and there, the control panel. Plotting the landmarks helped calm me, at least a first. The more I examined the space, though, the more I began to comprehend that there were no tools left behind, no extraneous bits of metal lying on the concrete floor, nothing that could be used to pry open a door or break a lock.

Again, despair washed over me, and I crumbled against the wall by the door, my back against the hot concrete. The heat was increasing, pressing the air out of my body. I had to tell myself to breath steadily, in and out, in and out. At the moment, focusing on my oxygen intake was the only thing keeping me sane. I felt like an animal trapped in a cage. My body trembled with fear. How long did I have before dehydration killed me?

I tried to think of everything I knew about dehydration. Like most desert dwellers, I respected what the arid, hot climate could do to the body. Water loss accelerates in desert conditions, especially if you're exercising, which causes you to perspire. This was not good. I was sweating profusely, and I'd been perspiring long before I landed in this prison. While driving with Brandon out to the turbine, my clothes had become saturated with nervous sweat. Then there was my futile flight across the desert to get away, and the subsequent fight with Brandon, during which I'm sure I sweated buckets. The worst part was that I didn't know how long I'd been unconscious in the turbine, sweating in the growing heat. Every hour that went by reduced my chances of survival.

How long had it taken for Cole to succumb? I tried to recall the details of his death. When Cole's body was found, the coroner estimated that he'd been dead four to five days. But he'd been missing for a day or two longer than that, which meant that Cole probably spent a day or two in the turbine before he died. How much of that time had he been unconscious? Hopefully, all or most of it.

I guessed the most I had was twenty-four to forty-eight hours. Maybe less, since I'd lost so much water already previous to my incarceration. How long had I been in the turbine? Five minutes? Five hours? I felt panic rise.

I began to inventory my symptoms to see how advanced the dehydration was. I vaguely remembered from a desert survival course I once took what to look out for, from headache to dizziness to delirium. I definitely had a headache and felt dizzy, but that could be the result of getting beat to a pulp or freaking out from being trapped in a small space. I was thirsty and fatigued, too, more symptoms of dehydration. My heart and respiration rates seemed high, but, again, that could be because of anxiety. Then again, it could signal that my body was gradually shutting down. Without enough water, my body would not be able to transport nutrients, oxygen, or white blood cells, nor would it be able to get rid of waste products. My very cells would lose cohesion, and the various chemical reactions needed to live would not take place. Eventually, I'd feel disoriented, sleepy, and then I'd blank out. Death would quickly follow.

Weirdly, I found this train of thought calming. Thinking was better than panicking, better than *feeling*. I tried to stay in the present, and, strangely, I never once thought about what would happen if I died. It never occurred to me to hope that I would be reunited with my mother and father in some otherworldly place. I suppose that would have been a comfort. But such solace was denied to me. I've never been a religious person, but I always considered myself open to the idea of God and transcendence. Being open to the idea, I learned, is not the same thing as believing in it. A person of faith in my situation might have prayed for deliverance. I just talked to myself, drew strength from thinking. And all I could think of was how much time I had left, and how I could get out.

After what seemed hours spent mapping my condition, precious time I could not waste, I roused myself. Find a way to get out, Sam, I said aloud through gritted teeth. I stood and held onto the doorknob as waves of pain washed over me. My breathing became ragged and my vision clouded. I pushed my weight against the wall to keep from falling, held on until the pain subsided enough for me to think. I glanced around my prison again, my gaze landing on the control panel. From what I remembered of the panel, it contained numerous copper and steel parts bolted onto a metal back. I limped over to the panel and opened the doors.

Rows and columns of circuitry, small fans, yards of rigid conduit, lots of bolts. I didn't know how to make heads or tails out of what I was looking at. But, I thought, Cole would have. Perhaps he knew how to remove or damage or adjust something in this box that would alert those monitoring the turbines at Mill Maintenance. He might have known how to shut the turbine down, which would send a warning message to some worker's computer screen that something was wrong. If Cole had known how to send such a message, for some reason he hadn't done it. I could only surmise that he'd never regained consciousness inside the turbine. I hoped that was true, hoped that he had been spared the agony I was now going through. Then a less comforting thought intruded: Maybe Cole had known there was no way to use the panel to get help.

It didn't really matter. I didn't know enough about the panel to know whether it could help me or not. Certainly, none of the components inside the panel were labeled "On/Off" or "If you need help, press this." Not to mention the fact that the entire panel looked like it was built to withstand a nuclear explosion, every piece battened down with bolts and clips. I felt hopelessness embrace me again. My heart seemed to constrict, and my legs buckled. As the walls closed in again, sweat began streaming from my face, which increased my sense of panic. Pain came in waves, at times so brutal I moaned. But pain at least kept me angry, and fighting.

I began to pull and push and twist each of the components inside the box. Precious sweat flowed out of me, making the scrapes on my palms and knees burn as if acid had been poured on them. The sharp metal edges of objects within the panel sliced my fingers as I worked at them. It was all in vain, nothing budged, I was trapped and I would die. But I kept at it because doing something was better than doing nothing. I slipped my fingers under conduit and pulled and wedged them behind circuits and pried at metal clips. On and on I went, trying to break free anything I could, ignoring the blood flowing from my hands.

The energy began to leak out of me and I could barely stand. I had tried every component within the cabinet with no success. I looked at the two metal doors, each of which attached to the cabinet with metal hinges. Small, circular fans had been installed in each door, presumably to cool the components inside the cabinet. From each fan, metal conduit ran down the door, terminating at a bit of flexible conduit, which ran into the bottom of the panel. I grabbed hold of the metal conduit on the right hand door and gave it a yank. Did I feel it give? Easing both sets of fingers under the clips holding the conduit to the door, I pulled with all I was worth. It moved! I could see the clips contort with the strain. I felt my heart pulsing. I placed my left foot on the door as a brace and pulled backwards on the conduit, putting all my weight into it. A brief screech split the air and then the metal gave way. The conduit ripped from the door, and I flew backwards from my own momentum and hit the back of my head against the other door, then dropped to the floor. The fan that the conduit had been attached to made a horrible screeching noise and then shut down, and a burning tar odor filled the chamber. My head throbbed where I had hit it, and my ribs pulsed with pain, but in my hand I had it, a five foot piece of metal I might be able to use to jimmy the door.

Elation flooded me. I lay on my back, looking up into the tower, at the ladder and cables snaking up into concentric circles of blue light until they narrowed and eventually faded from view, and I laughed. My laughter gurgled and hiccupped as though I were weeping, but I felt good. Energy rushed back into my body and propelled me to my feet. I hobbled to the turbine door and examined it for vulnerabilities.

The steel door looked impenetrable, like those hatches on ships engineered to withstand thousands of pounds of water pressure when closed. I felt the euphoria fade, and my body suddenly felt too heavy to hold up. Pain reasserted itself, so intense now it seemed to fill my head, to close off all other thoughts. The white space of my prison seemed to waver, all the objects and contours washing together into a sea of fog, smothering me.

Damn it, Sam! Wake up! I looked down at the conduit in my hand and hit the door with it as hard as I could, metal banging against metal. The shock waves reverberated in the hollow tube, making my heart thud. My arm ached from the blow, and shivers of pain flashed from my right shoulder. But my vision cleared, and air rushed back into my body as if I'd popped to the surface of a cold lake. I hit the conduit against the door again and again until the tip of it flattened. Examining my handiwork, I then wedged the flattened tip into the space between the door and the turbine and pried. But the conduit wasn't strong enough, it bent under the pressure. With a cry of anguish, I heaved it to the ground.

Once I had my breathing back under control, I studied the door with as much rationality as I could muster. With a burst of clarity, I saw that the weakest part of the door was the knob/lock assembly. Whereas the door itself was heavy steel, the lock looked like the kind used in the exterior doors of ordinary houses. Such locks were made to thwart burglars, of course, but compared to the turbine door, the lock looked flimsy. Besides, I told myself, I was working at it from the inside. Maybe it would be more vulnerable from that side.

I retrieved the conduit, raised it above my head, and brought it down with all my might onto the top of the door handle. The impact jolted through my hands and elbows and up into my shoulders. I nearly passed out as the reverberations coursed through my body. My ribs sent shock waves of pain throughout my torso, and blood began pouring from my shattered nose. My legs crumpled, and I wound up on my knees. But when I looked up, I saw that the doorknob was half off, hanging and bent. I thought one more strike might do it. But I could barely breathe for the pain—my mind was choked with it. Give it five minutes, Sam. Rest for five minutes.

I must have blacked out because I suddenly found myself lying in a fetal position underneath the doorknob in a puddle of sweat. My first thought was, good, at least I'm still sweating. That means I still have water left in my body. Then I remembered what I had been doing. I looked up and breathed a sigh of relief to see the lock as I had remembered it, damaged, nearly broken off. I got to my feet unsteadily, hanging onto the wall as my vision blurred. After a moment, my head cleared, and I grabbed hold of the conduit again. Unsteadily, I raised it above my head, took a deep breath, steeled my body against the pain that was coming, and brought the bar down again.

Before I passed out, I heard a metallic crack, but whether it was the doorknob or the conduit hitting the concrete floor, I couldn't tell.

I again awoke in a fetal position. I didn't want to move, I wanted to just lie there, my knees tucked up under my chin, my eyes closed. But the pain was so intense, every breath served to wake me further, until I was completely conscious. I opened my eyes and saw it: The doorknob lay on the floor about two feet from the door. Small metal springs and flat pieces of metal littered the concrete like the innards of a wounded robot. Adrenaline shot through me and chased all thoughts of pain away. I struggled to my knees and examined the hole where the doorknob had been.

I could see the rods from the knob on the other side of the door come through a metal plate that ran perpendicular to the hole. I started pushing and pulling at the flat plate, which I deduced held the mechanism that penetrated the door jam, thereby locking the door. No amount of pulling would move it. Then I realized that the shaft of the knob on the other side of the door was holding it in place. I pushed against the tip of the shaft, and the knob fell out the other side. Now, the only thing between freedom and me was that damned plate. I manipulated it until my fingers were numb, but it wouldn't give way, it held the door fast, its plunger deep inside the door jam.

I had come too far to let a stupid metal plate stop me. I picked up the conduit rod and began shoving it in and out of the hole where the knob had been, bashing at the plate with the blunt end of it. I felt such rage that I barely registered pain as I smashed at the mechanism repeatedly. At some point, I wasn't hitting the lock at all but Brandon, and I felt my arms retract and lash out, retract and lash out, striking with more force than I felt capable of. Eventually, I exhausted myself, and when I dashed the sweat out of my eyes, I saw that the metal plate was bent in the middle. My heart lurched. When I reached in for it, the damage had accomplished what I suspected: The crease in the metal had compressed the plate, drawing out the part of the lock that penetrated the doorframe. I pushed, and the door swung outward, revealing the desert stretching away before me.

I stood in the doorway, the blast of fresh air rocking me back on my heels, unable to believe it. I blinked in the bright light, looking out at the desert as if it were a mirage. I blinked and blinked, but the desert stayed just where it was. I was free! I had never been so happy to see sand and rocks and cactus in all my life. Blinking and teary, I stood on the threshold in the hot sun and held my arms up to the blue sky. I breathed in the dry air, filled my lungs to bursting. My body seemed to expand and float in the vast expanse as if I were floating in space. Laughter bubbled up, and I let it burst out of me. I stumbled out of the turbine, giggling and smiling.

As my eyes traveled over the miles of cholla and turbines shimmering in the late afternoon sun, though, a demoralizing thought intruded. What now? Stranded miles from town, what were the odds that a Mill Maintenance worker, or anyone for that matter, would find me? I was too weak to walk home. I had maybe another day before dehydration killed me. Pain made it hard to stay conscious, and I was exhausted. Would someone come looking for me? Here?

I was free, but what had freedom brought me? Just another place to die.

I slumped onto the sand in a heap, not even trying to reach the shade on the other side of the turbine. I rolled onto my back and looked up at the white tower where it pierced the blue sky hundreds of feet above. The turbine blades glinted in the sun as they spun round and round and round. I felt consciousness slip away, and I closed my eyes.

I would die out here, then. They would find my body, stripped clean by vultures and coyotes, and bury what remained of me beside my mother. She and I would finally be on the same page, I chuckled to myself. But then I thought, no, we wouldn't be on the same page at all. I hadn't put the killer away as I knew she would have wanted. I had failed her. Brandon had beat me.

How had he executed my demise so easily? My best guess was that the teen happened to be in the Mill Maintenance office when my call came in this morning. He overheard the receptionist call Van Dorn about my request to see him, and then listened when she called me to tell me the meeting time. After that, Brandon went away for a half hour or so and came back, waiting in the office until I came, his plan set. At that point, he feigned the call from Van Dorn and lied to me, saying the foreman asked Brandon to drive me out to the field. Brandon probably couldn't wait to get me in his vehicle and drive me out to a location where he knew no workers would be. He must have enjoyed the thought of killing me by this method, given my terror of enclosed spaces. I remember Brandon saying how he thought my fear of the turbine was "hilarious."

When I had set my plan in motion this morning, I was fairly sure that Brandon had killed his father, but I wanted to make certain. I wanted to clear both Van Dorn and Sampson before I took my theory to Trent. I figured a short talk with both men would be all it would take. My fatal mistake was getting in that truck with Brandon. Part of me had felt the danger; the other part had dismissed the fear as irrational. After all, it was broad daylight, at a business, in Desert Rock. I had truly believed that Van Dorn had called Brandon to ask the teen to drive me out to him. The receptionist was right there, her presence assurance that everything was copasetic. But I had underestimated Brandon. And overestimated my own wits. I had been arrogant and foolish.

Contemplating how easily Brandon had suckered me filled me again with rage. I couldn't let him win. I sat up, the sudden movement making my nose bleed again. It wasn't right! I would not die out here while he walked free. I stood up, my legs trembling, my brain swimming in my head. I needed to think, there had to be a way to save myself.

Maybe Brandon had thrown my purse out the window when he drove off! If I could find it, then I'd have my cell phone. Excitement energized me, I could feel strength flood back into my body. With steady strides, I began to walk in ever expanding circles around the turbine, searching for the handbag. In the back of my mind, a niggling little voice said it was unlikely Brandon would have disposed of the purse so close to the scene of the crime. He had probably driven ten miles into the empty desert to bury it where no one would ever find it. But the primitive part of my brain cried out that I had to try something, I had to act. I would give myself a half-hour to search for it, and if I failed to find it, I'd start walking for town. I'd crawl if I had to.

As I circled the area around the turbine searching for the purse, I started to crave the cell phone like it was water. My longing became so deep I hallucinated, I could actually feel the phone in my left hand, the fingers of my right hand touching the keys, my middle fingertip poised over the raised dot on the 5 key. I could see the device in my mind's eye, the shiny silver keys, the lighted blue face. I actually looked at the display, could make out the two bars indicating signal strength and battery status, both good. I felt my fingers press the 9, then the 1. When my index finger moved to press the final 1, my mind sent a reminder: Don't dial 3 like you did last time. Yes, the last time I tried to call 911, a big white truck was following me, practically driving over my car's bumper. I remembered how I dialed wrong, punching in 913 instead of 911. The memory broke into the hallucination, and my mind cleared. I was once again in the middle of the wind farm, thirst burning my throat, the sun sinking lower in the western sky.

The sudden clarity immediately following the hallucination ignited an epiphany. I replayed the memory of the night I was followed just to be sure. I saw myself laugh with relief when the truck turned off after I put the phone to my ear. I saw myself wonder why no one was answering my call. I looked down at the display and realized that in my panic I had misdialed. I saw myself laugh, turn the phone off, *then slip it into my pocket.* Yes! I no longer kept the phone in my handbag. I kept it in the pocket of my capris! Ecstasy coursed through me. I shoved my hand into the left pocket of my capris, and there it was,

I could feel the warm metal against my fingertips. I had had it the whole time!

I pulled the phone out and gazed at it as if it were a talisman. Instantly, though, doubts began to dim my excitement. What if the phone had been damaged during my struggle with Brandon? My fingers trembled as I pressed a key so the face would light up. The phone came awake with a chime, and the display turned blue. My emotions soared. I cradled the phone in my hand in exaltation and thanked the gods of technology. Getting my breathing under control, I dialed 911. Nothing happened. I tried again. Nothing. I stared at the device in my hand as if it had betrayed me.

I didn't understand. The phone didn't appear damaged. Van Dorn said cell phone reception was not a problem out here. What was wrong? Then, again, the image appeared in my mind of the night I was tailed. I saw myself dial 913 instead of 911. Panicking, I had dialed wrong. Simple operator error. That was it! I was dialing 911 this time, but I had forgotten to punch the call button afterwards. My heart thudded as I dialed again and punched the right button. The phone rang! And rang.

A 911 operator picked up on the third ring.

Chapter Thirty-Four

Connor pulled the knife from the drawer, its blade glinting.

I watched him test the knife's sharpness by running his thumb along the blade. "Do you know," I said, "that's the same knife I pulled out to use as a weapon the night Brandon tried to break into the house. When I yanked it out of the drawer, I remember saying to myself, 'This is the knife Connor uses to cut the back ribs.' Isn't that the strangest thing? Why would I think of that at that moment?"

Connor looked at the knife, then at me. After a moment, he said, "Maybe thinking of me made you feel less alone."

This was surprisingly philosophical—and sentimental—for my brother, whose ruminations usually run along the lines of trying to decipher whodunit in *Scooby Doo*. "Yeah," I said, "Or maybe it's because we'd just had a barbecue a couple nights previous and the memory just flashed into my head."

He laughed, as eager as I was not to walk down deep emotional paths.

We stood in my kitchen preparing dinner, the late afternoon sun brightening the yard outside the windows. Lacy, practically adhered to Connor's leg, watched my brother as he began slicing through a rack of ribs, the knife sliding between the bones, separating them cleanly. The image of me doing that to Brandon in my own house during a thunderstorm made me shiver.

I bent down and lugged out a ten-pound sack of russets from underneath the kitchen sink for potatoes-au-gratin. Seeing me, Connor dropped the knife, sped to my side, and with greasy hands grabbed the sack from me. "You shouldn't be lifting that in your condition," he said.

I rolled my eyes and took hold of the sack again. "It's been three weeks, Connor. I'm not an invalid." It was true. I had not been seriously injured during my battle with Brandon. The headache and thirst from the dehydration passed quickly, what with all the fluids the hospital gave me during my one-night stay. My broken nose, unfortunately, still hurt, and the swelling made breathing difficult. The bruised ribs were still sore, too, which made bodily activities I took for granted—sneezing, coughing, laughing, you name it— painful. Other than that, though, the various scrapes and bruises were healing nicely.

Connor tried to pull the potato sack from my hands. "You've got to take care of yourself." He grunted with the strain, his greasy hands losing purchase on the plastic.

Lacy whined, looked from Connor to me, then back to Connor, her forehead wrinkled in concern.

At this point, my effort to get the bag from my brother was having a deleterious effect on my ribs, but I'd be damned if I'd let him tell me what to do. I grabbed hold of the sack and yanked with all my strength. The pain made my eyes water, but the sack was now under my control. I grinned at my brother.

He gave up, went back to the ribs, and said, "You are the most stubborn person I have ever known."

While Connor poured bottled barbecue sauce over the ribs, I washed and sliced the potatoes for the au gratin. Lacy remained at her post by my brother, her body rigid with anticipation. She knew she'd get a rib to gnaw on after dinner, and she'd stick to him like glue until then.

While I felt fine (for the most part), I sure hadn't when the paramedics arrived at turbine 311. Lucky for me, each turbine is identified by a metal plaque bearing its numbered designation.

That number probably saved my life. Without it, how could I have told the 911 operator where I was? Would I have said, "Oh, I'm by some turbine out at CalWind, just drive around until you see me"? Fortunately, it hadn't happened that way. The paramedics got Van Dorn to locate turbine 311 for them, and I was rescued within a half hour of my call.

The moment they rescued me, I lost it. I didn't need to be strong anymore, and it felt delicious just to go under. I don't remember anything until I woke up in the hospital in the middle of the night, scared and disoriented. The nurse in attendance came (somewhat desultorily, in my opinion) when I pressed the help button, and she explained where I was and what had happened to me. I slept then until morning, and was released that afternoon. On Vanessa's insistence, I spent the first night at her house, and then Connor drove over from Temecula to stay with me at my own place. I had never been so happy to be home in my life, which is not to say that Vanessa didn't take good care of me. It's just that a person can stand only so much ordering about (take your medicine, drink these electrolytes, stop fiddling with those bandages).

I assumed Connor would take more of a hands-off approach, but he'd been a pain in the ass, too, as the potato sack incident clearly illustrates. Even Eddie's concern had been getting on my nerves. He'd been coming by several times a day to check on me, bringing lattes and donuts and Ming's take-out, treating me as if I'm dying or something. Connor, being typically oblivious to other people's feelings, went ahead and invited Eddie to our barbecue tonight despite my frequent complaints about our friend's doting.

To prove how hale I was, I ripped open a bag of shredded cheddar cheese with excessive force, sending cheese worms sprawling on the counter. After collecting the errant strands, I sprinkled them over the potatoes, and then liberally added flour and milk and lots of salt and pepper. Connor opened a bag of shredded cabbage and began preparing coleslaw.

While placing aluminum foil over the potato pan, I nearly sliced my hand on the foil when Lacy barked, leapt from Connor's side, and ran for the front door. She stood in the entryway, whining and wiggling and wagging her tail. Damn, Eddie had arrived. I braced myself for more of his doting, but it was worse than I thought: Vanessa.

"Yoo hoo!" she called as she flounced through the door. Lacy danced and pranced, and Vanessa got down on one knee to hug the dog. Connor and I looked at one another like we'd eaten sourballs.

"Well," my sister said, bustling into the kitchen, Lacy at her heels. "Someone's feeling better." She waltzed past that someone and lifted the foil off the au gratin pan, stirred the coleslaw bowl, and spooned more barbecue sauce over the ribs. "Having a barbecue?"

"No," I said, "we're performing surgery."

A giggle escaped Connor's nose. Vanessa glared at him, then turned to me. "You're lucky *you* didn't undergo surgery what with all your meddling, Miss Smarty Pants."

I sighed and eased around her to get to the refrigerator—I suddenly needed a beer.

Connor reached past me and placed the coleslaw inside the refrigerator. I noticed that he also grabbed a beer.

Vanessa saw this, too. She sniffed. "Well, it's very nice to be asked to join you in a cocktail. My goodness, Sam, where are your manners?"

Connor piped up, "Beer or wine? Do you want to stay for the barbecue? We have enough for Thomas and the girls, too."

I glared at him, but he was so busy sucking up he didn't notice. Probably hoping to win brownie points so Vanessa wouldn't ask him about the money he owed her.

My sister nodded at me. "See, now that's how one behaves when one has visitors. White wine, please, but Thomas and the girls can't come. They're having their monthly night out together. Don't you usually invite Eddie to these barbecues? Is he coming?" She looked at me expectantly, as if we might also have invited a justice of the peace so Eddie and I could finally tie the knot.

"He's coming," I said. "But if he asks how I am one more time, I'm going to kick his ass right out the door." I grabbed the au gratin pan, shoved it into the oven, and turned the temperature knob to 350.

"You ought to be ashamed, Sam," Vanessa said. "He's just worried about you. We all are. How are you feeling, anyway?"

Ug! They just didn't get it. "I'm fine. Really. We can all just get on with our regular lives now."

Vanessa said, "Sam, honestly, what on earth are you thinking? After you almost get yourself killed it's rather difficult getting on with regular life. Do you know what's happening with the Mintock kid?"

My sister and brother crowded around me, waiting for my answer. I could see that they would not leave me alone until I shared every detail. "Last time I talked to Trent, he said that Brandon is being held at Juvenile Hall without bail. Trent said that because the charges against him are so serious, Brandon will be tried in adult court, and if convicted, he'll get twenty-five years to life in prison, probably without the possibility of parole."

Connor asked, "Do you think they'll convict him?"

"They have a good case. Brandon tried to kill me, and he admitted to me that he killed his father. They'll have evidence, too, at least concerning my case. Of course, the feds could certainly screw things up, given how they handled Cole's murder."

"No kidding," Vanessa said. "It took my sister to get it right. How did you finally decide it was Cole's son? I thought you were convinced Richard Sampson did it."

Connor hoisted himself up and sat on the counter, something our mother strictly forbade. If he didn't mind barbecue sauce on his shorts, I didn't care. Vanessa and I leaned against the counter, sipping our drinks. I took a deep breath, said, "It was really a process of elimination. I always felt that Luke was innocent, and I quickly scratched Jillian off my list. That left Sampson and Brandon. To try to get a bead on which one killed Cole, I first looked at means. Toward the end of my investigation, I was fairly sure how the murder had taken place. The killer had asked Cole to meet him or her at the CalWind office. There, the murderer had knocked Cole unconscious, gotten him into his or her vehicle, driven out to the wind farm, and deposited the body inside the turbine. I figured the killer had to be someone whom Cole knew and trusted. The killer also had to have access to the turbine keys. Sampson was strong enough, and maybe he could have convinced Van Dorn to get him the turbine keys, but I doubted Cole would trust the man enough to meet him in the dead of night out at the wind farm."

"But Cole would have trusted Brandon," Vanessa noted. "Brandon was his son."

"Right, though 'trusted' is putting it too strongly. I'm not sure Cole trusted Brandon at all. But, as disturbed as Cole was about his son's behavior, I don't think he actually thought Brandon would physically harm him. So, Brandon had perfect means. He could get the victim alone without too much hassle. He had access to the turbine keys. He was strong enough to heft an unconscious body into a truck and drag it to a turbine."

I paused, drank some beer, and then went on. "The second thing I looked at was motive. Sampson had two reasons to want Cole out of the way. One, without Cole, the wind farm expansion might be stopped, and Sampson would still have his view, and he could possibly buy up the land. But that outcome had been extremely uncertain. I had a feeling the expansion would go through with or without Cole, and I suspected that Sampson thought so as well. Moreover, Sampson had too much to lose—his family, his reputation, his empire—to pursue a course of action that promised such unlikely gains."

Vanessa and Connor leaned forward, eager for me to go on.

"The second reason Sampson may have wanted Cole dead was to protect his name. Cole had apparently become aware at some point during their acquaintance that Sampson slept with men. Cole may have threatened Sampson with exposure if he didn't stop fighting the expansion. However, I doubted Cole would have followed through on his threat. He had kept that secret for years, and I didn't think he was the type of person who would expose someone to ridicule and censure. Most likely, Sampson, who knew Cole even better than I did, shared my opinion. I don't think he ever felt a need to silence Cole."

I leaned back against the counter and drained my beer. "Anyone for another drink?"

Both shoved their empties at me. I tossed Connor's and my beer cans into the recyclables bin and grabbed two more from the fridge. I refilled Vanessa's wine glass. Lacy looked as if she felt left out, so I grabbed a dog biscuit from the canister I keep on the counter and threw it to her.

"So," Vanessa said, "Sampson's motive was weak. What about Brandon's?"

By way of answer, I said, "One thing that always bothered me about the case was why the killer would stuff Cole's body in the wind turbine. I thought most people would have tried to hide the body where no one would ever find it. Instead, the killer placed the body where it would be found, to make a statement. Why? The only person I could see doing that was Brandon. Despite working at Mill Maintenance, Brandon hated the wind farm—he hated anything associated with his father, especially the plant. I think it amused Brandon to lock Cole inside one of his turbines. It expressed perfectly Brandon's view of the wind farm and his father's ideals."

Connor asked, "You're saying Brandon killed his dad just because he hated him?"

"I think so. You have to understand, Brandon is not a well person. The more I learned about him, the more he seemed capable of killing. For example, he enjoyed torturing and killing animals."

I waited a beat, letting Vanessa, the world's biggest animal-lover, recover after swallowing a mouthful of wine the wrong way. Eyes watering, she nodded for me to continue. I said, "Brandon took pleasure in terrorizing a young girl. He was a master at manipulating and dissembling, and he lied and got friends to lie for him—"

Vanessa interrupted. "You think Brandon is a sociopath. Sam, he was awfully young for that. Most sociopaths never kill anyone, and those who do, do so when they are older, not usually in their teens."

I nodded. "Very good. Since you're the psch. major here, perhaps you can tell us what might make someone so young kill his father."

My sister set her wine glass on the counter. After a moment, she said in a professorial tone, "The way you describe his behavior before the murder leads me to conclude that he had 'conduct disorder,' a group of behavioral and emotional problems in children and adolescents. The thinking on the disorder is that it is caused by any number of things, such as brain damage, child abuse, school failure, or traumatic events. Kids with the disorder act like bullies, they can be cruel to people or animals, they sometimes force other kids to have sex with them, they set fires and destroy property, and they lie and steal. Basically, they have difficulty following the rules."

Connor gaped at our sister. I laughed, said to Connor, "See, I told you Vanessa uses her degree even though she's not officially working."

"How do you remember all that stuff?" he asked.

Vanessa inflated. "Mom always said I had the world's best memory."

Before she could expound on this singular talent, I said, "Use that good memory of yours to tell us how a kid with conduct disorder winds up being a killer at age sixteen."

Vanessa thought about it, in no hurry to answer. You could tell she enjoyed being the expert, and she wanted to draw out the pleasure as long as possible. Finally, she said, "If kids with conduct disorder don't get treatment, they can become sociopaths later in life. Brandon was pretty young when he killed his father, but sometimes a major life event can trigger such behavior earlier than usual. From what I know of the case, it was probably a series of things. His father had an affair, his mother committed suicide, and then his father married the woman he had the affair with. I doubt Brandon killed his father out of some sense of revenge for his mother's death—sociopaths don't care about anyone but themselves—but something about that chain of events set him off."

Connor asked, "Are you saying that Brandon hated his father because of Jillian?"

I shrugged. "Cole's relationship with Jillian might have been a trigger, but Brandon's hatred of Cole went way back. I think Brandon hated his father in part because he couldn't manipulate Cole the way he did everyone else. I mean, Brandon manipulated everyone: his grandmother, his friend Garrett, Jillian. I can only imagine how Brandon treated his mother. Brandon knew she was mentally ill and therefore vulnerable. But Cole was a different story. He was too strong for Brandon to manipulate, at least to the extent the kid manipulated his mother. For the most part, Cole went about his life the way he wanted. Take the wind farm. Protecting the environment was his life's mission. No matter how Brandon mocked his father's efforts to help the environment, Cole just kept right on with his wind farm and his green committees and whatnot."

"Why was Brandon so down on the environment?" Connor asked.

"I think environmentalists represent everything that Brandon sneered at. Environmentalists believe that in order to ensure our own well being, we need to protect other life forms. That to survive, we must think of others. Brandon doesn't think that way. He thinks his rights, his wants, his desires, are the only things that matter."

"Wow," Connor said. "The whole thing makes our family's problems seem trivial."

Vanessa and I nodded. Connor didn't know how accurately he had echoed the thoughts I'd been having over the last three weeks.

Vanessa asked, "What will happen to the wind farm?"

I shrugged. "Jillian's intent on keeping it. She thinks Cole would want her to. But I suspect she'll get overwhelmed by the responsibility and sell it to G.E. or one of the other big energy companies."

"Would she sell that land to Sampson?" Vanessa asked.

"I doubt it. If Cole didn't want to, she won't either. Sampson, I'm afraid, is out of luck."

"Well," Connor said, tossing his empty beer can in the bin. "I better start that barbecue."

"What do you need me to do?" Vanessa asked. She opened the oven door and lifted back a corner of the aluminum foil covering the au gratins. The heavenly scent of melting cheese and roasting potatoes wafted out at us. She shut the door and turned the heat down.

The three of us, plus Lacy, tramped out to the patio, Connor holding the plate of ribs. He flipped back the lid of the gas barbecue and began arranging the ribs on the grill.

Vanessa drew Lacy's attention from the cooking meat by throwing the dog's beloved tennis ball across the yard. Lacy tore after it, spewing dirt in her wake. When she brought the ball back to Vanessa, my sister pried it out of her goopy mouth and tossed it again. Vanessa's laughter and Lacy's excited yips blended with the murmur of the wind in the trees. The air smelled like barbecue.

My family thus engaged, I found myself thinking about my brother's comment. He was so right: The Mintocks' problems made our family's issues seem minor by comparison. And the Mintocks were not the only ones I had encountered during the investigation who had troubles. So many of the people I met were dealing with serious problems—lies and betrayals being top on the list—and they weren't doing a whole lot to deal with them, either. They stuck their heads in the sand and soldiered forward, never facing the truth. That's what I had done with my mother, and look where it had gotten me.

How could I have been so blind? Distorted thinking is anathema to me. Creating clarity out of murk is my job. Why I never thought to apply rational analysis to my relationship with my mother is a mystery. Maybe it's simply easier to think dispassionately about issues that don't directly affect us than it is to evaluate those close to home.

As painful as it had been to discover that I had been wrong about my mother, I learned a valuable lesson. It's not wise to hold onto grudges. The past is just a story we tell ourselves about how it all went down. We are often wrong about it, constructing a fiction with no basis in reality. We feel angry or hurt or bitter because of events we remember that never occurred—at least not as we recall them—in real life.

The investigation also gave me a deeper appreciation for my job. Yes, the pay sucks, but I'm doing important work. To help young people see clearly, to help them avoid some of the pitfalls I'd seen people fall into while investigating Cole's murder, seemed an honorable calling. Besides, things were looking up where Vince was concerned. After I told him what had happened to me at the wind farm, he extended my deadline by three weeks. In exchange, he asked me to write a short blurb about my investigation that he can use to market my book. He wants to bill me as "the author who solved the Desert Rock wind farm mystery!" Well, if it helps sell my book, I'm all for it.

My thoughts about Vince were interrupted when Connor called, "Eddie's here!" The whoosh of the wind rushed into my consciousness again as if someone had just turned up the volume. As I came back to the present, I saw Eddie standing beside my brother, the smoke from the grill half obscuring him. He was listening to something Connor was saying, but he looked at me. He smiled, and I smiled back, the smoke like a screen between us. Good, safe Eddie. Despite his blasted doting, I was glad to see him.

Vanessa gave the tennis ball one last heave, sending Lacy after it on a dead run. As my sister and I made our way toward the barbecue, I pointed to the straggly weeds, piles of dried up leaves, and dead branches that littered Mom's yard.

"I'm finally going to clean this up," I told Vanessa. "If I do a bit each day, maybe I can get it whipped into shape. Although it's never going to look like Mom had it."

My sister looked over at me, her eyes wide. "You're going to stay in Desert Rock then?"

By this time we were standing by the barbecue watching Connor remove the ribs from the grill. He stopped when Vanessa asked the question, tongs held in mid-air. Eddie's gaze searched my face.

Ever since I had begun living in Mom's house I had done nothing but complain. I griped about Connor and Vanessa dropping in on me whenever they felt like it. I railed about how Mom never appreciated me. Every day I groused about the wind and heat. But the thought of leaving, selling the house, never again looking out at Mom's garden made my chest hurt.

Lacy came bounding up with the filthy tennis ball. I reached down and placed my hand on her head. "I think I'll stay. For now, anyway."